Fallen Heir

The Royals Series by Erin Watt

✦ ✦ ✦

Fallen Heir

ERIN WATT

Berkley Romance
New York

BERKLEY ROMANCE
Published by Berkley
An imprint of Penguin Random House LLC
penguinrandomhouse.com

Library of Congress Cataloging-in-Publication Data

Names: Watt, Erin, author.
Title: Fallen heir / Erin Watt.
Description: New York: First Berkley Romance, 2023. | Series: The Royals
Identifiers: LCCN 2023026682 (print) | LCCN 2023026683 (ebook) |
ISBN 9780593642191 (trade paperback) | ISBN 9780593642207 (ebook)
Subjects: LCGFT: Romance fiction. | Novels.
Classification: LCC PS3623.A8745 F35 2023 (print) |
LCC PS3623.A8745 (ebook) | DDC 813/.6—dc23/eng/20230626
LC record available at https://lccn.loc.gov/2023026682
LC ebook record available at https://lccn.loc.gov/2023026683

Fallen Heir was originally self-published, in different form, in 2017

Printed in the United States of America
1st Printing

Book design by Alison Cnockaert

To everyone who clamored for more Easton Royal. This book is for you.

Fallen Heir

One

"REMEMBER THAT NO matter what function you choose, the sum of the differences is controlled by the first and last," Ms. Mann concludes just as the bell chimes to signal the end of class. It's the last of the day.

Everyone starts packing up. Everyone but me.

I lean back in my chair and tap my pencil against the edge of the textbook, hiding a grin as I watch the new teacher desperately try to hold the quickly disappearing attention of her students. She's cute when she's flustered.

"Parts one-A and one-B for tomorrow!" she calls, but nobody's listening anymore. They're all racing out the door.

"Coming, Easton?" Ella Harper pauses at my desk, her blue eyes peering down at me. She's looking thin these days. I think her appetite left her around the same time my brother did.

Well, not that Reed *left* her. Big bro is still head over heels for Ella, our kinda sorta stepsister. If he didn't love her, he would've chosen to go to some fancy college far, far away from Bayview. Instead, he's at State, which is close enough that they can visit each other on the weekends.

"Nah," I say. "I got a question for Teach."

Ms. Mann's slender shoulders twitch as my words register. Even Ella notices.

"East . . ." She trails off, her pretty lips forming a frown.

I can see her winding up some lecture about how I need to clean up my act. But we're only a week into classes, and I'm already bored out of my mind. What else do I have to do but mess around? I don't need to study. I barely care about football. My dad has grounded me from flying; at this rate, I'll never get my pilot's license. And if Ella doesn't leave me the hell alone, I'm gonna forget she's my brother's girl and seduce her just for the hell of it.

"See you at home," I tell Ella, my voice firm. Ms. Mann has been flirting with me relentlessly since the first day of school, and after a week of exchanging heated glances, I'm going for it. It's wrong, sure, but that's what makes it exciting—for both of us.

It's rare for Astor Park Prep to hire young, hot female teachers. The administration knows there are too many bored rich boys in here looking for a challenge. Headmaster Beringer has had to cover up more than one teacher-student relationship, and I'm not even relying on the rumor mill for this, since one of those "inappropriate" relationships was mine. If you consider making out with my nutrition teacher behind the gym a *relationship*. I don't.

"I don't mind if you stay for this," I drawl to Ella, whose stubborn feet are rooted into the tile, "but you might feel more comfortable waiting in the hall."

She gives me a withering look. Not much escapes her notice. She grew up in shady places and knows shit. Or she just knows how deviant I am.

"I don't know what you're chasing, but I doubt you'll find it up Ms. Mann's skirt," she mutters.

"Won't know until I look," I quip.

Ella sighs and gives in. "Be careful," she admonishes in a tone loud enough to carry to Ms. Mann, who flushes and stares at the floor as Ella walks out.

I tamp down a swell of irritation. Why the judgment? I'm trying to live my best life here, and as long as I don't hurt anyone, where's the harm? I'm eighteen. Ms. Mann's an adult. So what if her occupation is currently "teacher"?

Silence fills the room after the door closes behind Ella. Ms. Mann fiddles with her pale blue skirt. Well, hell. She's having second thoughts.

I'm slightly disappointed, but it's all good. I'm not one of those guys who has to bang every girl I meet, mostly because there are so many out there. If one girl isn't interested, you move on to the next.

I bend down to grab my backpack when a pair of pretty heels show up in my line of vision.

"Did you have a question, Mr. Royal?" Ms. Mann asks softly.

I raise my head slowly, taking in her long legs, the curve of her hip, the indentation at her waist where her prim white blouse is tucked into her equally modest skirt. Her chest heaves under my examination, and the pulse at her neck flutters wildly.

"Yeah. Do you have any solutions to my in-class problem?" I place my hand on her hip. As she gasps, I run a finger along the waistband of her skirt. "I'm having a hard time concentrating."

She takes another deep breath. "Is that right?"

"Mmmhmmm. I think it's because every time I look at you, I get the feeling you're having problems concentrating, too." I smile faintly. "Maybe because you're fantasizing about getting bent over your desk while everyone in calc watches."

Ms. Mann gulps. "Mr. Royal. I don't have the slightest idea what you're referring to. Please remove your hand from my waist."

"Sure." I slide my palm lower, so that my fingers are dusting the hem of her skirt. "Is this a better place for it? Because I can stop altogether."

Our gazes lock.

Last chance, Ms. Mann. We're both acutely aware of how I'm ruining her skirt and possibly her reputation, but her feet are glued to the floor.

Her voice is hoarse when she finally speaks. "That's fine, Mr. Royal. I think you'll find that the solution to your concentration problem is in your hands."

I slide my palms underneath the skirt and flash her a cocky grin. "I'm trying to eliminate the problematic functions."

Her eyelids flutter shut in surrender.

"We should not be doing this," she chokes out.

"I know. That's why it's so good."

Her thighs clench under my hands. The naughtiness of this scene, knowing we could be caught anytime, knowing that she's absolutely the last person I should be touching, makes this a million times hotter.

Her hands fall to my shoulders and her fingers dig into the two-thousand-dollar Tom Ford–designed school blazer as she tries to balance herself. My own fingers work their magic. Small, muffled sounds fill the empty classroom until there's nothing but her heavy breathing.

With a satisfied sigh, Ms. Mann backs away, smoothing her hands across her wrinkled skirt before lowering herself to her knees.

"Your turn," she whispers.

I stretch my legs out and lean back. AP Calc is absolutely the best class I've ever taken at Astor Park.

When she's done giving me my extra credit, a hesitant smile settles on her face. Her hair brushes the tops of my thighs as she leans close to murmur, "You can come over tonight. My daughter is in bed by ten."

I freeze. This could've ended in many directions, but I was really hoping to avoid this one. A dozen excuses race through my mind, but before I can get one out, the classroom door opens.

"Oh my God!"

Both Ms. Mann and I whirl toward the doorway. I catch a glimpse of ink-black hair and the navy Astor Park jacket.

Ms. Mann shoots to her feet and stumbles. I jump forward to catch her. She's weak-kneed as I help her brace herself on a desk.

"Oh God," she says numbly. "Who was that? Do you think she saw . . . ?"

Saw Ms. Mann on her knees, saw that my pants are undone and Ms. Mann's clothing is rumpled? Um, yeah. She saw.

"She saw," I say aloud.

The confirmation only freaks her out more. With an anguished moan, she drops her face into her palms. "Oh God. I'm going to get fired."

I finish putting myself together and reach for my bag, hastily shoving my stuff in it. "Nah. It'll be fine."

But I don't say it with much confidence, and she knows it.

"No, it won't be fine!"

I shoot a worried glance at the door. "Shhh. Someone's gonna hear you."

"Someone *saw* us," she hisses back, panic filling her eyes and trembling in her voice. "You need to go find that girl. Find her and do your Easton Royal thing and make sure she doesn't say anything."

My Easton Royal thing?

Ms. Mann hurries on before I can ask what the heck she expects me to do. "I can't get fired. I *can't*. I have a daughter to support!" Her voice starts shaking again. "Fix this. Please, just go and *fix* this."

"Okay," I assure her. "I'll fix it." How, I have no frickin' idea, but Ms. Mann is two seconds away from a nervous breakdown.

She lets out another low moan. "And this can never happen again, do you understand me? Never again."

I'm totally cool with that. Her panic attack killed the mood, as well as any interest in a repeat performance. I like my hookups to end as pleasantly as they begin. There's nothing sexy about being with a girl who has regrets, so you gotta make sure at the start that she's fully into it. If there's any question about her interest, it's a no-go.

"Gotcha," I say with a nod.

Ms. Mann stares at me with pleading eyes. "Why are you still here? Go!"

Right.

I shoulder my backpack and exit the classroom. Out in the hall, I take a quick survey. It's more crowded than it should be. Why is everyone loitering in the halls? School's over, for Chrissake. Go home, people.

My eyes skip over Felicity Worthington, who flips her platinum-blond hair over one shoulder. Claire Donahue, my ex, spears me with a pair of hopeful blue eyes—she's been itching to get back together since school started. I avoid meeting her gaze and move on to Kate and Alyssa, the Ballinger sisters. Neither of them has black hair. I scan the rest of the hallway but come up empty.

I'm about to turn away when Felicity leans over to whisper something in Claire's ear, and in the space previously occupied by Felicity's head, I spot *her*. The girl's face is in her locker, but her hair is unmistakable, so black it's almost blue under the fluorescent lighting.

I stride forward

"Easton," I hear Claire say.

"Don't humiliate yourself," Felicity advises.

I ignore them both and keep walking.

"Hey," I say.

The girl looks up from her locker. Startled gray eyes collide with mine. A set of pink lips part. I wait for her smile— the response I get from ninety-nine percent of women, no matter their age. It doesn't come. Instead, I get a face full of hair as she whirls and sprints down the hallway.

Surprise stalls my response. That and I don't want to draw an audience. Nonchalantly, I close her locker before following her fleeing figure down the hall. Once I hit the turn, I run, too. With my much longer legs, I'm able to catch her in front of the locker rooms.

"Hey," I say, planting myself in front of her. "Where's the fire?"

She stops hard, nearly falling over. I grab her shoulder to make sure she doesn't do a header into the tile.

"I didn't see anything," she blurts out, shrugging away from my steadying hand.

I glance over her shoulder to make sure we don't have an audience, but the hallway is empty. Good.

"Sure, you didn't. That's why you ran away like a kid caught with her hand in the cookie jar."

"Technically, you're the one with the hand in the cookie jar," she retorts. And then slams her lips together as she realizes what she admitted. "Not that I saw a thing."

"Uh-huh." What to do with this cutie? Too bad I'm supposed to scare her into silence.

I move forward. She edges sideways.

I keep going until she's backed up against the wall. I lean down until my forehead's about an inch from hers. So close I can smell the spearmint of her gum.

Fix this, Ms. Mann had said. And she's right. What happened in that classroom was supposed to be fun. That's all I want—to have fun, not ruin people's lives. It was fun doing something dirty and wrong. It was fun toying with the idea of getting caught.

But Ms. Mann losing her job and her kid being homeless? Not in the fun category.

"So—" I start in a low voice.

"Um, Royal, right?" the girl interrupts.

"Yeah." I'm not surprised she knows me. Not that I'm proud of it, but the Royals have run this school for years. Thankfully, I've avoided any leadership role. Ella's the Royal in charge now. I'm merely her enforcer. "And you are?"

"Hartley. Look, I swear, I didn't see anything." She holds up her hand as if pledging allegiance to the truth.

"If that was true, you wouldn't have run, Hartley." I turn

her name over in my head. It's an unusual one, but I can't place it. Or her face, for that matter. Astor doesn't see a lot of new faces. I've been with most of these assholes for as long as I can remember.

"Seriously. I'm a monkey." Hartley continues her feeble defense, folding one hand over her eyes and another across her mouth. "See no evil, speak no evil. Not that what you did was evil. Or what you *may* have been doing. Not that I saw anything. Evil or good."

Charmed, I tap the hand over her mouth. "You're babbling."

"New-school nerves." She straightens her school-mandated blazer and juts out her chin. "Maybe I did see something, but it's none of my business, okay? I'm not going to say anything."

I cross my arms, my own blazer drawing tight over my shoulders. She looks like she wants to fight. I love it, but flirting with her isn't going to generate the results I need. I inject some menace into my voice, hoping fear will curb her tongue. "Thing is, I don't know you. So how am I supposed to take your word for it?"

The menace works, because Hartley visibly gulps. "I . . . I won't say anything," she repeats.

Instantly, I feel bad. What am I doing scaring a girl like this? But then the fearful face of Ms. Mann pops into my head. Ms. Mann has a kid, and Hartley is just another rich prep school classmate. She can handle a little warning.

"Yeah? And what if someone—Headmaster Beringer, maybe—asks you about it?" I slant my head in challenge, my tone getting more and more threatening. "What then, *Hartley*? What would you say?"

Two

AS HARTLEY CONTEMPLATES my question, I mentally catalogue her. She's a tiny thing—probably a foot shorter than my six-foot, one-inch frame. There's not much to brag about in the boob department, and down below she's wearing a pair of really ugly loafers. Footwear is the only thing that isn't dictated by the school's dress code—the one expression of individuality we're allowed. The guys run around in sneakers or Timbs. Most girls opt for something fancy like a Gucci flat or red-soled heels. I guess Hartley's statement is *I don't give a fuck*. I can appreciate that.

Everything else about her is ordinary. Her uniform is standard. Her hair is straight and long. Her face isn't striking enough to draw the eye. Ella, for example, is drop-dead gorgeous. My ex, Claire, was recently named debutante of the year. This Hartley girl has manga-big eyes and a wide mouth. Her nose kind of tips up at the end, but none of her features are going to be gushed over in *Southern Coastal Quarterly*.

Said nose wrinkles as she finally responds. "Well, let's think about what I *actually* saw back there, right? I mean . . . technically, I saw a teacher picking up something off the floor.

And a student was, um, holding her hair out of the way so she could see better. It was very sweet. And kind. If Headmaster Beringer asked, I'd tell him you're an upstanding citizen and nominate you for student of the week."

"Really? That's what you're going with?" The urge to laugh is strong, but I figure that will ruin the effectiveness of any threat I need to dish out.

"Swear to God." She holds a small hand over her chest. Her nails are short and missing the picture-perfect manicure that most of the Astor girls sport.

"I'm an atheist," I inform her.

A frown mars her face. "You're being difficult."

"Hey, I'm not the one playing Peeping Tom."

"It's school!" Her voice rises for the first time. "I should be able to peek into any classroom I want!"

"So you admit to watching me." I struggle to keep the smile off my face.

"Okay. Now I see why you have to get it on with a teacher. No normal girl would want to put up with you."

At her exasperated outburst, I give up on the intimidation because I can't hide my grin any longer. "You won't know until you try."

She stares at me. "Are you seriously flirting with me now? Hard pass."

"Hard, eh?" I lick my bottom lip. Yes, I am flirting, because as ordinary as she might look, she intrigues me. And, I, Easton Royal, am bound by the laws of the universe to pursue all things interesting.

There's a flicker of fascination in her eyes. Brief, but I've always been able to tell when a girl thinks I'm hot, when she's imagining what it'd be like to hook up with me.

Hartley's totally thinking about it right now.

Come on, baby, ask me out. Take what you want. I'd love to see a girl grab me by the metaphorical and literal balls and tell me she wants me. Straight up. No games. But despite the whole girl-empowerment thing, I find that most chicks want the guys to chase them. Bummer.

"Ew." She tries to inch away. "Seriously, Royal. Move."

I plant both hands against the cool wood on either side of her head, effectively trapping her. "Or what?"

Those gray eyes glint, piquing my curiosity again. "I might be small, but I have the lung capacity of a whale, so if you don't move, I'm gonna have to release the oral kraken until the entire school is in this hallway rescuing me from you."

I crack up. "The oral kraken? That sounds pretty dirty."

"I'm thinking everything sounds dirty to you," she says dryly, but a smirk toys with the corners of her lips. "In all serious-ness, I only opened that door because I'm trying to transfer into Ms. Mann's calculus class. But I'm going to keep your little secret, all right?" She spreads her hands wide. "So what's it going to be? Oral kraken or stepping aside?"

Threats aren't likely to work with Hartley, mostly because I don't think I could carry one out. Intimidating girls isn't my style—making them happy is. So I'm going to have to take her word for it. For now, at least. Hartley doesn't seem like the narcing type. And even if she does spill the beans, I can fall back on the wallet. Dad might have to endow another scholar-ship to get me out of the Ms. Mann mess, but he's already done it once for Reed and Ella. I think I'm due for a little be-quest in my name.

Grinning, I move aside. "Listen, if you want to take AP

Calc"—I gesture to the room at the end of the hall—"I recommend you talk to her now. You know . . ." I wink. "Catch her when her defenses are down."

Hartley's jaw drops. "Are you saying I should blackmail her? Tell her I'll only keep my mouth shut if she approves my transfer?"

I shrug. "Why not? Gotta look out for yourself, right?"

She studies me for a long, long moment. I'd give a lot to know what's going through that head of hers. She gives me nothing.

"Yeah, I guess so," she murmurs. "Later, Royal."

Hartley brushes past me. I amble behind her, watching as she knocks on the door and then enters Ms. Mann's classroom. Will she go the blackmail route? Somehow I doubt it, but if she does, her transfer will be approved in no time; Ms. Mann would do anything to stop Hartley from ratting us out.

Even though I've successfully executed my orders to "fix this" (or at least I think I have), I don't leave the hallway. I want to make sure nothing bad goes down between Hartley and Ms. Mann. So I cool my heels outside the classroom, which is where my friend and teammate Pash Bhara finds me.

"Yo," he says, rolling his eyes. "You're supposed to be giving me a ride home. I've been waiting downstairs for, like, fifteen minutes."

"Aw shit, man. I forgot." I shrug. "But we can't go just yet—I'm waiting for someone. You okay to wait a few more minutes?"

"Yeah, it's cool." He comes to stand beside me. "Hey, did you hear about the new quarterback they're trying to bring in?"

"Really?" We lost our first game of the season on Friday,

and based on the way our offense played, we should get used to it. Kordell Young, our starting QB, busted his kneecap on the second play, leaving us stuck with two underclassmen who are in the running for Dumb and Dumber.

"Coach thinks with the injuries and all, we'll need someone."

"He'd be right, but who's going to come here after the season's started?"

"Rumor has it that it's either someone from North or Bellfield Prep."

"Why those schools?" I try to remember the quarterbacks from either school but draw a blank.

"They run the same type of offense, I guess? The guy from Bellfield is cool. I've partied with him a few times. Straight-laced but decent."

"I don't see a problem there. More booze for us," I joke, but I'm starting to feel antsy. Hartley's been in there a long time. It would take Ms. Mann all of five seconds to scrawl her name on the transfer slip.

I peer through the small window on the door, but all I see is the back of Hartley's head. Ms. Mann is out of view.

What's the holdup? There's no way that Ms. Mann doesn't immediately agree to Hartley's request.

"Agreed." Pash's gold-plated phone buzzes in his hand. He checks the text and then wiggles his phone at me. "You going out tonight?"

"Maybe." But I'm not really paying attention to him. I twist around to take another look in Ms. Mann's window. Pash notices this time.

"Dude, seriously? Ms. Mann?" he says with arched brows. "You tired of the Astor girls already? We can take your dad's plane to New York. Fashion Week is starting up and the city is gonna be thick with models. Or, we can wait for the new QB to come and hook us up with some locals. Although"—he nudges me—"there's nothing like doing something you shouldn't, right?"

Irritated that he guessed right, my answer comes out terse. "Wrong. She's too old."

"Then who is it?" Pash tries to peer past me as I use my big frame to block his view.

"No one. There's some chick inside and I'm waiting for her to leave so I can make sure I have the assignment correct."

"The assignments are online," he says unhelpfully.

"Ah, that's right." But I don't move.

Naturally, Pash is only more intrigued. "Who's in there?" he demands, trying to shove me aside for a look.

I decide to move and let him investigate, because otherwise he won't stop bothering me.

Pash presses his nose against the window, takes a long look, and concludes, "Oh. So you *are* here to see Ms. Mann."

"I said I was." But now I'm confused, because why was he so quick to dismiss Hartley as the focus of my interest?

He checks his phone again. "Okay, this is boring. I'll meet you downstairs in the parking lot."

As he starts to take off, curiosity gets the better of me. "Why not the other girl?" I call after him.

He turns around and, as he walks backward, says, "'Cause she's not your type."

"What's my type?"

"Hot. Hot, stacked. Hot," he repeats before disappearing around the corner.

"Wow," a dry voice remarks. "I'm totally crushed that your friend thinks I'm cold and flat."

I nearly jump five feet in the air. "*Jesus.* Can you make a little noise when you move around?"

Hartley grins at me and adjusts the strap of her backpack as she walks. "That's what you get for lurking outside the door. Why are you still here, anyway?"

"Did you get everything taken care of?" I ask, falling in beside her.

"Yes." Hartley makes a face. "I guess she figured out it was me who saw you guys, because she was embarrassingly willing to do everything I asked. I feel bad."

"You shouldn't. Teach made a mistake, and now she's paying for it." It's meant to be a quip, but it comes off callous, and I recognize it the moment Hartley frowns deeply at me.

"She didn't fool around with herself, Royal."

"No, but that would've been hot," I try to joke again, but it's too late.

"Whatever." Hartley pushes open the stairwell door and ducks through it. "Either way, our business here is done. Nice chatting with you."

I hurry after her, practically chasing her down the steps. "Aw, come on, don't be like that. We're just starting to get to know each other. We were *bonding.*"

Her snort bounces off the stairwell walls. "We were not, nor will we ever be, *bonding.*" She quickens her pace, taking the steps two at a time in order to get away from me faster.

"Never? Why so absolute? You should get to know me. I'm charming."

She pauses, hand on the railing, feet ready to take flight. "You are charming, Royal. That's the problem."

And with that, she scampers down the rest of the stairs.

"If you wanted to make me less interested, this is not the

way to go about it," I tell her retreating back. Her ass looks fine under her pleated Astor Park uniform skirt.

Only when she reaches the other side of the lobby does she stop to spare me an amused look. "I'll see you around, Royal." With a little wave, she waltzes out the huge oak doors.

My gaze stays glued to her petite body, and I find myself smiling at nothing and no one.

Yeah . . .

I think I'm going to bang that girl.

Three

"ELLA TOLD ME you fooled around with a teacher today," my older brother says over the phone a few hours later.

I balance my cell on my shoulder as I strip out of my swim trunks and let them drop to the bedroom floor. I spent the past hour in the pool channeling my brother Gideon. Gid's the swimmer in the family, but I haven't been able to stop thinking about Hartley since I got home, and I was hoping a few laps or thirty would help clear my head. Didn't help at all. I'm still thinking dirty thoughts about that girl, except now I'm also wet and cranky.

"Easton," Reed growls. "You there?"

"I'm here."

"Did you do your teacher or what?"

"Mmmhmmm, I did. So what?" I answer flippantly. "I've hooked up with teachers before."

"Yeah, but you're a senior now."

"So?"

"So grow up. Ella's going out of her mind worrying about you."

"She should concentrate on making sure you don't stray."

There's two beats of dead silence while Reed tries not to yell at me. His throat must ache.

I smirk into the phone. "Anyway, thanks for calling, Grandpa. It's nice to know I can count on Ella to narc me out if I do something wrong."

"East." His tone sharpens, then softens. "She cares about you, that's all. We all do."

"Aw, I feel so loved." Rolling my eyes, I grab a pair of jeans from my dresser drawer and yank them up my hips. "We done here, Reed? Dinner's ready."

"No, we're not done," he says, and even though I can easily hang up the phone, I instinctively wait for him to continue because he's my older brother, and I've always followed his lead. "How's the new QB working out?"

"He's not. That busted knee was worse than we thought— he's out for the season. And his backups are two sophs who can't throw a decent pass to save their lives."

"Shit."

"Yup. I had no idea that anyone at Astor who played sports could be this bad. Why didn't they just flunk Wade?"

"He would've left anyway. Is Val broken up?"

"Nah, she said he was her rebound guy. Besides, she doesn't think guys can be faithful when couples are separated." Can't blame the girl. Her first boyfriend did her dirty the minute he stepped foot on a college campus.

Reed's sigh is heavy in my ear. "I know. She's had a run of bad experiences. I hope her attitude doesn't rub off on Ella. Keep an eye on that for me, would you?"

"No can do. I have zero desire to keep tabs on Val Carrington. Besides, it's your responsibility to make sure that Ella's happy. Not mine."

I hang up before he can say another word. Reed's always called the shots when it comes to the two of us, but he's not here anymore. He's got a fresh start at college, playing defensive end for one of the best college football programs in the country, and a girlfriend who adores him.

Me, I'm grounded here in Bayview. Literally grounded. Dad told the airfield that I'm not allowed to fly. He says I need to prove that I'm sober and responsible. It's my senior year of high school—what's the point in being sober and responsible? Besides, I'm not going to fly drunk. I know better than that, but he doesn't believe me.

Thanks to my grandparents, I have a trust fund big enough to buy a sleek little Cessna, but there aren't enough air traffic controllers who would cross my dad and allow me up in the air. It's a bitch of a situation and it puts me in a constant bad mood.

I'm stuck doing the same old shit—which includes walking downstairs to have dinner with my family, a tradition that stopped after my mom died and started up again when Dad brought Ella to live with us. After Ella's biological father, Steve O'Halloran, was arrested for murder, these family dinners became nonnegotiable. We're not allowed to skip them, even when it's obvious nobody is in the mood for quality family time.

Like tonight. We're all somewhere else. The twins, Sebastian and Sawyer, look exhausted, probably from a tough lacrosse practice. Ella looks preoccupied. Dad looks weary.

"You couldn't find a shirt in that big closet of yours?" my father asks politely. Since Ella joined our family, Callum Royal has perfected the Disapproving Dad look. He never cared about what we did or wore before, but now he's all over us.

I glance down at my bare chest, then shrug. "Want me to go up and find one?"

He shakes his head. "No, you've kept us waiting long enough. Sit, Easton."

I sit. We're eating out on the patio that overlooks the huge, kidney-shaped pool. It's a warm night, and the breeze is nice. The table feels kind of empty with just the five of us, though. It's weird now that both Gid and Reed are gone.

"Looking a little pale there," Sawyer jokes. Despite being the younger twin, he always leads; Seb once said it's to make Sawyer feel better for being born last. Seb's quiet but has a wicked sense of humor.

Seb smirks. "It's his pecs. He's been skipping Chest Day, so he looks pale and small."

"You little shits. I'll show you who's small and weak." Grinning, I rise halfway out of my chair and shake my fist at the two twerps. "I've crapped out logs bigger than you."

"Yeah, well, there's two of us and—"

"All right, that's enough," Dad hastily intercedes before Sawyer can give us a rundown of the twins' bowel movements. "Food's getting cold."

The mention of food is enough to divert our attention. Our housekeeper, Sandra, prepared roasted potatoes, garlic carrots, and a shit ton of barbecue sauce–laden ribs. The twins and I dig in like the animals we are, while Dad and Ella take their time, chatting with each other as they eat.

". . . chance you'll have to testify at Steve's trial."

I'm not paying much attention, so when the conversation shifts toward Steve O'Halloran, I'm caught off guard. These days, Dad goes out of his way to not bring up Steve when Ella's around.

At her seat, Ella's back goes stiffer than the flagpole on Astor Park Prep's front lawn. "I thought the lawyers said Dinah's testimony would be enough." Dinah is Steve's shrew of a wife, which makes her Ella's shrew of a stepmother.

"Most likely, you won't be called to the stand," Dad assures her. "But when I spoke to the DA on the phone this morning, he mentioned it's still a possibility. I only bring it up because I don't want you to be blindsided if it happens."

The tension doesn't leave Ella's body. I don't blame her for being upset. The twins are wearing identical expressions of disgust.

Steve was charged with murder months ago, but he hasn't spent a second behind bars. He paid his five-million-dollar bond, surrendered his passport and flight license, and, unfortunately, has abided by the terms of his pretrial release. Money and good lawyers mean you don't serve a day until you're convicted and maybe not even then. Dad's lawyer says that as long as the judge is convinced he's not a flight risk, he's free as a stinkin' bird.

The whole innocent-until-proven-guilty thing is a crock of shit if you ask me. We all know he's guilty, and it drives us nuts that Steve's not in prison for what he did. Not just killing a woman, but also not stepping forward when the cops tried to pin it on Reed.

Granted, the victim was Brooke Davidson, the evil viper who was trying to take down my family, but still. Brooke was a bitch, but she didn't deserve to die.

"Hey, Dad?" Sawyer says warily.

Dad shifts his gaze to his youngest son. "What is it?"

"When Steve's trial starts . . ." Sawyer pauses for a second. "Are they gonna bring up all that stuff about Steve and, um . . ." He trails off and closes his mouth, deciding not to finish that sentence.

Nobody else finishes it for him, but everyone's expressions become strained, including mine. Seb reaches over and squeezes his brother's shoulder. My dad takes Ella's hand in his. She closes her eyes and takes a few calming breaths.

I watch my family as they all try to get a grip on their emotions.

I hate thinking about my mother these days. After Steve killed Brooke, it came out that Mom cheated on Dad with Ella's dad. That's some incestuous shit right there.

Thing is, I can't even be angry at Mom for cheating. Dad was hardly ever around. He was too focused on Atlantic Aviation, the family business, and while he was away for long periods of time, Steve poisoned Mom's mind with ideas that Dad was cheating on her.

But I am angry at her for dying, for taking those pills. Reed says there's no way it could've been the same pills I was stashing in my room, but he doesn't know for sure. I was hooked on Adderall and Oxy back then. The stimulant prescription was completely legal at first, but when I needed more, there was a ready supply at school. My Adderall supplier suggested I take some Oxy as a way to escape. He was right. It helped a lot, but the high didn't last.

When Mom found my stash and threatened to send me to rehab if I didn't straighten out, I promised to right my ship. And I didn't question what she did with the pills. I handed over the bottles because I was a fifteen-year-old who would've cut off his arm if she'd asked. That's how much I adored her.

Chances are, I killed my mother. Reed claims I didn't, but of course he's gonna say that. He'd never tell me straight out that I killed her. Or rather, my addiction did. Is it any wonder that I'm a self-destructive screwup?

I'm off the pills now. Mom's OD scared the shit out of me, and I promised my older brothers I wouldn't touch that junk anymore. But the addictions don't go away. It means I have to feed the thirst in other, safer ways—booze, sex, and blood. Tonight, I think I'll choose blood.

"Easton." I find a worried Ella studying my face.

"What?" I ask, reaching for my water glass. The subject of conversation has shifted away from the trial, thank God. Dad and the twins are now engaged in an animated conversation about soccer, of all things. We've never been a soccer family. Sometimes, I wonder if the twins are even Royals. They play lacrosse, watch soccer, aren't fans of fighting, and have zero interest in flying. That said, they have Mom's features and the Royal blue eyes.

"You're smiling," Ella accuses.

"So? Smiling is bad?"

"It's one of your bloodthirsty smiles." She sneaks a peek across the table to make sure Dad isn't paying attention to us. Then she hisses, "You're fighting tonight, aren't you?"

I drag my tongue across my bottom lip. "Oh yeah."

"Oh, East. Please don't. It's too dangerous." She presses her lips together in concern, and I know she's remembering the time Reed got stabbed at one of those fights.

But that was a total fluke that had nothing to do with the actual fight. Daniel Delacorte, an old enemy, hired someone to take Reed out.

"That won't happen again," I assure her.

"You don't know that." Determination gleams in her blue eyes. "I'm coming with you."

"No."

"Yes."

"No." I raise my voice, and Dad's sharp gaze swings toward us.

"What are we arguing about?" he asks suspiciously.

Ella smirks, waiting for me to field that one. Dammit. If I keep arguing with her, she'll tell him I'm going to the docks, and we both know Dad's not too keen on that idea anymore, not since Reed was knifed down there.

"Ella and I can't decide what movie to watch before bed," I lie. "She wants a rom-com. I obviously want anything but."

The twins roll their eyes. They know bullshit when they hear it. But Dad buys in. His deep chuckle washes over the patio. "Give it up, son. You know the woman always gets her way in the end."

Ella beams at me. "Yeah, Easton. I always get my way." When I get up to fill my glass, she follows me. "I'm going to stick to your side like glue. And when you go to the fight, I'm going to make the biggest scene ever. You'll never be able to show your face there again."

"Can't you go pick on the twins?" I complain.

"Nope. You have my sole and undivided attention."

"Reed's probably throwing a party because he's not under your thumb." I hear her breath hitch, and I look up to see her cheeks turn from pink to white. Oh, crap. "I didn't mean that. You know he can't stand to be away from you."

She sniffs.

"Seriously. He was on the phone with me before dinner crying about how much he missed you." Silence. "I'm sorry," I say, and I am, truly sorry. "My mouth runs ahead of my brain. You know that."

Ella raises one eyebrow. "You should stay in to make it up to me."

Check. Mate.

"Yes, ma'am." Meekly, I follow her back to the table.

"Giving in without a fight?" Sawyer murmurs when we take our seats.

"She was going to start crying."

"Damn."

After dessert, I nudge Ella with my foot and nod toward the twins. She nods back and then turns to my dad. "Easton and I have calculus homework, Callum. Do you mind if we go?"

"No, of course not." He waves us off.

Ella and I escape inside, leaving the twins to clear the table. We used to have staff to do that for us, but Dad fired everyone after Mom died. Except for Sandra, who cooks for us, and his driver, Durand. There are maids who come in a couple times a week, but those aren't live-in positions.

As Ella and I desert them, Sawyer and Seb grumble about how they're going to be late to see Lauren, the girl they're dating. I feel no sympathy. At least they have plans tonight, instead of staying home.

Upstairs, I get comfortable on my king-sized bed and flick the TV on. The football season hasn't started yet, so there's no Monday night game. ESPN is playing highlights from preseason, but I'm not paying attention. I'm too busy scrolling through my phone contacts. I find who I'm looking for and press Call.

"'Sup, Royal," comes Larry's deep baritone.

"'Sup, nerd," I say cheerfully. Lawrence "Larry" Watson is a two-hundred-and-eighty-pound offensive lineman, a good buddy, and the biggest computer geek I know. "I need a favor."

"Hit me." Larry's the most easygoing guy in the world. He's

always down to help out a friend, especially if he gets to use his hacking skills in the process.

"Can you still hack into the mainframe at Astor Park? I've got a pair of Tokyo Twenty-threes chilling in their box."

"The Air Jordan Fives that were only released in Japan?" He sounds like he's about to cry. Larry's a huge sneakerhead and he's always wanted this pair that my dad picked up during a business trip to Tokyo.

"The same."

"What do you want? Grades aren't out yet."

"Just some student information. Full name, address, phone number, that kind of stuff."

"Dude, that's just basic contact info. You ever heard of Google?"

"I don't even know her last name, asshole."

"*Her*, eh?" He laughs in my ear. "Shocker. Easton Royal's looking to score."

"Can you help me or what?"

"What's her first name? Maybe I know her."

"It's Hartley. She's a senior. She's about five foot nothing. Long black hair. Gray eyes."

"Oh sure," Larry says instantly. "I know her. She's in my AP Gov class."

I perk up. "Yeah? You know her last name?"

"Wright."

I roll my eyes at the phone. "Right as in you know it, or riiiiight, as in why would you ever know it?"

"Wright."

Impatience jolts through me. "Right what?"

A loud boom of laughter thunders over the line. "*Wright*,"

Larry wheezes out between chortles. "W-R-I-G-H-T. Her name is Hartley Wright. *Damn*, son, you dumb."

Oh. Okay, I'm dumb. "Sorry, man. Got it. Hartley Wright. Do you know anything else about her? You got her number?"

"Why would I have her number, bruh? I'm with Alisha." Larry once again uses his *are you from Planet Stupid?* tone. "Give me five minutes. I'll get back to you."

He hangs up. I kill time by watching sports highlights. It's closer to ten minutes, not five, when my phone beeps in my hand. I check the screen, grin widely, and shoot Larry a quick text.

> You da man

I kno, he texts back.

> Ill bring sneaks tmrw

I waste no time sifting through the intel Larry sent me. It includes a phone number, an address, and a link to an article from the *Bayview Post*. I click the URL and discover that Hartley's father, John Wright, made a run for mayor a few years back, but he lost the race. Also according to the article, Mr. Wright is the assistant district attorney of Bayview County.

I scan my brain, thinking of the last time I was in a courtroom. It was when Reed's murder charges were dropped followed by Steve's arraignment. Had the prosecutor's name been Wright? No. It was . . . Dixon or something. And I'm pretty sure he was the DA and not an assistant.

I scroll through the article until I reach a picture of the Wright family. Posing in front of a huge plantation-style mansion, John Wright is wearing a gray suit and has his arm around a hot MILF who the caption says is his wife, Joanie. The couple's three daughters are next to their mother—they all inherited her raven hair and gray eyes. Hartley seems to be the middle daughter. She looks about fourteen in the picture, and I grin at the very prominent zit on her forehead.

I'm digging through my backpack before I even realize I'm doing it. I pull out the notebook that contains all my calculus notes. Hartley's missed a week's worth of classes, so that makes her a week behind. When she shows up to class tomorrow, she's going to be totally lost . . . unless someone is nice enough to tell her everything she's missed. I mean, that's the least someone could do, right?

I tug on a loose T-shirt and duck into the upstairs office that I share with my brothers and Ella, well aware that I'm acting like a desperate loser. It's not like I *have* to make photocopies. This isn't the olden days. I can just take pics of the calc notes and message them directly to Hartley. I have her number now, after all.

But nope. I make actual copies, which I staple together and shove in a file folder I find in one of the desk drawers.

"Where are you going?" Ella intercepts me as I'm leaving the office. Her blue eyes are narrowed, her tone thick with suspicion.

"I'm dropping off some homework for a friend." I hold up the folder, then flip it open so that my nosy stepsister can see there's real schoolwork in there.

"At eight o'clock at night?"

I mock gasp. "Eight o'clock?! Holy fuck! It's so late! We should turn in!"

"Stop yelling at me," Ella mutters, but she looks like she's fighting back laughter. Eventually, it comes out as a snorted giggle. "Okay, I'm being ridiculous."

"Yup."

She squeezes my arm. "Just don't go to the docks afterward, all right? Promise me that."

"I promise," I say dutifully, and then I dart off before she can keep bugging me about it.

The drive to Hartley's house doesn't take long at all; Bayview isn't that big. The Wrights live inland, in that plantation mansion from the article picture. It's a nice house. Not as big as mine, but then again, the Wrights aren't the Royals.

I'm about a hundred yards away from the Wright joint when a familiar black Rover careens around a sharp curve. I swerve onto the shoulder and lay on the horn. Sawyer waves merrily at me from the driver's seat, while Sebastian holds up his fingers in the shape of devil horns.

Those two assholes. In the backseat is Lauren, who I guess lives around here.

I park on the curb in front of Hartley's home. My palms are weirdly clammy as I hop out of my truck, so I wipe them on the front of my ripped jeans. Then I wonder if maybe I should've changed my clothes before coming here. Showing up in a threadbare T-shirt and jeans with holes in them doesn't exactly make a good impression, especially since I might run into Hartley's folks.

On the other hand, what do I care about impressing Hartley or her family? I want to bone down the girl, not ask her to marry me.

It's Hartley's mom who opens the front door after I ring the bell. I recognize her from the picture. "Hello," she greets me, her voice slightly chilly. "How can I help you?"

"Hi. Uh . . ." I shift the file folder from one sweaty hand to the other. "I'm here to, uh . . ." Dammit. This was a stupid idea. I should've just texted her a pic of my abs or something. What kind of idiot shows up on someone's doorstep unannounced—

No. Screw all this self-doubting. I'm Easton fucking Royal. What do I have to be insecure about?

So I clear my throat and speak again, this time clear and confident. "I'm here to see Hartley."

Joanie Wright's eyes widen. "Oh," she squeaks, then nervously glances over her shoulder.

I can't see who she's looking at—is it Hartley? Is she standing out of sight mouthing for her mom to get rid of me?

Mrs. Wright turns back to me. "I'm sorry," she says, and her tone has turned to ice again. "Hartley isn't here. Who are you?"

"Easton Royal." I hold up the folder. "I've got some math notes for her. Should I leave them with you?"

"No."

"No?" I wrinkle my forehead. "Then what should I do with—"

I don't get to finish that sentence.

Hartley's mother slams the door in my face.

Four

SINCE I WENT to bed early and my body is ache-free because I didn't fight, I actually wake up on time the next morning. For once, I'm able to drink a coffee and scarf down a bagel for breakfast. At school, I stop by Larry's locker and slam my hand next to the lock. When the door pops open, I shove the box of sneakers inside. Then I head for the locker room. I'm even uncharacteristically *not* late for our six a.m. practice. My teammates note this rare occasion by breaking out in applause when I stride in.

"Holy shit," Larry exclaims. "It's ten to six and Royal is here."

Someone snickers. "Guess hell has frozen over."

"Maybe he lost a bet," someone else suggests.

I roll my eyes and head for my locker. I spot Coach Lewis standing near the equipment room door, talking to a tall guy with a buzz cut.

Even though I'm ten minutes early, I'm still the last one to show. Coach claps his hands when he sees me and says, "Good. We're all here."

I glance over at Connor Babbage, who's leaning against his

locker, and give a discreet nod toward Coach's new friend. Connor shrugs as if to say *no idea who that is.*

Coach steps forward. "Men, this is Brandon Mathis—he just transferred to Astor from Bellfield Prep. He's our new quarterback."

Everyone in the room—myself included—exhales in relief. Nobody even spares a consolatory look at the two sophomore backups. They've already proven to be absolutely useless, and they look equally relieved by the news.

"Mathis," Coach barks. "You got anything to say to your team?"

The new guy smiles at everyone. Tall, decent looking, and friendly? I can already hear the Astor girls' panties dropping to the floor. "Just that I'm looking forward to getting to know y'all and taking home that trophy."

Several players nod their approval. Me, I'm still sizing Mathis up.

Coach's gaze shifts in my direction. "What about you, Royal? You good with this change-up?"

Now that Reed has graduated, I'm the unspoken leader of the defense. If I welcome Mathis, the other guys will follow my lead. Coach knows this.

"Aw, Coach, look at you, taking my lil' ol' feelings into consideration." I wipe away a nonexistent tear. "I'm touched."

"I don't give a flying hoot about your feelings, kid. I just know how difficult you Royals can be." He arches his bushy eyebrows. "But you're not going to be difficult today, are you, Royal? You're going to welcome your new quarterback with open arms, isn't that right?"

I pretend to think it over.

"Royal," he warns.

A grin breaks free. "Nah, I'm not gonna be difficult." I spread my arms wide and beam at Mathis. "Come in here for a hug, big guy."

A few of my teammates snicker.

Mathis looks startled. "Um. Yeah. I'm not much of a hugger."

My arms drop to my sides. "Dammit, Coach, I welcomed him with open arms—*literally*—and he rejected me."

Babbage busts out with laughter.

Coach sighs. "It's a figure of speech, kid. Just shake his damn hand."

Laughing, I step forward and slap my hand against Mathis'. "Good to have you on board," I tell him. And I mean it. We desperately need a QB that can throw the damned ball.

"Good to be here," he replies.

Coach claps his hands again. "All right, boys, get changed and hit the weights."

I strip out of my clothes. Dominic Warren is beside me, putting on a pair of basketball shorts.

"Yo, Mathis," Dom calls across the room. "What's the tail situation over at Bellfield?"

"Tail situation?" our new QB echoes.

"Yeah, tail. You know. Chicks." Dom flops down on the bench and bends over to lace up his sneakers. "I'm thinking of finding myself a Bellfield girl—I'm tired of these Astor chicks."

Mathis grins. "Hey, from what I've seen so far, Astor Park girls are smokin'."

"Yeah, they're easy on the eyes," Dom agrees. "But they've got sticks up their asses. Their daddies are billionaires, you know? Most of them act like they're doing you a favor just by talking to you."

"They don't all have sticks up their asses," I disagree, thinking of Ella and Val, the two coolest chicks I know.

I'd add Hartley to that list, too, except I don't know her well enough yet. Her mom, however, definitely had a stick or two up her ass last night. What the hell was up with that woman? I've met a lot of prissy, snooty rich bitches, but even the snootiest of them have a default code of manners. We're Southerners, for Chrissake. You're invited inside and insulted over a glass of sweet tea and a slice of cake. Doors are not slammed in your face.

Dom rolls his eyes. "That's another thing you should know," he says to Mathis. "Royal here has hooked up with every chick at this school."

"I'm a stud," I confirm, shoving my feet into my sneaks. "Stick with me, QB, and you'll get laid no problem."

Chuckling, Mathis wanders over to me. "Gee, thanks, Royal—was that your name?"

"Easton Royal," I confirm.

"Which one do you prefer?"

"Whichever. What do you prefer—Mathis or Brandon?"

"Bran, actually."

"Bran? Like the stuff in cereal that makes you shit?"

Mathis throws his head back in laughter. "Yeah, like the stuff that makes you shit." He claps me on the shoulder. "You're a funny guy, Royal."

Don't I know it.

He's still laughing as we file into the gym. Normally I partner up with Pash or Babbage, but since I wouldn't mind getting to know my new quarterback, I offer to spot him.

"Sure," Mathis says gratefully.

He lies on the bench. I stand at the head of it, my hands hovering over the heavy barbell. I study his arms—they're long, muscular but not too bulky. I hope he's got a decent throwing arm.

"So . . . Bellfield Prep, huh? Means you were living over in Hunter's Point, right?" I ask, referring to a town about twenty minutes west of Bayview.

"Still living there, actually. My folks weren't about to pack up and move just so I could be fifteen minutes closer to Astor. My mom loves her garden too much to give it up."

"What does your family do?"

"What do you mean?"

"Where did the Mathis fortune come from?" I clarify in a dry voice. "Oil? Exports? Transportation?"

"Oh, ah, there's no fortune. We're middle class, I guess? My mom's a teacher and my dad is an accountant. I'm here on scholarship or I wouldn't be able to swing it. Tuition's about ten times the cost of Bellfield." He sets the bar in place and takes a couple deep breaths. His face is red from the strain of lifting.

"Ah. Gotcha." I feel a little stupid for making the assumption, but Mathis is a cool guy. He didn't bat an eyelash over my questioning or look offended or embarrassed by his social status. Not that I go around bragging that my dad's part of the three-comma club, because what does my dad's money got to do with me?

The conversation keeps flowing even as we switch places so I can lift while he spots me. He tells me that he started for Bellfield last year during the regular season, but a broken wrist kept him off the field for the playoffs. His backup lost them the first playoff game by throwing three interceptions, which is why Astor Park never played Bellfield Prep in the postseason. They've never made it there and are apparently pissed that Bran left them for Astor.

"But Astor opens doors, you know?" he says. "Better curriculum, better connections."

I wouldn't know. I've never moved outside the Astor social circle. If you're part of that world, you went to St. Mary's School for Boys and Girls, even if you weren't religious. After St. Mary's, you were shuttled to Lake Lee Academy. Finally, you ended up at Astor.

We're a breeding ground of privilege with our trust funds, luxury cars, and designer clothing. And private jets, if you're a Royal.

"What's the social scene like at Bellfield?" I ask. Judging by the guys I fight and gamble with, the only difference between an Astor Prep punk and a kid from the dock is the price of the liquor we drink. We bleed the same, hurt the same.

"I'm not much of a partier. I don't drink."

"Like during the season?"

"At all. My parents are really strict," he admits as I hop off the bench after my set. "My dad's a football fanatic. As in, football is life. He monitors my food and drink intake. We have a nutritionist who comes to the house once a week with new diet plans. I've had a personal trainer since I was seven."

That sounds like a nightmare. I can't imagine my dad monitoring all the toxins I put in my body. There'd be too many of them for him to keep up with. The only thing he really puts his foot down about is flying. But as much as it bugs me that I'm banished from the cockpit, I know it probably has something to do with the lawsuit Dad dealt with a while back. One of the test pilots for Atlantic Aviation died, and the post-accident investigation turned up a drinking problem. Dad's been strict on the *no bottle to throttle* rule ever since.

"That's brutal," I say sympathetically.

Bran shrugs. "Football's my ticket to a better life. It's worth the sacrifice. Plus, your body is your temple, right?"

I grab a towel and use it to mop my sweaty neck. "Nah, man," I answer with a grin. "My body's a playground. No, wait. It's an amusement park. Eastonland. Chicks come from far and wide to experience those wild Eastonland rides."

Mathis hoots. "You always such a cocky bastard, Royal?"

"Always!" Pash confirms from the other side of the weight room.

"Seriously, it's fucking annoying," another teammate, Preston, chimes in.

"They're just jealous," I explain to Mathis. "Especially Preston." In a stage whisper I add, "Poor guy's still a virgin. Shhh. Don't tell anyone."

Preston flips up his middle finger. "Screw off, Royal. You know that's not true."

"Nothing to be ashamed of," I assure him, enjoying the way his face gets redder and redder. Preston's so easy to needle. "Someone's got to be around to exchange purity rings with the debutantes."

The jokes and trash-talking go on for the rest of practice, and even though it's fun, I'm disappointed we're only lifting today. I would've liked to let out some aggression on the turf, but Coach takes strength and conditioning as seriously as field drills.

After a quick shower, I change into my uniform and march across campus with one destination in mind: Hartley Wright's locker.

The first thing I see when I get there is Hartley's butt. Well, kind of. She's standing on her tiptoes, straining to reach something on the top shelf of her locker. Her skirt rides up, revealing a hint of bare thigh.

She didn't hem the skirt, I realize. All the other chicks at this school hem their skirts to the shortest length that Beringer lets them get away with. Hartley leaves hers long, just above her knees.

"Lemme get that for you," I offer.

She starts in surprise and bangs her head on the underside of the locker shelf. "Ow!" she exclaims. "Dammit, Royal."

I snicker as she rubs her head. "Sorry. Was just trying to be helpful." I lean past her and grab the textbook she was reaching for. "PS, maybe don't put stuff on the top shelf if you're too short to get it?"

Hartley scowls at me. "I'm not short."

"Really?" I arch a brow and peer down at her.

"Really," she insists. "I'm just vertically challenged."

"Uh-huh. Let's call it that, sure." I place the book in her waiting hands, then rummage around in my backpack. "Speaking of me being awesome and helpful—"

"Nobody said you were awesome *or* helpful," she interjects.

I ignore that. "I made copies of my calc notes for you. You're starting class today, right?"

Hartley nods slowly. She looks a bit suspicious as she accepts the notes from me. "This is very . . . nice of you."

I get the feeling she'd rather punch herself in the face than compliment me, which triggers a huge smile. "You're welcome."

"I didn't say thank you."

"You said I was awesome—"

"Didn't say that, either."

"—which is the same as saying thank you." I move closer and pat her on the head. She bats my hand away. "So, you're welcome. By the way, I went over to your house last night and—"

"You what?" she screeches.

"I went over to your house." I stare at her. "Is that not allowed?"

"Who answered the door?" she demands. "Was it my sister? How'd she look?"

How'd she look? She's acting like she doesn't even live there. "I don't know. Your mom answered and when I asked if you were home, she said no and slammed the door in my face. What's up with that?"

"My mother's not the nicest" is all she says, sounding resigned.

"No shit."

Around us, the hallway is starting to get crowded. I notice Felicity and a couple of her friends lurking five feet away. They look mighty interested in my conversation with Hartley. I angle my body to block their view.

"So. Where were you?" I ask. "Hot date?"

"No. I don't date." Her tone is absent, and she's gnawing on the side of her thumb.

"Like ever?"

"Like now. I don't have time for dating."

I frown. "Why not?"

She looks at me. "You're super cute—"

I perk up, but she's not done.

"—and in another life I'd jump all over the chance to date you, but I don't have the time or energy to be with someone like you."

"What the hell does that mean?"

"It means I'm going to class." She slams her locker shut.

"So we'll see each other at lunch, then."

I don't get a response. But then again, I'm Easton Royal. I don't really need one. I know she'll come around. They all do.

Five

I WASTE TEN minutes of my lunch period waiting for Hartley to show up. When my stomach starts growling, I trudge into the dining hall. What's her deal, anyway? She admitted that I'm "super cute" and that she wants to be with me. End of story. Why she keeps running makes no sense. Doesn't have time for me? Like I'm some high-maintenance boyfriend who needs nonstop attention? Ha.

"Easton! Over here!" A high-pitched voice hails me.

I cringe. Claire refuses to let me go, even though we haven't dated for a year. Unlike Hartley, I know it's not nice to ignore people, but I also know that when I give Claire even the smallest bit of attention, she takes it the wrong way. A hello in the hallway becomes a prom proposal in her head. If I eat lunch with her, she'll be sending out save-the-date notices for an impending engagement party.

Gritting my teeth, I grab a tray and load it up with food, then make my way across the cafeteria. With its oak-paneled walls, round tables, and floor-to-ceiling windows, the massive room looks more like a restaurant in a private club than a cafeteria. But that's Astor Park Prep for you. Wealth and excess is the only way we roll.

I think the reason I'm interested in Hartley is because I'm bored. I've seen every face here at Astor for the last three years. Some of them, like Felicity Worthington, I've known since I was in diapers. She was just as irritating at the age of five as she is now.

School is boring. I already know all the stuff that Ms. Mann is teaching. My grades aren't great, but that's because the subject matter is too easy. It's not like I need good grades to test planes, as long as I know what I'm doing. And I do. I just can't be bothered to show it right now.

Hartley is a nice distraction. A puzzle whose pieces don't all fit together. And to be fair to her, I'm a good time. She'd be lucky to have me. So really, I shouldn't let it go. For her sake and all.

Ella and her best friend, Val, are already at our usual table when I walk up. So are my twin brothers and their girl, Lauren.

Yeah, Sawyer and Seb share a girlfriend, but who am I to judge? I hooked up with my calc teacher yesterday.

"What's wrong?" Sawyer asks when I park my ass in the chair next to Ella's.

"Nothing," I lie.

Across the table, Val's dark eyes twinkle mischievously. "You're lying."

"I am not," I lie again.

"You totally are. I always know when you're lying." She shoves a strand of dark hair behind her ear and leans toward me. "You get this little crease right here—" Val's index finger traces a line across my forehead. "Sort of like, 'It's painful for me to lie, but a man's gotta do what a man's gotta do.' Know what I mean?"

I capture Val's hand before she can snatch it back. "Always looking for any excuse to touch me, eh, Carrington?"

She snickers. "You wish, Royal."

"I do," I answer solemnly. "I wish it so hard. Every night when I'm lying in bed all alone."

"Poor baby." Val pinches the center of my palm until I release her hand. "Keep wishing, Easton. All this goodness"—she gestures to herself with a flourish—"is off-limits."

I roll my eyes. "Why? Are you keeping yourself pure for your nonexistent boyfriend?"

"Ouch." But she's grinning. "And no, I'm not staying pure for anyone. I'm just not into *you*."

"Ouch," I echo, but we both know I'm not broken up about it, either.

"I honestly can't believe you two never hooked up," Ella says with a laugh. She's got a plate of chicken penne on her tray, but she's just moving her fork around the pasta without taking any bites. "You're like the same person."

"Which is why we never hooked up," Val answers.

"Not true," I object. "We made out once."

Ella's jaw drops. "You did?"

Val looks like she's about to deny it, but then she bursts out laughing. "Oh my God, we totally did. Mara Paulson's Sweet Sixteen party! I forgot about that."

I sigh. "Okay, that one hurt. You forgot we made out?"

Ella is grinning at us. "But you didn't go out?"

Val shakes her head. "We decided we were better off as friends."

"Too bad," Ella remarks, her face falling. "Think of all the double dates we could've gone on."

I watch my stepsister move her fork around some more. Reed asked me to watch out for her while he was away. So I'm always watching her. Like, right now, I'm watching how she's yet again not eating.

I'm also watching the way her skirt rides up as she leans forward to rest both elbows on the table. Unlike Hartley, Ella does have her skirt hemmed short. Reed always liked it that way. I can't say I disagree.

"East . . ." It's the softest of warnings, courtesy of Sawyer. My younger brother noticed where my gaze had wandered.

Ella notices, too, and she reaches over to smack my arm. "Easton! Stop looking up my skirt!"

I fake innocence. "I was doing no such thing."

"Bull," she accuses.

"Bull," Sawyer, the traitor, echoes. Seb nods silently beside him. Those two little shits are always ganging up on me.

I drop the act and flash Ella my best little-boy smile. "Sorry, sis. Habit."

Val laughs. "Habit?"

"Yeah, habit." I shrug. "I see a girl in a short skirt and I wanna know what's under the skirt. So sue me. Besides . . ." Waggling my eyebrows, I tug a strand of Ella's blond hair and twirl it around my finger. "Reed can pretend it didn't happen all he wants, but the first Royal lips you ever tasted were mine. We all know that."

"Easton!" Her cheeks turn beet red.

"It's true," I tease.

"That doesn't mean we have to talk about it. Ever." She

glares at me. "And anyway, you know I was just using you to forget about Reed."

I slap a hand over my heart. "Wow. And I thought Val was the evil one."

"Hey!" Val objects, but she's still laughing.

"Oh whatever," Ella says, waving a hand. "You said you were into someone else, too."

I furrow my brow. "Did I?"

"Yes."

I shove a few French fries into my mouth, chewing slowly. "Was I drunk when I said that?"

Ella thinks it over, then nods. "Wasted."

"Thought so. I say lots of dumb things when I'm wasted." And I'm pretty sure that when my lips were on Ella's, I wasn't pretending she was anyone but herself. Ella is hot. I wanted to hook up with her, badly, before she got with my brother.

Nowadays, it'd feel incestuous, but I still have fun teasing her about it.

"Some chick is staring at you."

The observation comes from Sawyer, who's looking behind me in amusement.

I twist around, and just like that, my spirits rise higher. Hartley is sitting at a table near the window. Her guarded gray eyes meet mine for one brief moment before breaking contact.

"Who is that?" Lauren asks curiously, taking a sip from her Evian bottle.

"My new best friend." I wink at the table full of shocked faces before I leap to my feet and make my way to Hartley.

Without waiting for an invitation, I plop down in the chair across from hers and steal a roll off her plate.

Hartley sighs. Loudly. "Don't you get tired of following me around?"

"Don't you get tired of playing hard to get?"

"I can see how that would bother you if I was actually playing hard to get, but in reality, which you apparently have a very thin grasp of, I'm just not interested."

I thrum my fingers on the table. That's possible. There are girls who haven't been interested in me. Maybe. I guess, theoretically, that's true.

"You look stumped."

"To be honest, I've never had anyone turn me down. I'm not saying that to be braggy, but it's the truth. I've got a good sense about this sort of thing. Besides, you already admitted you think I'm hot."

"I used the word 'cute' and I also said that even if I were in the market, I wouldn't pick you. You had your hand up our teacher's skirt yesterday."

I ignore the teacher jab and focus on the positive. "Cute. Hot. It's the same thing. We might as well hook up. I'm free tonight."

Hartley exhales again. Louder. "Easton," she starts.

I fold both hands on the tabletop and lean closer. "Yes, babe?"

Exasperation fills her silvery eyes. "You know what? Forget it." She reaches into the messenger bag on the empty chair beside her. "I've got some reading to do for Lit."

I sit there, slack-jawed, as she pulls out a book and proceeds to eat one-handed while she reads. She tunes me out. Completely.

I'm fascinated with her. She's attracted to me, but she's not going to do anything about it?

"I'm not dating anyone."

She doesn't respond.

"You got a man?"

Silence.

I tap my fingers against the table. Another guy is a complication, and ordinarily I don't do complicated. But if she had a boyfriend, that's something she would've brought up within the first five minutes of talking. At least, if she had a boyfriend she was serious about. And then the light bulb turns on.

"Tough breakup, huh? Aw. Good thing I've a nice shoulder here for you to cry on." I give said shoulder a pat.

This earns me another long, heavy sigh. "I'm not suffering from any tough breakup. I don't have a boyfriend, not that it's any of your business, and I would still like for you to leave me alone."

This is all rattled off rapid-fire. She doesn't even bother to raise her gaze from her book. I don't think she's reading, though. Her eyes are fixed on one spot.

I decide to call her on her bullshit. "You'd be more believable if you were actually reading."

She flushes slightly and flips the page. The one she's been reading for the last minute or so. I finish the roll and grab a carrot stick from her plate. Her lips smush together, but she doesn't say anything. I proceed to demolish the rest of her lunch. I mean, if she's not gonna eat it, I don't want it to go to waste.

When there's nothing left but her water, I consider leaving.

"Why is everyone looking at us?"

Hartley's irritable remark stops me. I glance around the room. I hadn't noticed we'd become the center of attention. The hyenas are salivating, smelling fresh meat. Felicity

Worthington is at a table with a few other senior girls, their heads all bent together as they whisper about this latest development. Easton Royal sitting with a girl in the dining hall? Huge.

Claire also watches us, and she isn't pleased. She's glaring daggers at Hartley, but her expression softens when it meets mine. She gets this wounded doe-eyed look that one of Reed's obsessive exes used to give him after he dumped her. I really need to find a way to nix this Claire thing.

Blanching, Hartley picks up her water bottle and takes a nervous sip. "Seriously, this is dumb. Why are they staring?"

I shrug. "I'm a Royal."

"Lucky you."

"Is that sarcasm I detect?"

"Absolutely," she says cheerfully.

Rolling my eyes, I swipe her water from her hand and take a long swig. I hear an audible gasp from Claire's direction. Okay, my ex needs to chill. Like really.

"Sounds like you're the one with the bad breakup," Hartley murmurs, still pretending to read her book.

"It wasn't at the time. We both agreed we weren't interested."

"So why is she offended you're drinking out of my water bottle?"

"I guess she forgot that she was tired of my shit?"

This generates a choked laugh from Hartley. "What'd you do? Sleep around?"

"Nah. I think I didn't pay much attention to her. She mentioned something about me being a bad boyfriend."

"Nothing that comes out of your mouth convinces me you'd be a good one."

"Ouch." I pass the bottle back to Hartley. "I probably just need more practice."

"Pass."

"You ever have a boyfriend?" I ask, genuinely curious. Hartley's more tight-lipped about her past than a clam out of water.

"Yes, I've had a boyfriend." She lays her book down and takes a swig of water.

"What happened? He dick you over? You get tired of him? Get too busy? What?"

She leans forward, her eyes narrow. "What does it matter?"

"I'm curious." A voice clears behind me. I ignore it. "You're interesting, and I'd like to know more about you."

The throat clearing gets louder. Hartley's eyes widen, and the corners of her mouth tip up. "I think someone wants your attention."

"I'm having a conversation with you."

"*Easton.*" Footsteps close in on me, and then Claire's fingers curve over my shoulder. "Didn't you hear me?"

I swallow a sigh. *Manners*, I remind myself. "Yeah, but I'm having a conversation—"

"I'm done. You can have my seat." Hartley stands up and waves at her chair.

Claire beams. "Thank you."

"Wait a sec." I grab for Hartley's wrist, but she steps out of reach. Annoyed, I turn to Claire. "Hartley and I need a moment."

"We really don't," Hartley says. A second later, she skips away.

"We aren't done." I hop up and hurry after Hartley.

Behind me, Claire calls out my name again. I keep walking. I ignore the amused glances of Ella and the others. I'm focused solely on Hartley, who I manage to catch at the entrance to the dining hall.

"It's cruel of you to leave me alone with Claire," I joke. "Don't you have a heart?"

Hartley rubs a finger along her forehead, and I notice a thin white line on her left wrist. It looks like a surgical scar. Must've been a real bad break if she needed surgery for it.

"Here's the deal, Easton. I don't like being the center of attention and clearly you do." She gestures toward the crowd of faces turned in our direction. "I'm trying to lay low this year. I don't want—and can't afford—to have all this attention pointed at me."

The cryptic statement summons a frown. "Why not?"

"Because" is all she says.

But she doesn't move away.

I edge closer.

Still, she doesn't move. It's as if her feet are stuck to the floor.

I lower my head until my nose is inches from the top of her adorable ear.

I'm so close that I can feel the heat of her skin right through the starchy material of her skirt. My fingers find her wrist. Her pulse is beating wildly. Or maybe it's me.

She smells fantastic, fruity and fresh. I want to shove my nose against her neck and breathe her in. And then maybe lick my way up her jaw until I reach her pouty lips. Then I'd lick those, too, before sliding my tongue in her mouth.

And now I have a hard-on in the middle of the cafeteria.

Hartley's gaze lowers to where my hand is touching hers. "Royal," she warns.

"Mmm?" I'm too distracted by how dark her hair is, how it curls so neatly around her ear. The image of Hartley's hair hanging like a curtain around my face flashes through my head, and I almost groan out loud.

"There's no way you don't feel this," I say, my voice sounding low and husky to my ears.

Her eyes widen slightly. "Feel what?"

The heat. The *I want you so bad* rush that's jolting through me right now.

"This," I mutter, and before I can stop myself, I move even closer.

My mouth zeroes in on hers.

I hear several gasps this time. A flurry of whispers. I ignore them. I'm fixated on Hartley. Two more inches and our lips will touch. One more inch and my tongue will be in her mouth. Half an inch and—

Something cold and wet soaks my face.

I jerk back in surprise, one hand reaching up to touch my cheek. Water?

For Chrissake, she just dumped the entire contents of her water bottle over my head.

"What the hell!" I say in outrage.

Hartley looks as mad as I feel. "You're such an asshole," she hisses.

My jaw falls open. "Me? You're the one who threw water at me!"

"I *just* told you I don't want the attention and you tried to *kiss* me in front of the whole school! But you don't care what anyone else wants, right, Easton? Only what *you* want matters, because you're a Royal, remember?"

She slaps my hand away, and I watch in dismay as she storms off.

"Easton?" a plaintive voice says.

I drop my head against the doorframe. Fucking great. I can't get rid of my ex, and I keep alienating the girl I want. My senior year isn't going the way I thought it would.

Not at all.

Six

"DO YOU THINK I'm an asshole?" I ask later that night. Glum, I poke one of the apples on the counter as I watch Ella slice one up for me.

"What kind of question is that?" She drops the slices into a bowl and slides it down the counter.

"So the answer is yes?"

"Of course not." She pushes on her tiptoes and pats me on the head, like I'm a little puppy. I don't like that feeling—the one that makes me wonder if Ella thinks I'm five years old.

"Why do you treat me like I'm a kid when I'm three months older than you?"

"Because you act like one."

"I do not."

"Yes, you do. You totally act like a little kid."

I bristle. "Is that why you never saw me like you saw Reed? Because I'm a *little kid*?" I might've been Ella's first Royal, but Reed has always been first in her heart. And that bugs me.

Everyone's always loved me best. Mom, girls at school. Hell, old ladies get stars in their eyes anytime I come into their orbit. Reed's face wears a perpetual scowl and Gideon never had the time of day for anyone but Savannah Montgomery. I'm the golden child, yet lately I keep losing.

I catch a reflection of myself in the glass cupboard. I'm still as good-looking as ever. I'm charming and hilarious. My body could be on the cover of a magazine, partly thanks to good genes, but I work on it, too—lifting and football. Claire can't stop chasing after me and it's been ages since we went out.

Nah, I haven't lost it. Ella got hooked by Reed early on for some inexplicable reason, and Hartley Wright just has a rod up her ass. She's antisocial.

"I'm not a kid," I mutter.

Ella sighs. "Okay, what's really going on here? Is everything all right?"

I avoid her concerned gaze. "Why wouldn't it be?"

"Are you sure? Because you've looked bummed ever since that girl dumped water on your head at lunch—what's her name again?"

I manage a half-hearted grin. "Hartley, and I'm not bummed about that. I'm Easton Royal and the world's my oyster. Besides, she'll come around eventually." I pinch Ella's cheek. "Gotta go, little sis. Don't wait up for me tonight."

She stiffens. "No fighting."

"No fighting," I echo with the roll of my eyes.

"Easton . . ."

"I'm serious." I hold up my hands in an innocent gesture. "It's Tuesday, anyway. No fights on Tuesdays."

Ella doesn't look entirely convinced. "So then where are you going?"

"Somewhere that good girls shouldn't be seen." I grab the rest of the apples and walk out.

"Easton!" she yells after me.

I give her a wave but don't turn around. I don't want Ella following me tonight. She'd be full of disapproval and that would take the shine off my glow.

Upstairs, I throw on my favorite pair of jeans. The rips in the knees are getting larger and are starting to look less like a fashion statement and more like I stole them from a dumpster, but I don't like throwing shit out. Besides, where I'm going, it doesn't pay to look like you have money. I find a hoodie on the floor and shrug that over my favorite black tank.

Palming my keys and a few hundred dollars, I take the back stairs to avoid Ella, Dad, and all the other prying eyes. In the garage, I pull the tarp off the splurge that I'm hoping Dad hasn't noticed. The motorcycle is used, but I couldn't swing a more expensive one without setting off warning bells in the accounting office. Any purchase over ten grand is flagged these days. I'm kinda glad of that anyway, because some of the places I've been going, something pricey would stand out and likely get boosted.

I roll the black-and-silver Yamaha halfway down the drive before climbing on and gunning it the remainder of the way. It takes thirty minutes to reach my destination.

Outside the run-down house, there are a half-dozen people smoking—cigarettes, of course, because weed's not legal here and probably won't be until the entire country okays it. Inside is a different story. Not only is there weed, but a whole drugstore of choices. I didn't come for that, though. I'm trying to stay away from the drugs, although it hasn't been easy.

Just seeing a joint can make my mouth water and my tongue tingle. I force my eyes away from the group who are cutting white powder at the table and make myself tromp down the stairs. It's hard, but I promised my brothers, and after seeing what it did to my mom, I've tried to eliminate that one addiction. I don't have a death wish. I just want to have a good time. The pills helped settle me down, mellowed me out enough to enjoy life, but I know that too much of a good thing can lead to disaster.

At the bottom of the stairs, a guy with a gut large enough to be seen from the Pacific greets me with a finger salute. "Royal."

Tony's size is deceiving. He looks soft, but he's the one guy down here you don't want to piss off. One swipe from his paw and you'll be out cold.

I clasp the bouncer's hand and go in for a manly side hug. He gives me a bone-rattling back slap before moving aside. In the dimly lit cement box, four tables are set up. No smoking is allowed down here due to the fact that it's already a fire hazard. There's only one exit and that's up the stairs.

There's plenty of booze. Three of the tables are already filled, but the fourth has empty chairs. Although the dealer is new to me, I still throw my five-spot into the middle.

"Long time, no see, Royal," says the guy next to me.

"Hey, Nate Dog." We slap hands. His is coarse from working on the docks. I met him after a fight once and he invited me to one of these games. I think it's because he knew I had money and wanted to relieve me of some of it. Whatever the motivation, this place is a good way to blow off steam. I don't mind losing, and, for the most part, I break even.

Despite me having at least three inches on him, I still feel small around Nate D. It's not just his age but the way he carries himself. He knows who he is. Gotta admire that.

The third player lifts his chin in my direction, acting like a tough guy. He straightens his shoulders under the oversized hoodie designed, I guess, to give him more bulk than he really has.

"You got a problem with me?" the kid asks, jutting his chin out.

"No. Why?"

"You were staring," Nate D informs me.

"Yeah, look at your own cards." The kid is getting on my nerves.

"You're just so cute that I can't help myself," I say.

Nate D covers his mouth with his arm to stifle a laugh, and even the stone-faced dealer cracks a smile.

The kid doesn't think I'm amusing. Too bad the punk has no sense of humor. Someone hands me a bottle of beer as the dealer whips out the first hand. I chug half the bottle before coming up for air.

I might've given up one addiction, but I can't shake all of them. I told Ella once that it's part of my genetic makeup. I get obsessed with shit. That's just how I'm built and I'm not going to be sorry for it. I don't hurt anyone—or, at least, I try to avoid it.

I pick up my cards and start playing. Not only does the punk have no sense of humor, but he's bad at cards. He doesn't pay attention to the ones that have been played and he makes reckless bets.

After five quick hands, he's lost all the money in front of him while my pile keeps growing.

"You're lucky tonight, son," Nate D sighs, throwing his three sixes on the table in frustration.

"That's your second straight in five hands." The kid scowls at me. "You're cheating, aren't you?"

I pause in the middle of raking in the kitty. "I don't even know the dealer's name, so how am I supposed to be cheating?"

"I was winning until you got here. It's real suspicious," he says.

I roll my eyes.

"Play your cards," Nate barks.

The punk grits his teeth but backs down.

I look down at my cards and pull out two. "Two, please," I tell the dealer.

"Please? Like we're in some country club," scoffs Tough Guy, who folds his cards together. "I pass. My hand's a winner."

He ends up losing to Nate. We cycle through another deck with Tough Guy losing another two grand. I take his last hundred in a major bluff where I have jack shit. Nate folds and Tough Guy follows suit.

"Let's see your cards," he growls.

"No." Maybe if it was with Nate and a few others, I wouldn't mind, but this guy's been an ass all night. I'm not in a friendly mood and haven't been since lunch. Ella was right—getting reamed out by Hartley *did* upset me.

"I want to see your cards!" He reaches across the table to grab them, but I flick them toward the dealer, who smoothly slides them into the discard pile.

"Sit down," I order.

"This is bullshit!" Tough Guy slams his fist on the table.

"Take off your clothes." He lunges forward as if to snatch my hoodie off my back.

I scramble out of the way while Nate arm-bars Tough Guy back into his chair. "Settle down," Nate warns, flicking a finger in my direction.

Sullenly, Tough Guy crosses his arms. "I'm not playing another dime until he takes off his hoodie. I'm not bad at cards."

I snort.

"I'm not," he insists.

Nate tugs on the back of my sweatshirt. "Just do it so we can play."

In other words, shut up so we can take more of this easy mark's money.

I shrug out of the dockworker's grip. "No. I'm not cheating and I'm not taking my clothes off because some dipshit who can't bluff tells me to."

Nate gets to his feet. "His money's green. Just take it off, Royal."

Talk about bullshit. Nate is so hungry for cash that he's gonna throw me under the table? Forget that.

"Take it off, cheater," Tough Guy taunts. He's all false confidence now that Nate's backing him.

I smile humorlessly. "No."

Nate tugs on my arm, and I whip forward out of his grip. I'm not sure where it all goes wrong, but after that, it's a blur. The table tips over. Money falls to the ground. Knuckles come out of nowhere and connect with my jaw, spinning me around.

I jump up with my fists flying. I don't know who I'm fighting or even why, but it feels good. I take a kick in the gut and two punches to my upper body, but I land even more. I fight even though sweat and blood are clouding my eyes and filling my mouth. I fight until a stream of cold water blasts across my face. Huh. More water. Second time in one day.

"Enough!"

I find myself on my back looking up into Tony's angry face. He's got the end of a hose in his hand. My ears ring from his shouting or maybe a blow to the skull. I give my head a rough shake, but the ringing doesn't go away.

"Time to go, Royal."

I pick myself off the ground and blurrily take in the scattered tables, the floor littered with cash, and the bodies lying around.

"I didn't start it," I slur.

"Don't care. Night's a bust thanks to you. Get out."

I plaster on a smile, even though it hurts like hell. "Aren't you blaming the wrong party here? Who was that guy, anyway? I've been playing here for—"

"Are you deaf, son? I told you to get your pretty-boy ass out of my basement. And don't come back." He roughly shoves me toward the stairs.

The ringing persists. I stagger toward the exit, dragging myself up the steps. Man, my head *kills*.

The house is mostly empty. Outside, there're a few people hanging out on the porch. I give a hasty wave and stumble down the steps.

The sidewalk shifts in front of me. I hold out my hand to steady myself but find nothing except air, and my forward momentum causes me to trip over my own feet. I fall to my knees.

Laughter lights up behind me. Assholes.

I push to my feet and then straighten. My bike is only a block away. Once I get there, I'll be fine.

I lurch down the sidewalk, weaving and tottering, but I make it to my bike. I throw a leg over and try to start it. The motor rumbles but sputters out after a few seconds. I slam my hand on the tank and restart it. This time it roars to life. Good boy.

"Easton?"

I swing my head toward the familiar voice. What the hell?

Hartley Wright's face appears in front of me, except there are like three of them. Three Hartleys to yell at me and be mean to me and soak me with water for having the nerve to want to kiss her. Awesome.

"Are you following me around?" I mutter.

"You wish." The three Hartleys turn to leave.

I ease off on the clutch and the bike rolls forward.

"Wait." She and her two doppelgangers return. "Come on. I'll take you home."

"You live around here?" Even with my shitty eyesight, I can see it's a place where no Astor Park kid lives. Not even a scholarship student would come from this shithole, right?

"Come on." She tugs on my sleeve. "If you drive off in this condition, you'll hit some kid and ruin an entire family's life."

"Thanks for your concern for me," I say sarcastically, but a sudden bone-deep weariness washes over me. She's not wrong. My head's ringing, I'm seeing double or triple, and my entire body aches.

Slowly, I back the bike against the curb and flip the kick-stand down.

Or try to. I make four attempts before she leans down and pushes my foot aside.

"Why are you helping me?" I mumble.

"I have no clue."

"You were a bitch to me at lunch."

"You deserved it."

She might've said something else, but my entire view turns black.

Seven

THE DEEP BASS of Kendrick Lamar's "Humble" pounding between my ears has me searching for the snooze button. I hate early-morning practices. Eyes still closed, I fumble on my nightstand for my phone, but instead of a hard wood surface, I find nothing but air.

I reach out farther and end up dumping myself on the floor. The impact wakes me up.

As I scrape myself off the carpet, I realize that I'm not home. There's a dingy carpet underneath my feet and a ratty sofa behind me. Two folding chairs sit at a small wooden table to my right. Just beyond that is a tiny space housing a refrigerator, stove, and sink.

The need to piss grips me. Two strides and I have the sole door in the joint open. The bathroom, like the rest of the place, is miniscule. A small sink, stand-up shower, and toilet fill the space.

I use the can, wash my hands, and dry them on a surprisingly nice hand towel. I fold it in half and hang it on the ring where I found it.

Back in the living space, I begin remembering last night's

events. I drove out to the slums on my Yamaha, played a few hands of cards, and then got into a fight.

I must've blacked out from a punch to the head. No, wait. Something happened before that.

Hartley.

Hartley brought me here right before I passed out. I dimly remember her ordering me to move my ass and then climbing an unholy number of steps.

But if I slept on the sofa, where did she sleep? This place doesn't have another bedroom, and the sofa's not big enough for two. She would've had to literally sleep on top of me. Given her aversion to me, I'm guessing she slept on the floor.

Crap.

I drag a hand through my hair. No, I'm not going to feel guilty about this. I never asked for her help, and I certainly didn't ask to sleep on her couch even if I did need a place to crash last night.

I find my shoes and my sweatshirt on the table. Inside my sweatshirt is about three grand, which means she found my money and didn't take a dime. She should've taken a finder's fee.

I peel off a few bills and leave them on the table. Under my shoes there's a note with a key taped to it.

Lock up and put the key in this envelope and stick it in the mailbox downstairs.

I tap the note against my chin. This girl is a mystery. Her parents live in an expensive mansion. Her dad is a big-shot prosecutor. Hartley, meanwhile, lives in the worst part of Bayview, where the walls are so thin I can hear the music her downstairs neighbor is playing, and yet she attends the best school in the state. What the heck is up with that?

I figured my senior year was going to be boring as hell. Ella spends most of her time talking to Reed on the phone, texting Reed, or visiting him up at State on the weekends. The twins are busy with their lives. Gideon's at college, and when he does come home, he only wants to chill with Savannah.

I'm the odd man out and have been my whole life. Before Gid left home, it was the oldest two and the youngest two, with me futzing around in the middle.

Mom said that this developed my individualism and self-sufficiency. I could always find something to do. I didn't need my brothers. Plus, I made friends easier than any of them. I had dozens of friends. My contact list was full of them.

Yet . . . I didn't call even one person on that list last night. Instead, I tried to get on my bike and ride home like some dumb asshole whose brain is smaller than his ballsack.

I leave Hartley's apartment and lock up, but I pocket the key instead of sliding it into the envelope. Practice is in thirty minutes, which means I'm going to be late. So much for setting a precedent with yesterday's early arrival.

My cell phone shows a bunch of texts from Ella.

> Where r u
> Callum looking for u

Shit. At this rate, I'm never going to get in the air again. I really need to work on my decision-making skills in the future.

> I covered for u. Told him u left already

I walk toward the stairs. The alley next to Hartley's building smells like cat poop and dog piss and—well, it pretty much reeks like every bad animal smell you can think of. It's brutal.

I text back, Thanks

✦   ✦   ✦

EVERYONE'S STILL IN the locker room by the time I arrive. Practice this morning consists of drills, clubbing and running, bull rushing, and combo bag drills. My legs feel like jelly at the end of it.

Now that Bran Mathis is heading up the offense, Coach is no longer taking it easy on us. I think he'd given up once our QB situation got so dismal, and didn't want to risk injuring any of his remaining players for what was bound to be a write-off season. Now, all bets are off.

Pash throws me a water bottle and then chugs his own. "Damn, I'm out of shape," he gasps. "I did too much drinking and smoking this summer."

"Same." I guzzle the bottle, toss it aside, and throw myself back on the grass.

Pash collapses beside me. We both lie there staring up at the cloudless sky.

Bran, looking fresh as a daisy despite the grueling practice, saunters past and chuckles at us. "You guys need to hit the gym more. I feel great."

I weakly manage to lift one hand—so I can give him the finger. "You only feel great because you're straight-edge."

He laughs harder. "Is that an insult? 'Cause seems to me being straight-edge means I'm not the one dry-heaving on the turf."

This time Pash joins me in flipping Bran the bird.

Eventually, we're able to haul our asses off the field and

into the locker room, where I take a quick shower. I transfer Hartley's apartment key from my jeans to my uniform trousers, then head over to the admin office.

Mrs. Goldstein is there. Her wiry, tinted-blue curls halo above her small round face. Pink glasses are perched on the end of her nose.

I prop an elbow on the counter. "Mrs. G, you look fine today."

She sighs. "What do you want, Mr. Royal?"

Ignoring her obvious impatience, I tap the top of her monitor. "I stopped in because there's a mistake in my class schedule. I went to first period and apparently I'm not in that class anymore. Some kid named Wright transferred in, and when he did that, he took my spot."

The drawn-on eyebrows above her glasses crash together. "That's highly unusual."

Aka I'm full of shit. Which I am.

But I go all in on the lie. "I know, right? All I can say is, Mr. Walsh was like, 'You're not in this class anymore, Royal.' And I was like, 'What? How could this Wright person just take my spot?' And he goes, 'Well, why don't you go to the office and ask.' And—"

"All right!" she cuts in, visibly exasperated. "Just stop talking. Let me have a look."

I hide a grin. "Thanks, Mrs. G. I really think the Wright kid is in the *wrong* class."

I wink after making my terrible pun. Mrs. G likes it, though. She presses her thin lips together to keep from laughing.

"Let's see what we can do." She types a few things on her keyboard.

I twist toward the monitor to watch what she's doing—

she's just pulled up a record labeled *Wright, H.* Pushing her spectacles up to the bridge of her nose, she starts to read the schedule.

Smooth operator that I am, I lean over the counter and quickly tap the Print Screen button.

"Mr. Royal," she yelps, jumping out of her seat.

But she's not fast enough for me. I vault over the counter with one hand and land right in front of the printer.

"Thanks for printing this." Beaming at her, I snatch up the paper and jog around the end of the desk.

She grabs for me. "I didn't print it for you. Easton Royal, you get back here!"

"Your perfume smells great, Mrs. G," I call over my shoulder.

Outside the admin office, I look at the printout. There's not one overlap, except for last period. In fact, most of *Wright, H*'s classes are at opposite sides of the building as mine.

That's going to change after today.

I take the stairs two at a time. The lecture has already started by the time I breeze into Hartley's first-period class. All the chairs next to her are taken. She's surrounded by a bunch of potted plants—the kids that suck up all the oxygen because of their self-importance. I walk over to one I know and don't like much.

I bend down at her desk. "Your car's on fire."

"Omigod!" Cynthia Patterson yelps and sprints out of the classroom without a backward glance.

With a smug smile, I pull out her abandoned chair and settle in.

"Mr. Royal, what are you doing in this class?" the teacher asks.

I have no clue who she is. Based on the lines on her forehead that she's trying to Botox away, she's in her forties. Too old for me.

"I'm here to learn. Isn't that what everyone else is doing here?"

"It's Feminist Thought."

I cock my head. "Then I don't know why you're discriminating against me. If we want more gender equality, shouldn't this class be mandatory for males?"

Teach makes one last effort to kick me out. "You don't have the books necessary for the class."

"No worries. I'll share with Hartley for now. We're old friends." I pick up my desk and move it right next to hers.

"What are you doing?" she demands under her breath.

"You have an amazing ability to whisper-shout, do you know that?" I drag one of her books onto my desk.

"You have an amazing ability to piss me off."

"I've been perfecting this skill since I made my first appearance in the world." I kick my legs out. "My momma told me that I came out punching. Thanks for helping me out last night."

Reaching into my pocket, I do a quick examination of the room, then slide my hand under the table and nudge Hartley's thumb with her key.

She startles for a second, glances down, and tenses. "I told you to leave it in the mailbox," she mutters.

"Figured this would be easier."

She searches my face. "You must have a deal with the devil. It's the only way you look this good after a night of drinking and getting your ass kicked."

"I didn't get my ass kicked."

"Really? Is that why you blacked out? You didn't get hit so hard in the head that you couldn't see straight?"

"That's right."

I get nothing more than a headshake after that. Her jaw remains stiff. At the front of the room, the teacher is droning on about third-wave feminism. She's oblivious to the fact that hardly anyone is paying attention.

"Why are you here?" Hartley finally says.

"Oh, didn't I mention? I'm in all your classes now."

Her head swivels toward me. "Oh my God."

"Well, except for music. I'm tone-deaf."

"Oh my God," she says again.

"I knew you'd be excited."

She groans so loudly that everyone turns in our direction. "What was that, Ms. Wright?" the teacher asks pleasantly.

Hartley is visibly clenching her teeth. "I just can't believe that even in this progressive modern society, drug trials are still primarily based on male subjects, endangering the lives of women every day. It's shocking."

"Shocking!" agrees our teacher. "And yet true!"

The moment she resumes her lecture, Hartley scowls at me. "Switch your schedule back to whatever it was before, Royal."

"Nah."

She clutches the edge of the desk with both hands, as if fighting the urge to punch me. "Fine," she mutters. "Then stop talking to me. I'm trying to learn something."

"What's there to learn? Women deserve the same rights as men. End of story."

"Do you really believe that?"

I raise both eyebrows. "Doesn't everyone?"

"Obviously not."

I wink. "So does that mean you like me now because I'm super enlightened?"

But my charm goes unnoticed, because her eyes narrow suspiciously. "I don't know why you're following me around, but you need to stop. I'm not interested in you and will not be interested in you in the future. And from what I hear, you have a line of girls about ten deep who are ready and willing to be whatever you want, so just . . ." She makes a shooing gesture with her hand. "Just go away."

I ignore everything she said except for the obvious. "You've been asking about me, have you?"

She shuts her eyes and spins back to face the front.

"What else have you heard? I like hearing gossip about myself." I nudge her arm.

She moves it away from me and remains silent.

"My favorite rumor is that I've got a magic tongue— because it's true. I'll be happy to demonstrate for you at any time."

Hartley crosses her arms, still not saying a word to me.

I glance down at the schedule. "I can't wait for us to go to British Lit together," I whisper gleefully.

Her jaw tightens.

This is fun. This is really fun.

Eight

HARTLEY IGNORES ME all throughout Lit and then in Government, another class I'm not actually enrolled in but that I attend because it's on her schedule. The teachers don't even bat an eye at my presence; they just assume that if I'm there, then the office must know and is cool with it. Kind of irresponsible of them, if you ask me.

I guess technically what I'm doing can be considered stalking, but it's not like I'm hurting her or being extra gross about trying to get in her pants. She's just fun to bug.

Not that I'd be against getting in her pants. Or, rather, under her skirt, which covers the ass I'm currently admiring. It's lunch, and I'm lurking behind Hartley in the cafeteria line. Her cute behind juts toward me as she reaches up to grab an apple.

Yeah, I'd tap that.

"Are you for real?" She spins around with indignation, and I realize I'd said that out loud.

I'm not about to apologize, though. I'm Easton Royal. I say dumb shit all the time. That's part of my charm. "What? You should be flattered," I assure her. "I'm a hot commodity at this school."

Hartley purses her lips. I can see a hundred angry retorts flying through her head, but she's a smart girl—she's already figured out that arguing with me is absolutely pointless. I only get a kick out of it.

So she turns around and continues to pile food onto her tray.

I amble after her, doing the same. Astor Park's cafeteria choices are serious shit, and totally unnecessary. A celebrity chef is hired each semester to create a menu full of poached fish and tarragon chicken for a bunch of teenagers who would rather have burgers and fries. The cafeteria is as overdone as everything else in this joint.

"You want to sit together in Photography?" I ask her. "I heard we're pairing up this afternoon and taking pictures of our seatmates." I lean closer and murmur in her ear, "I'll show you mine if you show me yours."

Hartley plants a hand on my arm and gives me a small shove. "We're not showing each other anything. And you're not even in that class! Stop coming to my classes!"

I smile broadly at her. "And deprive you of my awesomeness? Never."

She blinks. Then blinks again. Then she stares deep into my eyes. "Easton. Do you have a . . . problem? Like . . . upstairs?" She taps the side of her head.

I burst out laughing. "Course not."

"Okay. So then you're just so full of yourself that you don't listen to a word anyone else says. Got it."

"I listen," I object.

"Uh-huh. I bet you do."

"I do!" My solemn expression lasts for about a second before a grin breaks loose. "Like, when chicks say 'Please, Easton, more!' and 'Omigod, Easton, you're the best!' I'm listening one hundred percent."

"Wow."

"I know, right? Wow."

"I don't think we're wowing about the same thing." She sighs heavily, then shuffles forward and grabs a serving spoon.

As she heaps a mountain of roasted potatoes onto her plate, I glance at her tray and realize she's taken an insane amount of food. Sure, maybe she has a big appetite in general, but she's so tiny that I can't see where she's putting away all this food. She either exercises like crazy, or . . . she's a binge-and-purge type of girl.

That would be a damn shame. I hate it when girls are afraid of their own curves. Curves make the world go 'round. Hell, the world is round because it has curves. Curves rock. Curves—

I blink myself out of my thoughts. I go on tangents sometimes, not just out loud but in my head. These are the times when I want to smoke a joint or pound some booze, calm down the frenetic thoughts that race through my mind.

I've always been a bundle of energy, though, and it was even worse when I was a kid. I was on a perpetual sugar high even when I hadn't had any sugar, bouncing around and around and around until I finally crashed, much to my parents' relief.

"You want to do something tonight?" I ask Hartley.

She stops in her tracks.

I nearly slam into her, darting backward just in time. "Is that a yes?"

Her tone is matter-of-fact. "Look. Royal. I don't know how much clearer I can make myself. I'm not interested in you."

"I don't believe you."

"Of course you don't. You can't *possibly* understand why someone might not want to be around you."

I feign a hurt look. "Why don't you want to be around me? I'm fun."

"Yeah, you are," she agrees. "You're fun, Easton. So fun that you get beat up by a bunch of degenerates on Salem Street. So fun that even when you're about to black out, you still think it's a good idea to get on your motorcycle and drive home—"

Shame pricks my chest.

"So fun that you crash at some random girl's apartment with a wad of cash in your pocket. I could have robbed you blind if I wanted to." She shrugs. "I don't have time for that kind of stuff. It's too much of a burden."

A burden?

"I didn't ask to stay over," I remind her, a bit stiffly. "And I left you cash for your trouble." I lift a pious brow. "A thank-you is all that's necessary."

"Why would I thank you? I slept on the floor while Prince Royal got my bed. I deserve to be compensated for that. I woke up with a cockroach crawling up my arm, you know."

I shiver in horror. I hate bugs. Especially cockroaches. They're the worst. And once again, I'm torn between annoyance and guilt. Because while I didn't ask for her help, she *did* help me. And she did give up her bed—well, her sofa—so my sorry, beaten-up ass would have somewhere to sleep.

"Thank you for giving me a place to stay," I say sheepishly.

Someone nudges us, so we shuffle forward again, moving toward the dessert bar. I'm not surprised when Hartley takes not one but two pieces of cheesecake.

I feel a pang of concern. I really hope she doesn't have an

eating disorder. It's bad enough that Ella's lost her appetite since Reed left. I don't want to spend the whole school year monitoring the diets of the women in my life.

"You're welcome," Hartley tells me. "But just so you know? You only get one favor from me. That was it."

Before I can inform her that I'm very much looking forward to returning the *favor*, Felicity Worthington interrupts us.

"Hi, Easton."

A few feet away stand a couple of her friends: the one who has a headband permanently attached to her head, and her blond companion in four-inch heels. The two girls whisper to each other behind their hands as Felicity stands there eyeing me like a predator.

"What's up, Felicity?" I ask lightly.

"Bonfire at my place next week," she answers sweetly. "I wanted to personally extend the invitation."

I swallow a laugh. The Worthingtons live a few houses down the shore from my house, so I've been to a ton of their parties, always hosted by Felicity's older brother, Brent. But the last one I went to ended up with Daniel Delacorte stripped naked and trussed like a pig at a luau, courtesy of Ella, Val, and Savannah Montgomery. They were punishing the asshat for drugging Ella at a different party. And then, after Daniel got free, he ran down the beach and into Reed's fist.

Needless to say, the Royals haven't been invited back since. But Brent graduated last year, so I guess Felicity's in charge now.

"Yeah, maybe," I say noncommittally. "It all depends on whether my girl wants to go." I wink and turn toward Hartley, only to find her gone.

Dammit. She's walking across the polished floor toward

the French doors that lead to the outdoor eating area. As I watch, Hartley makes a beeline for one of the farthest tables on the patio and sits with her back to the dining hall doors. Of course. Eating alone, like the antisocial princess she is.

"What girl?" Felicity narrows her eyes. "Do you mean Claire? Because she was telling Melissa the other day that you guys are back together—"

"We're not back together," I interject. Fuckin' Claire.

"Oh. Okay. Good." Felicity looks more than a little relieved. "Anyway, about the party, you don't have to text that you're coming or anything. Just show up. You're always welcome at my place."

"Yeah, maybe," I say again.

She reaches out and curls her fingers around my upper arm, lightly caressing my bicep over my shirt. "No maybes. Please come. I'd love to spend some quality time with you."

As she flounces off to rejoin her giggling friends, I have to wonder if there's even a bonfire. Maybe it's just a scheme to get me over there so she can have her way with me.

But Felicity's party is what Val and Ella are talking about when I walk up to our usual table. I knock fists with several of my teammates before sinking down in the chair next to Ella.

"I already told you, I don't want to go," she's saying to Val. "Felicity's fake sweetness gives me a toothache."

Val laces her fingers together. "Me too, but you've got no choice. You have to make an appearance, especially now that we know what they're up to."

"What who is up to?" I ask with a frown.

Val glances over at me. "The nobles are planning a revolt against the crown."

My frown deepens. "What do you mean?"

Ella notices my worried expression and reaches over to squeeze my arm. "Ignore her. She's being melodramatic."

"I am not," Val maintains. "Easton, back me up here."

"I would, babe, but I still don't know what we're talking about." I stick my fork into one of my beef empanadas and take a huge bite.

Connor Babbage, who plays cornerback for the Riders, pipes up from my other side. "That chick you were just talking to—Felicity? She wants Ella's head."

"Does she?" I turn to grin at my stepsister. "You gonna beat her up after school, little sis?"

"Hardly," Ella says in a dry voice. "But, according to Val, that's what Felicity wants to do to me."

I shrug carelessly. "Don't worry. You can take 'er."

"Catfight after school?" Babbage says hopefully.

"Keep it in your pants, Con." Val waves a hand at him before refocusing on Ella and me. "This isn't a joke, Easton. I sit behind Felicity and her bitch coven in Art History and all they do is whisper about how Felicity is going to put Ella in her rightful place."

"How's she going to do that?" I ask.

"She's not going to do anything to me," Ella insists.

Val shakes her head. "Babe, these girls don't like that you're the Royal in charge. It'd be different if it was Easton."

I fold my arms across my chest. "I'm way too lazy for that."

Val goes on as if I hadn't spoken. "But you're the interloper. The one who got Reed. The one who tamed Jordan. The one who reunited Gideon and Savannah."

"I had zero to do with Gid and Sav," Ella protests.

"It doesn't matter. It's all perception. They don't like being upstaged by you," Babbage chirps before wandering off to return his empty tray at the counter.

I slouch lower in my chair. Fucking Reed. No. This is all Gideon's fault. If he hadn't started ordering people around in his senior year, the Royals wouldn't have to do anything for Astor. We could pretend to be as blind and as oblivious as the majority of these students. Instead, because of Gideon's stupid interference, the entire school thinks we're all wired like him—ready to lead.

I want to fly, drink, fight, bang hot women. In that order. "Why are we wasting our time talking about stupid people? Can't we just enjoy our senior year?"

Val kicks me under the table. "No, you can't. You and Ella should do something. Make the kids afraid of you. It's better to be feared than loved. Yada yada yada."

"You want us to tape someone up to the outside of the school?" I say, referencing something that Jordan Carrington, Queen Bitch, did last year.

"No. Just throw your weight around. That's why I think Ella needs to go to Felicity's party. You too, Easton. You guys should start rounding up your allies now."

"We're not NATO, Val. We don't have to get allies and enemies."

She sighs. "God, I'd expect Ella to be naïve, but I thought better of you, Easton."

Whatever. I have no desire to get involved with the social politics of this stupid school. I'll back Ella up if she needs me, but from the sound of it, she doesn't want to deal with this crap, either. Can't say I blame her.

As I take another bite of my empanada, my gaze drifts to

the huge patio doors. Hartley's still sitting outside. I can't see her tray, but I doubt she's even made a dent in her mountain of food.

"What are you looking at?" Ella's curious gaze follows mine. Then she laughs. "Has she agreed to go out with you yet?"

"Of course," I lie, but both girls see right through me—they smirk, and I cave. "Fine, she hasn't. But whatevs. It'll happen. It's just a matter of time." I focus on the back of Hartley's head, noting the way her jet-black hair looks nearly blue in the sunlight. "Besides, I'm not in chase mode. I'm trying to figure her out."

Ella frowns. "What's there to figure out?"

"I don't know." I chew my lip in frustration. "She goes to Astor, right?"

Val mock gasps. "She *does*?"

"Quiet, woman." I swipe Ella's water bottle and take a long swig. "So she goes to Astor, and I know for a fact her family's got money. I've seen their house."

"I'm not following," Ella says.

"So if she's got money, then why does she live in a shoebox on Salem Street?" I furrow my brow as I think of Hartley's suffocating, crappy apartment. She doesn't even own a bed, for Chrissake.

Ella and Val look startled. "You were at her apartment?" they say in unison.

"When?" Ella demands.

I wave a dismissive hand. "That doesn't matter. All I'm saying is, she lives in a rathole while her family lives in a mansion. It's weird. And when we were in line before, she got like three lunches' worth of food. You'd think she hasn't eaten in days."

Beside me, Ella starts chewing on her lower lip, too. "Do you think she's in trouble?"

I hand over the water bottle. "Maybe? But you guys think it's weird shit, too, right?"

Val nods slowly. "Yeah. Kind of."

Ella's expression conveys worry. "It's definitely weird."

The three of us turn our heads in Hartley's direction again, but sometime during our discussion she got up and left. Her table is empty and her tray is gone.

Nine

I DON'T SEE Hartley for the rest of the day.

She's not in Photography, so I'm stuck there alone— and I'm not even enrolled in the damn class.

She's not in Music Theory, leaving me to sit beside Larry, who chirps to me about how I'm in *lurrrrrrve*. And when he's not talking about love, he's talking about those stupid Jordans. Fuckin' Larry. Also, who the hell takes Music Theory? What kind of class is this, anyway? There are physics to sounds? I zone out after a math equation for the relationship between wavelength, frequency, and speed is thrown up on the whiteboard.

And she's not in calc, a class she was so desperate to get into that she personally begged the teacher for a transfer.

Not gonna lie—I'm worried.

After I'm done with my strength and conditioning session with the Astor Park trainer, I decide to text her and hope that she doesn't ask how I got her number.

Skipping out on classes is my thing.
Where ru

No reply.

At home, I quickly eat and do my homework before heading out. Thankfully no one is around, so I don't have to answer any stupid questions. Mostly because I don't have good answers.

I don't know why I'm driving to Hartley's place with a burrito in my passenger seat. I don't know why it bugs me that she doesn't text me back. I don't know why I'm so fucking curious about her.

I park a block down so she can't see my truck and then gingerly jog up the exterior side stairs to her door. The wooden steps are so dilapidated, I'm scared they're going to peel away from the side of the two-story house at any given moment.

"Delivery," I call after knocking sharply.

Nothing.

I call her phone and press an ear to the door. There's no ringing inside. I bang a few more times.

Footsteps below me catch my attention, but when I look down to the ground, I see only a squat, bald guy waving a spatula in the air.

"She's not home, you dumbshit."

I trot down the stairs. "Where is she?"

"Probably working." The man narrows his eyes at me. "Who are you?"

"I'm a friend from school. She forgot a homework assignment."

"Hmmph," he grunts. "Well, she's not home, so you should git, too."

"I don't want her to get a bad grade. Do you mind if I wait?"

He grunts again. "So long as you keep it down, don't care what you do."

"Yessir."

He grumbles under his breath about fool kids and their fool tasks before disappearing into the side door of what must be a first-floor apartment. This small house with its wood siding and peeling paint doesn't look like it'd last through the next hurricane season. Again, I'm struck by the incongruence of an Astor Park kid living in this neighborhood, in this type of house.

I settle on the bottom step with the food bag at my side and then I wait. And wait. And wait.

Hours pass. My phone battery gets dangerously low from all the candy I'm crushing. The sun goes down and the crickets start singing. I doze off, waking when the warm autumn air turns chilly. My phone says it's past midnight.

I tuck my arms close to my side and text her again.

> Your food's cold

"What food?"

I nearly drop my phone in surprise. "Where the hell did you come from?" I ask Hartley.

"I could ask you the same thing."

She stalks forward, and I get a whiff of . . . grease? She's wearing some type of uniform: black pants, a white short-sleeved shirt that's wrinkled and wilted, and sturdy black shoes.

"Working?" I guess.

"What? You don't think this is a fabulous club outfit?" She waves a hand down her side.

"It's the most fabulous." I grab her dinner and gesture for her to go up the stairs. "You look dead tired, though. Whatever amazing stuff you did this afternoon and evening must've worn you out."

"Yup." Sighing, she places a foot on the first step and then looks up the stairs as if the climb is insurmountable.

Good thing I'm here.

I lift her into my arms.

"I can walk," she says, but the protest is feeble and she's already looping her arms around my neck to hold on.

"Uh-huh." The girl hardly weighs a thing. I take the stairs slow, though. It's the first time she's let me touch her and I like it. Way too much.

The inside of her apartment is as cramped and depressing as I remember it being. It's tidy and smells clean, and she's put a clear vase of daisies on the narrow windowsill, but the flowers do little to de-ugly the place.

Hartley's gaze follows mine. "I thought a splash of color might help brighten things up," she says dryly.

"Not sure that's even remotely possible." I walk to the small counter and open the microwave door. Wow. I didn't know microwave models this old still existed. It takes me a second to figure out how to work the stupid thing.

I heat up the burrito while Hartley ducks out to use the bathroom. As I wait for her, I open the cabinets in search of a snack. All I find is a box of crackers. The rest is canned food.

"You finished snooping?" she grumbles from the doorway.

"Nope." I peek inside the mini-fridge—this sad excuse for a kitchen isn't even big enough for a regular-sized fridge—and study the meager selection of staples. Butter, milk, a small carton of orange juice, some veggies, and Tupperware containers full of already-prepared food.

"I cook all my meals for the week on Sunday," Hartley explains awkwardly. "That way I don't have to worry about what to eat."

I pick up one of the clear containers, study it, and place it back. "These are only dinners," I note.

Hartley shrugs. "Well, yeah. Breakfast is usually a granola bar or some fruit, and I eat lunch at school. On the weekends, I work and there's usually no time for lunch."

It clicks now, why she's always loading her tray at Astor with like four meals. Clearly money is super tight for this girl. She's struggling. Guilt pricks me as I recall how I scarfed down her entire lunch the other day.

I check the microwave countdown. Twenty more seconds. Plenty of time for me to bite the bullet and ask, "Why aren't you living with your family?"

Her whole body stiffens. "We . . . don't see eye to eye on things," she replies, and I'm surprised I even got that much out of her.

I want her to elaborate, but, of course, she remains stubbornly silent. I'm not dumb enough to press for details. The microwave beeps. Steam rises from the burrito as I open the little door, and I use a paper towel to pick up the edge of the plate so I don't burn my hand.

"Let's give this a minute to cool down," I suggest.

She looks slightly aggravated, as if the delay is unacceptable to her because it means she has to spend more time with me. I've never met a chick who's less interested in hanging out with me.

Hartley walks over to the sofa and sits down to unlace her shoes. Then she kicks them away as if they committed some heinous crime. She's silent for a few seconds. When she speaks again, her tone is riddled with defeat. "Why did you bring me food, Easton?"

"I was worried about you." I grab a knife and fork from the cutlery drawer. Not that she needs an entire *drawer*—she owns two forks, two knives, and two spoons. That's it. "Why did you ditch school in the middle of the day?"

"My boss texted me," she admits. "A shift opened up, and I couldn't say no."

"How long are these shifts?" I ask, because she left Astor around noon and didn't get home until midnight. She was gone twelve hours. That seems like a really long shift for a part-time waitress.

"It was a double," she says. "Doubles suck, but it's hard for me to get hours. There are two other waitresses with young kids and they need the hours more than I do."

I think about her bare cupboards and debate the truth of that statement. She *does* need those hours. Pretty badly.

Or maybe she doesn't. I mean, I've got money. I'm not sure how much this dump costs, but it can't be even a tenth of my monthly allowance. I wouldn't lose a wink of sleep if I parted with some of that cash.

I place her dinner on the coffee table, along with a napkin and a glass of water, and try to think of a way to offer her money without pissing her off. When Hartley doesn't make a move to pick up her fork, I sit on the other end of the couch and cross my arms.

"Eat," I order.

She hesitates.

"For God's sake, I didn't poison it, dumbass. You're hungry. Eat."

It doesn't take any more coaxing after that. Hartley cuts into the burrito with the enthusiasm of a kid on Christmas morning. She devours nearly half the thing before slowing down a little, proving that she must've been starving.

She has a hard time accepting a ten-dollar burrito from me. How am I going to convince her that she should take a few grand?

"How come you don't tell anyone that you're working?"

"Because it's nobody's business. Yeah, I wait tables at a diner. So what? Why is that something that needs to be spread around school? It's hardly a big deal."

Frustration has me leaning forward. I rest my forearms on my knees and study her intently. "Who are you, Hartley?"

Her fork pauses halfway to her mouth. "What do you mean?"

"I mean, I looked you up—"

Just like that, her shoulders snap into a straight, angry line.

"Oh, relax," I say. "It's not like I found any deep, dark secrets. All I know about you is that your dad ran for mayor and lost."

The mention of her father casts a shadow across her face, and I find myself scanning her arms for bruises. Did her dad beat her and she ran away?

I try to fish for more information by saying, "And I found an article that says you have two sisters."

Rather than confirm or deny that, she simply stares at me with the most tired expression I've ever seen. "Easton." She pauses. "Why are you looking me up?" Another pause. "Why are you buying me dinner?" And another. "Why are you *here*? Why would you leave your big fancy house and spend your entire night waiting around for me? I'm surprised you weren't robbed out there."

I have to laugh. "I can take care of myself, babe. And to answer your question, I'm here because I like you."

"You don't even know me," she says in frustration.

"I'm trying to!" Feeling that same frustration, I slam my palm against my thigh.

Hartley flinches at the loud smacking sound. Fear darts across her gaze like a skittish rabbit.

I quickly raise both hands in a signal of surrender. "Sorry. I didn't mean to startle you."

Holy hell, maybe she *was* being abused at home. Or being abused now, by someone else. Should I call my dad?

"Is someone . . . hurting you?" I ask cautiously.

"No," she answers. "No one's hurting me. I live here alone and I don't need help. I'm managing fine on my own."

"This doesn't look fine to me." I wave my hand around the apartment.

"Really? And you wonder why I don't tell people at Astor where I work? Or where I live? I like my place here." She shakes her head in annoyance. "It's not fancy, but it's mine. I provide for myself and I'm damn proud of it."

"You're right."

My admission catches her off guard. "What?"

"Hey, I can admit that I made a mistake. I actually admire the hell out of you. If I didn't, I sure as shit wouldn't be following you around, bringing you food."

She relaxes, but her expression doesn't entirely lose its guardedness. "You're not the kind of person I want to hang around, Easton."

Something jolts up my chest and stabs me in the heart.

"I know that sounds harsh." She's totally oblivious to the effect her words have on me. "But I keep trying to tell you—you're too much trouble. I don't have time for that."

Despite the burn of indignation in my blood, I know she's right. I *am* trouble. I'm the Royal screwup who gets into fights and drinks too much and pisses everyone off all the time.

But even though it hurts to find out that she clearly views me as completely unsubstantial, I appreciate her honesty. She's not like Claire or the other girls I've been with, who fawn all over me and forgive me no matter what I do, since Easton Royal can do no wrong in their eyes.

Hartley isn't afraid to tell me everything she doesn't like about me. And I can't even be mad at her, because all these bad things she sees in me are the same things I hate about myself.

"All I care about is making sure I have somewhere to sleep every night, which means making money," she says frankly.

"If you need money, I'll give you money."

Fuck. Wrong thing to say.

Her fork clatters to the plate. "Did you *seriously* just say that? What, you think if you hand over some cash, I won't have to work as much and therefore I'll have more time to spend with you?" She sounds incredulous.

"I'm sorry. That was a dumb thing to say." Shame tickles my throat, because that's how we Royals fix problems—by throwing money at them.

But at the same time, the judgment in her storm-gray eyes needles at me. She's not like Ella, who grew up dirt poor. Or Valerie, who comes from the less-well-off Carrington side and is forced to accept handouts from her aunt and uncle in order to attend a good school.

Hartley's family is rich. She might not be living with them right now, but she sure as hell lived with them before.

"I've been to your house, remember?" I find myself snapping. "You might not have a steady cash flow right now, but your family comes from money. So don't look at me like I'm a spoiled brat and you're a hardened coupon clipper who's been struggling her whole life. For fuck's sake. You were at some fancy boarding school up until a few months ago."

Those gray eyes, rather than blaze with anger like I thought they would, once again convey exhaustion. "Yeah, I did have money before. But I don't anymore. And I've been in this apartment since school ended last May. That's only four months, long enough for me to realize that I used to take everything for granted. Life isn't about boarding schools and fancy clothes and mansions. I learned a hard lesson when I came back to Bayview." She looks me over. "I don't think you've learned that lesson yet."

"What?" I scoff. "How to be poor? Is that what it'll take for you to be nicer to me? If I trade in my ride for a bus ticket and see how the other side lives for a while?"

"I'm not asking you to do that. I don't care what you do, Easton. I'm not here to help you or hold your hand while you learn various life lessons. I'm just trying to take care of myself." She takes a quick sip of water. "Ninety-nine percent of the time, you don't even cross my mind."

Ouch.

That fucking stings.

But the painful sensation fades once I register something—

the false note in her voice. The way she's studiously avoiding my eyes.

"I don't believe you," I declare. "I *do* cross your mind."

She puts down her glass and rises unsteadily to her feet. "It's time for you to go, Easton."

"Why? Because I'm getting to you?" With a look of challenge, I stand up, too.

"You're getting on my nerves, that's what you're doing."

"No. I'm getting to you," I repeat.

I step closer, and although she tenses up, she doesn't move away. I don't miss the way her breathing quickens, and I swear I see her pulse throbbing in the base of her throat. And the need in her eyes. She wants me, or she at least wants what I can give her, but she's too proud or stubborn or frustrated to ask for it. Because she thinks she doesn't need affection or closeness or connections.

I'm starting to figure her out. Not her past. Not the problems with her family, but what makes her tick.

When she's scared and hurt, she lashes out. Someone less stubborn than me would've left by now. But that's why she's alone—because she doesn't have anyone in her life willing to stick it out with her.

I know what it's like to be alone. I know what it's like to want and not have. I don't want Hartley to feel that way. Not anymore. Not while I'm around.

"I'm gonna do it," I say softly.

Her gaze whips up to meet mine. "Do what?"

"Kiss you."

Her breath hitches. The air stretches thin between us, like when you're up high in the clouds with nothing but a couple inches of metal between you and the big blue sky. Excitement spreads through my veins as I look into her eyes. I see the same anticipation in response.

"Easton—" she says, but I don't know whether it's a warning or a plea.

And it's too late. My mouth is already on hers.

She gasps in surprise, but her lips soften under mine. Holy fuck, she's kissing me back.

My head spins and my stomach's in my throat and it has everything to do with this girl. Her lips are unbelievably soft. So is the skin at the nape of her neck, which I'm stroking with my thumb. I pull her closer to me, wanting to feel the full weight of her. My tongue dives through her parted lips and touches hers, and that's when she shakes out of my grasp.

It's over so fast I don't even have time to blink. Disappointment crashes over me, summoning a low curse from my throat. "Why'd you stop?" I practically groan.

"Because I don't want this," she says hoarsely, backing away from me. "I told you, I don't have time to date. I'm *not* interested."

"You kissed me back," I point out. My pulse is still racing from that boner-inducing kiss.

"Moment of weakness." Her breathing sounds labored. "I don't know how many different ways I can say this, Easton. I don't want to go out with you."

I swallow my frustration. *I don't get this girl. Why kiss me back, then? Moment of weakness? Screw that. She likes me. She's attracted to me. So why can't we just do this?*

Do what? a voice in my head taunts.

That gives me pause, because . . . what *do* I want here? To sleep with Hartley or to actually date her? I was planning on playing the field for my senior year, didn't want a girlfriend tying me down. There are plenty of girls I can sleep with, but I'm drawn to Hartley in a way I haven't ever been drawn to another person. There's something about her that makes me happy when I'm with her.

A crazy idea occurs to me.

"How about if we're friends?" I ask slowly.

She looks startled. "What?"

"Friends. It's a seven-letter word meaning individuals who have a mutual attachment."

"I know what it means. I just don't understand what you're saying."

"I'm saying we should be friends. Since you're not interested in me and all." I wink. "It's either that or I keep hitting on you and trying to kiss you."

Hartley makes an exasperated noise. "Why does it have to be either one of those? Isn't there a third option?"

"Nope." I offer a crooked grin. "Come on, Hartley Davidson—"

"Hartley Davidson?"

"I'm workshopping nicknames for you. Best friends give each other nicknames." I shove my hands in the back pockets of my jeans. "Honestly, I like this idea. If we're not gonna hook up, we might as well do the friendship thing. I've never really had a close female friend, so this would be a good experience for me."

Hartley sinks back down onto the couch. "From what I can tell, you have tons of friends."

"I don't," I blurt out.

Almost immediately, I'm hit with a rush of guilt, because what does that make Ella and Val? My brothers don't count—they *have* to be in my life. I do consider them friends, but blood has a way of binding you to someone, taking away your choice in the matter. I chose to be friends with Ella and Val.

So I correct myself, saying, "I have *some* friends. But I want another one. I want a Hartley Wright."

She rolls her eyes. "Is this the part where I say I want an Easton Royal?"

"Yup." I grow enthusiastic. "We'll hang out after practice. Do our calculus homework together. Not gonna brag, but I'm pretty good with the school stuff if I want to be."

"The school stuff," she repeats dryly.

"Yup. Fact is . . ." I hesitate and then confess, "I'm kind of smart."

"I know." She stretches out her legs, flexing her toes.

"You do?"

"Yeah. The notes you wrote out are pretty amazing. Only someone who really understood the subject could explain it like that."

"Huh."

"But you enjoy playing dumb, so I won't ruin it for you."

"I'm not playing dumb, I'm just not . . . interested. School's a drag."

"If I agree to this—"

I break out in a grin.

"*If* I agree," she says, stern this time, "there will be some rules."

"Hard pass. I don't do rules."

She smiles sweetly. "Then I hard pass on this friendship."

I grumble under my breath. "Fine. Whatever. Let's hear the rules."

"You're not allowed to try to fool around with me."

"Fine," I say with a nod, because I already said I wouldn't.
"You're not allowed to flirt."

"Negative. That happens naturally and I can't stop it." I
hold up my hand in compromise. "But if I do it, you're allowed
to tell me to stop."

"Fine."

"What else?"

She thinks it over. "No sexual innuendo."

"Impossible. Also comes naturally . . . that's what she
said." I sigh. "See, you're asking too much of me. My counter-
offer is that you ignore any and all innuendo. My dad always
says if you don't give something your attention, then it didn't
actually happen."

I can see her fighting a laugh. "Your dad says this. Really,"
she drawls. Her voice is full of skepticism.

"Uh-huh. Or maybe it was Gandhi. Someone smart, anyway. We should have a handshake," I tell her.

She arches an eyebrow. "A handshake."

"Yeah. LeBron James has a special handshake for each
one of his teammates. That's how you know they've bonded.
Let's do one of those."

"I'm never going to remember some complicated handshake. I vote for a song. You can sing me a song every time we
meet." Her eyes drift shut.

Poor girl is so tired. I grab a blanket draped over the back
of the sofa. "I already told you I'm tone-deaf," I remind her as I
drape the blanket over her legs. "But what song do you propose?"

She draws the covers up to her chin. "I was kidding."

"I'm up for any challenge."

"I'm learning that."

"If songs and handshakes are out, we're down to a secret knock."

She doesn't respond. I watch as her chest rises and falls in a slow and steady pace. I slide off the sofa and pull her legs up onto the cushion I abandoned. She doesn't wake up even after I stick the pillow under her head.

As much as I want to stay, I know that Hartley would prefer to wake up by herself. So I let myself out.

I don't know why I latched on to the idea of being friends, but it sits right with my gut. I want Hartley in my life and if being friends is the way that happens, then friendship is what we'll have.

It's different, but maybe that's not a bad thing.

Ten

Where u at, BFF

We're not best friends

U agreed

To FRIEND. Not BEST

I grin at my phone as I walk down the hall of the arts building that's tucked away on the east side of campus. I've never actually had any classes here. I'm not too creative.

NEway, I text back, where u at

None of your beeswax, Hartley replies, punctuating the message with a smiley face.

"It's a good thing I know your schedule," I say aloud. "Morning, sunshine."

Hartley jumps in surprise as I approach her from behind. She was about to walk into one of the music rooms, but now she spins around.

"What the hell!" She makes the cutest little growling sound. "No way, Easton. I only get three solo practice hours a week and I'm not letting you spoil it! Go away."

I mock pout. "But I was so excited to hear you play the . . ." I slant my head. "What do you play again?"

"Violin," she says grudgingly.

"Fancy." I reach around her and open the door. "Let's go."

"You're really going to listen while I practice?"

"Why not?" I give her a little nudge. "I've got nothing better to do."

She hesitates but then enters the room. While she pulls her instrument out of its small black case, I take stock of the tiny practice space. It's not much wider than the piano shoved up against the wall. Other than the bench under the piano, which Hartley pulls out, and a black metal stand to hold her music, the place is empty.

"Will you kill me if I sit on the piano?"

"Yes," she says without looking up from the violin.

"Thought so." I drop to the floor. "I prefer rubbing my ass against the dirty tile anyway. Builds up my immune system and all."

"Good for you."

"I don't sense much sympathy over in your corner of the room."

"Isn't helping you be healthy something that a best friend would do?" she says as she arranges a few sheets of paper on the music stand.

"Aha! You admit we're besties." I close my eyes, lean back against the wall, and cross my arms over my chest. I wait for some retort, but instead I hear the mournful wail of music.

The notes are thin at first, just a few slow reverbs hanging in the air followed by a few more, but she builds the sound in layers, until the chords are played almost on top of each other and the music is so full that I can't believe it's only one instrument.

I open my eyes and find that Hartley has closed hers. She's not even looking at her instructional sheets. And she's not playing the violin with just her fingers—her whole body is into it. That's why it sounds like there's a full orchestra in the room.

The music fills me up, quieting all the extra noises in my life, making my heart swell larger and larger until there's nothing left of me but ears and a soul.

And that scares me half to death.

I pop up to my feet. "I'm going to wait outside," I mumble.

Hartley doesn't acknowledge me as I leave.

Outside the practice room, I rub my hands over my bare arms. I actually have goose bumps. Now that my lungs aren't filled with her melody, I can breathe again.

I slide down the wall until my ass hits the floor. The sounds she creates with her violin seep out the cracks of the door I can't quite bring myself to close entirely.

It's as if with every pass of the bow across the strings, she's trying to flay me open and expose me. I'm not deep. I'm not affected by music. I'm Easton Royal, superficial and only interested in how to have a good time.

I don't want to look deep into my being and see the bottomless, black, boring pool of nothingness. I want to live in blissful denial.

I should leave right now. Get up and go find someone to fight or to— Actually, if I want to do the latter, I have Hartley.

I don't need to go anywhere. I just need to convince her that this friendship thing would be so much better if we were naked during our alone time.

And I have just the way to get that done.

I slip back into the cramped room, steeling myself against Hartley and her magic violin. Luckily, I'm able to make it through the rest of the practice without a breakdown.

I'm not affected by the way her fingers fly over the strings. I don't notice the light sheen of sweat that breaks across her forehead. I don't care that all the features I previously marked as plain make her look like some sort of goddess when she's in this musical trance.

None of that bothers me. Not one bit.

"Done already?" I ask when she sets the violin on her lap.

She points her bow at a light above the door. "Time's up." The light is flashing red at her. "We're only allowed an hour."

An hour has passed already? It barely felt like ten minutes. "I can't believe it's already been an hour," I remark, frowning.

"You didn't have to come in or stay."

The frown deepens as I watch her pack away her instrument, an unruffled expression on her face. She truly doesn't care whether I was here or not.

The itchy feeling between my shoulder blades is because it's only going to be that much harder to get in her pants, not because I'm disappointed that she doesn't seek my approval or praise.

I take the case from her and drape her book bag over one shoulder.

"So why the violin?" I ask as we leave the room. I nod to a couple of my classmates, who give me a wide-eyed look of surprise as I meander down the hall next to Hartley.

She, of course, ignores them.

"Music was a requirement in my house. My older sister took piano, my younger sister plays the flute, and I picked the violin. It seemed like a cool idea when I was five." She hesitates, just for a second, and maybe somebody who wasn't paying as close attention as I was would've missed it. "My dad played it. I thought it was amazing."

A curiously sad smile plays around her lips. I wonder what it means.

"I can see that. I wanted to fly planes after my—" It's my turn to break off. "A guy I knew took me up as a kid."

Hartley doesn't miss my hesitation, either. "A guy you knew?"

I scratch the back of my neck. "You know much about my family?" The Royal drama was all over the papers last spring, but she wasn't here then. Gossip has died down a little.

"Like the legal stuff?"

I give a brief nod.

"I read some stuff online, but I figure a lot of it isn't true."

"If the story you read said that my dad's business partner killed my dad's girlfriend and tried to pin it on my brother, then it's pretty accurate."

"And the guy you knew is that business partner?"

"Yup."

"So now you're trying not to love flying and planes anymore because you're afraid that it makes you too much like him?"

Her summation hits way too close to home. "I'm not anything like that asshole," I say tightly.

Except . . . I am.

I'm way more like Steve than like my dad. The rest of the

Royals take after Callum, but I'm reckless and thoughtless, and those are classic Steve O'Halloran traits.

"You can be passionate about the same things as someone you don't like," Hartley says softly. "Like, just because I play the violin doesn't mean I'm going to drink myself to death like other famous musicians. Flying planes doesn't mean you're going to steal your best friend's girl."

"He didn't steal his friend's girlfriend. He killed someone," I say through gritted teeth. My words come out louder than I intend, catching the attention of a couple students passing by.

Hartley shrugs off the mention of Steve's actions. "There are lots of things I think you're capable of, Easton, but killing someone isn't one of them. Not even if you fly a plane."

"I thought that about Steve, too," I mutter under my breath.

Hartley doesn't say another word until we reach her locker. "Thanks for coming to practice with me, even if you didn't enjoy it." She tugs the backpack off my shoulder.

I lean against the locker next to hers and watch as she stows her instrument away and pulls out her books for the next period. "Who said I didn't enjoy it?"

"You left after the first passage."

"You noticed?" She hadn't moved a muscle when I left the room or when I came back in.

"Of course."

"Well, I liked it." Way too much. "I liked it so much I might take some lessons." I reach over her head and grab the case out of the locker, then tuck the entire case under my chin. "What do you think? Good look for me?"

I strike a pose. When she doesn't respond, I shove the case back in her locker.

"Whatever," I say carelessly. "Violin's kind of boring. I think I'll go for the guitar. Easier to pick up chicks that way."

"You're being an ass right now."

Again, there's an itch between my shoulders. The feeling that I need her approval, and how much I hate it when I don't get it. It makes me lash out. "Does that mean we're no longer friends?" I mock.

She tilts her head. "I almost like it better when you're this way. At least I know there's some genuine emotion behind your scorn. It's better than your fake good humor."

The itch turns into heat. "Fake good humor? What the hell are you talking about?"

"I'm talking about the fact that you're full of it most of the time and that you're more interesting when you're angry, like now. Or when you're being genuine, like when you were talking about being scared of flying because you're worried it makes you too much like the guy you used to admire but who turned out to be a terrible human being. I know exactly how that feels."

I open my mouth to unleash a torrent of insults, beginning with how she couldn't possibly know how I feel because she's a nobody and I'm Easton Royal, but I'm saved from my own stupidity by Pash, who slaps me on the back as he runs to his next class.

"What day is it, son?" he yells.

"Game day!" Dominic yells back.

Hartley twists around to watch the two players race by. "You have a game today?"

I pluck my jersey away from my chest. "You think I wear this for the hell of it?"

"What do I know? I went to an all-girls school for the last three years."

"Hmmm."

"Hmmm what?" she asks suspiciously. "Ugh. Are you thinking something dirty?"

"Nope, I was thinking how that's the most information you've ever willingly shared about yourself."

"I let you listen while I practiced," she protests.

Time to put my plan into motion. I really want her to come to a game so that she can see I'm good at something like she is. That there's more to me than my smart-ass comments and my looks. Besides, even though I promised not to hit on her, I think if she sees me in my football gear she'll be like every other female on the planet who loves a man in uniform.

I'm playing the odds here. There's no such thing as platonic friendship between guys and girls. Eventually the clothes are gonna come off. So, really, I've just got to be patient.

"Well, since I listened to you practice," I say, "that means you have to come to the game tonight. You owe me."

I brace myself for a bunch of excuses, but she surprises me.

"If we're doing quid pro quo then I should come to a practice, not an actual game."

"Look at you with the fancy Latin. Sure then, come and watch me lift. I get it—you want to see me without my shirt on. You know what? Let me give you a sneak peek. It's awesome, by the way. You might want to close one eye to reduce the effect."

With a wide grin, I pull up my jersey to expose my abs.

"Royal! Pull your shirt down," barks Headmaster Beringer, who chooses that moment to walk past us.

I sheepishly tug my shirt down.

Hartley's cheeks are pink, but she plays it cool as she says the words I want to hear. "Fine. One game."

◆ ◆ ◆

I ARRANGE FOR Hartley to sit with Val and Ella so it's easy to spot her when I run out of the tunnel. I don't want to brag, but I play awesomely. So does the rest of the team. Bran, in particular, shines. He's a real asset, and I have no problem telling him that in the locker room after the game.

"You played great, man." I slap him on the back as we head for the showers.

"Thanks. The defense made it easy for me." He grins. "I don't think I had to drive farther than sixty yards to get a touchdown tonight."

Everyone else is jubilant, too. There's a lot of towel-snapping and ass-slapping as we shower and ready ourselves for some postgame fun.

"After-party's at Dom's house tonight," Pash yells.

A loud cheer fills the locker room.

"You going?" Connor Babbage asks as we shuffle out of the steam-filled shower area.

"Probably. Gotta check in with my peeps, though." I plop my towel-clad butt on the bench and grab my phone.

U still here, I text Hartley.

Yeah

Good. Meet me in the parking lot

OK

The parking lot is packed with students. With so many headlights on, it's nearly as bright as day.

Bran falls in step with me as I walk toward the girls. "Going to Dom's?"

"Maybe." To be honest, the last thing I want to do is go to another high school party where I see all the same people and do the same thing I've done for years. It's nothing more than music, mixed drinks, and making out with girls I don't really like.

"That sounds like an enthusiastic yes." He rolls his eyes. "I'm going. Seems like it'll be a good place to get to know my classmates."

"Why? They're all assholes," I say sourly.

Bran cocks his head. "Including you?"

"I'm the worst of them all." I don't know why I'm in such a foul mood. We won, for Chrissake. I let out a short breath. "Sorry. I don't think I got enough hits in during the game. You spent too much time on the field."

"Get used to it," he says cheerfully, unfazed by my bad attitude. "I plan to spend a lot of time out there."

"Good game!" Ella cheers as we get close, saving me from responding.

I look to Hartley, who echoes the praise with a single thumbs-up. Would it kill her to show a little more admiration? Two thumbs maybe? Jeez.

"Hi," Ella greets Bran. "I'm Ella."

"Bran." He sticks out his hand. "I think we have Spanish together."

Ella nods enthusiastically. "Yeah. You sit in the front row."

"The front row? Nerd," Val teases, waggling her eyebrows at Bran.

"This is Val," I tell him, gesturing to Ella's best friend.

"And Hartley." I jerk my head at the girl who thinks one thumbs-up sums up how amazingly I played tonight.

"Confession time." Bran makes a little gesture with his finger and all three girls lean in. Even Hartley. "I actually don't mind school."

Hartley mock gasps. "Well, since we're baring our souls and all . . . Me neither."

The two exchange a grin that makes me want to gag.

"School is how those in power train young, malleable minds into enforcing the status quo," I bite out.

Everyone wears varying looks of surprise. Bran wrinkles his forehead. Val's and Ella's brows crash together. Hartley looks utterly dumbfounded.

"Um, okay," she says.

Ella pats me on the back. "Don't mind him. He's mad because he only got to sack the quarterback once."

Bran nods. "That's what he was saying before. Sorry, bro. Next time I'll make sure to score quicker so you can have more opportunities on defense."

"Bran!" someone shouts. "You coming?"

Our celebrated quarterback raises a hand. "On my way. See you at the party, folks."

The girls wave at him as he jogs toward a souped-up Nissan GT-R. Those are Dom's wheels. Bran's having no problem fitting in, apparently. I should be overjoyed by that, but the prospect of going to the party and watching him and Hartley—who barely gives me the time of day—flirt with each other makes me want to punch something.

"What's wrong?" Hartley asks warily.

I shove my hands in my pockets to hide my fists. From the

corner of my eye I see that Ella is also watching me, but rather than suspicious, her expression is resigned. She knows me well enough to figure out what's going on.

"Easton?" Hartley presses.

I shrug a few times, because my shoulders feel like moving. "I don't know, I just get like this sometimes. Like there's all this energy rushing through my blood." I shrug about five more times. "It's fine. I'll settle down."

"How?"

"I just need to expend some energy."

Ella frowns.

"What?" I say defensively. "She asked."

Hartley leans against the passenger door of my truck. "Okay. So how do you do that?"

I give her an overly lewd look that includes a lot of eyebrow waggling.

"No way, Royal. Remember the rules."

Val snorts. "What rules?"

"Har-Har over here—"

"'Har-Har'?" Hartley growls.

"New nickname," I say, waving a dismissive hand before turning to Val. "Anyway, Har-Har gave me a list of friendship rules. It's the only way she'll grace me with her presence."

"And one of those rules is that he's not allowed to hit on me," Hartley explains.

"How do I sign up for that?" Val asks eagerly.

"Hey, I wasn't hitting on anyone," I protest. "You asked how I like to unwind, and that's the answer." Well, there's another answer, too, but I'm not going to say it out loud, not with Ella still watching me like a hawk. She knows exactly what I'm hoping to do tonight, and she doesn't like it.

"Why don't we all go to Dom's place in your truck?" Ella's tone sounds overly cheerful. "I'll leave my car here and get it later."

Yup, she's in babysitter mode. "Sorry, sis. That's a dumb idea," I say just as cheerfully. "You're not leaving a convertible in the Astor parking lot where those asswipes from Gatwick can get to it. We crushed them tonight, and they're petty."

"He's got a point," Val says, backing me up. "When we beat them last year, they spray-painted the south lawn neon yellow. Let's take your car to be safe."

Ella knows when she's beaten. "All right. Val and I will meet you there." She stares at me. "Right?"

"Of course," I assure her.

I'm lying through my teeth.

The second the four of us part ways and Hartley and I are alone in my pickup, I turn to my passenger and say, "Mind if we take a little detour?"

Eleven

I CAN TELL Hartley is confused and a little nervous, but she's being a good sport about this. She hops the fence at the edge of the shipyard without a single complaint, and she doesn't say a word as we dart through the dark maze of shipping containers. It's not until we reach our destination that she turns to me with concern in her eyes.

"What is this?"

"Fight night," I explain happily. Adrenaline is burning in my veins, and my fists haven't even struck flesh yet.

Except then I look around and am a bit disappointed. There's not much of a crowd tonight, which is weird, because it's Friday and the weekend fights are usually packed. I guess people are still scared to show their faces after that bust that happened a while back.

But oh well. I'll just have to live with the smaller turnout. I don't need to beat the crap out of thirty dudes. Just one'll do.

"You're planning to fight?" Hartley asks anxiously.

I take her arm and lead her toward a stack of crates away

from the action. In the middle of the circle, two big dudes are already at it, fists swinging and insults flying. I don't want Hartley to accidentally get jostled by any of the cheering onlookers.

"Why don't you sit down," I suggest. "I've got to take care of something."

Hartley sits, although she looks reluctant.

I strip off my shirt and toss it on the crate next to her. I don't miss the way her eyes widen slightly. Is she checking out my chest? Guess she didn't get enough of my abs earlier. I reach above my head and make a show of stretching. Hartley twists her head to avoid looking at me. I grin. Girl is smitten.

"Yo, Royal! Buy in!"

I reach into my back pocket. "Here," I tell Wilson, the shaved-head dude who oversees the exchange of cash.

I slap a stack of bills in his meaty hand. It costs a lot to fight, but I'm a Royal. I can afford it. There's potential to win a lot, too, but now that Reed's not fighting, I've got nobody to bet on. I can't bet on myself—that's no fun, especially since I already know the outcome.

"Blondie over there called dibs on you the moment you got here," Wilson tells me, flashing a toothy grin.

I peer past his huge shoulder toward the tall, blond gym rat standing with a group of three or four other guys. Ah yeah. I recognize them as the douchey frat brothers from that party I went to last weekend. I think I might've banged one of their girlfriends.

"Royal!" one of them snaps. His face is red, eyes narrowed. "You ever come near my girl again and I'll end you!"

Guess it was his girlfriend. I give Tomato Face a little wave. "How about you try to end me right now?" I gesture to the center of the circle that's blocked out for the fights.

"Gonna let Mike do it for me," he sneers, patting his buddy on the back.

Pussy. He's relying on his muscleman friend to punish me for hooking up with *his* girl? Whatever happened to fighting for your girl's honor?

Hartley watches this exchange with increasing concern. "You hit on that guy's girlfriend?"

I wink at her. "Who, me?"

"Easton." Her voice lowers to a whisper. "I don't like this."

"What, that I flirted with his girlfriend or that I'm going to fight him?"

"The fighting."

It's hard to tell in the shadows, but I think her face is getting paler. I guess she's afraid for me? That's okay. She'll realize soon enough that there's nothing to be scared of. I can handle myself.

"Can you please be careful?" she pleads.

Nope. Careful isn't fun. Careful is boring.

"Of course," I lie, and she looks relieved by that.

But the moment I step into the ring, I charge recklessly at Muscle Man Mike, because I'm craving his uppercut. I want the pain that jolts through my jaw and rattles my teeth. I want the blood that I spit onto the pavement. Another thing my brother and I have in common, other than our taste in chicks, is our thirst for violence.

I let Mike pound me until I get bored. Then I take him out with two swift blows that send him onto his ass, and lazily wander over to Hartley, who's staring at me in horror.

"You're covered in blood!"

She's right. It's dripping down my chin and chest, and I can taste its metallic flavor in my mouth. I don't care, though. I feel so fucking good right now. I feel wired. Alive.

"Wilson," I call out, ignoring Hartley. "I want some more."

"Easton," she says miserably. "Can we leave now? Please?"

"Anybody else want a go at Royal?" Wilson asks the group, grinning from ear to ear.

There are about fourteen dudes littering the pavement. Nearly all of them volunteer to fight with me.

Guess I've got beefs with more people than I thought.

"Sit tight," I tell Hartley. "Lemme just take on a few more."

"*No.*" The one word snaps out fast and sharp.

She hops off the crate and gets right in my face, and now that she's standing closer to the lights, I can see that her skin *is* pale.

"What's your deal?" I demand. "It's just harmless fun."

"How is this fun?! A bunch of guys trying to kill each other? That's not fun!"

Her vehemence has me rolling my eyes. "Okay, chillax. Nobody's trying to kill anyone. We're letting out some aggression, that's all."

"Well, I don't want to watch it!" She crosses her arms tightly. "Take me home."

I raise an eyebrow. "I honestly never expected you to be this uptight."

"I don't like seeing people get hurt, so that makes me uptight?" Her voice is high and shaky, but her gray eyes are blazing. "Why did you bring me here? Why would you ever think I'd enjoy this?"

A frown forms between my brows. I haven't brought a

chick to these fights before. Ella, yeah, but that's because she followed Reed and me here without our knowledge. Other than that, these late-night visits to the shipyard are just for me. Mine alone. Easton's world.

So why'd I invite Hartley into my inner world?

"I thought you'd like it," I finally respond, but the words don't sound right. That's not why I brought her along. I . . . don't know why I did.

Hartley is quick to call me out. "No, you didn't. Nothing you do is for anyone else. It's for you, always." She scowls at me. "Do you get off on me watching, maybe?"

"No. That's stupid."

"*That's* stupid?" Her voice rises another octave. "You and these idiots—"

"Hey!" someone protests, and that's when I realize we've got an audience.

"—come out here at night and spend hundreds of dollars to play some idiotic version of *Fight Club*. If that's not stupid, I don't know what is."

"Then leave, sweetheart!" one of the guys in Muscle Man Mike's crew calls out irritably.

"Yeah! Quit shrieking like a banshee and get lost!"

"Royal, muzzle your bitch!"

I whirl around, seeking the moron who threw out that last remark. The moment he sees my expression, he takes several nervous steps backward.

"You," I tell him, jabbing my finger in the air. "You'll fucking pay for that comment."

He takes another step back.

"What, you're gonna hit him, too?" Hartley says in disgust. "Is that how you solve your problems, Easton? With violence?"

"I'm not gonna let some brainless motormouth run you down."

"I don't care. He can say all the bad things he wants about me. I don't care."

"Well, I do."

"Then you're fighting for yourself, not for me. I want to leave," she says stiffly. "And I want to leave now. So here's how it's going to be: you're either going to put your shirt back on"— she reaches behind her, and then she's slapping my T-shirt against my bare pecs—"and take me home. Or"—she holds up her cell phone—"I'm going to call the police and get this little party broken up."

"Narc!"

"Yo, bitch, ever heard the phrase 'snitches get stitches'?"

"Your girlfriend sucks, Royal."

Both Hartley and I ignore the shit flying in our direction. We stare each other down. Her eyes are on fire, a dark, stormy gray that sends a chill up my spine. She's furious with me.

I screwed up, I guess. But I honestly didn't think a few bare-knuckle matches would get her this upset. Ella was kind of squeamish when she came along with us, but I think she actually liked seeing Reed go all animalistic.

"Easton," Hartley says, low and threatening.

I find myself swallowing hard. "Yeah?"

"Take. Me. Home." She gives me a look so cold it freezes the sweat on my bare chest. "*Now.*"

Twelve

I'm really, really, really sorry. 3 reallys!
That's how u know I mean it ☹

After I send the text, I lie in bed for a good thirty minutes staring at my phone and willing Hartley to respond. She doesn't. Just like she hadn't responded to any of the other messages I'd sent between nine thirty and noon today. A total of eight unanswered texts fill our chat history.

There's a weird weight in my chest that won't go away. I feel bad, I guess. The look on Hartley's face at the fights? That wounded look? I can't seem to erase it from my head. Worse, I don't know what to do to fix it. She didn't say a single word on the drive home from the docks last night, not until we reached her apartment. When I tried to get out of the truck to walk her to her door, she glared at me and said, "How does walking me upstairs benefit Easton Royal? It doesn't. So don't do it." Then she jumped out of the pickup and slammed the door hard enough to rattle the frame.

It bugs me that she thinks I'm a selfish prick.

Biting the inside of my cheek, I pick up my phone and type another message.

> Plz, H, just talk to me. otherwise
> I'm coming over to apologize
> in person

I don't know if it's the threat that does it or if she suddenly decided she's in the mood to answer. Either way, I get results—I see the three gray dots indicating she's typing something.

Thank fuck.

> Don't you dare come over

> I will if u don't stop ignoring me. I don't
> like it

> I don't like getting dragged to some
> illegal fight club and then being told
> I'm uptight

Guilt arrows into me. And my stomach feels queasy, but that might be thanks to the bottle of tequila I sucked down when I got home after dropping off Hartley. Arguments like that almost always send me right to the liquor cabinet.

> How many more times do I need
> to say Im sry in order for u to
> forgive me

No response.

Frustrated, I sit up in bed and bang my head against my padded headrest a few times. Then I type a follow-up.

> Bcuz I AM sorry, Hartley. I feel like a shit
> for taking u there, and then trying to
> force u to stay when u asked to go home.
> U have every right to be mad at me

More silence.

> What do u want from me

Realness, is the reply I finally get.

Realness? What the fuck is that? I drag a hand across my jaw as I stare at the phone. I *am* sorry. That's as real as it gets. The fact that I even feel regret is a new thing for me. Why can't she see that?

My fingers hover over the screen. What do I say? What will be convincing?

> Im as real as they come bby

I read it over once more before I send it. And then read it again. On the third pass, it occurs to me that it's the worst response in the history of mankind. I'm not good at this texting thing. If she were here in person, she'd be able to see how sorry I really am.

> Come over, u can see im serious

Now you are

What the hell does that mean? She's like an advanced flight formula, and, unfortunately, there's no cheat sheet or app to help me out.

Cant be srs all the time. Wld be boring

Sometimes boring is good. It's in the
quiet you hear the heart beat

Is she quoting song lyrics? I don't even know with this girl anymore.

I tap my fingers against the sides of the phone, trying to come up with the best one-liner I can. All the usual suspects aren't going to work, so . . .

Be real, she says. The reason I can't think of anything good to write is because those lines are hollow. Be real. I let my fingers tap against the screen.

I don't want to lose your friendship.
I like u

As I press Send, I realize that this might be the first time I've ever actually said that to a girl.

I like you.

I've said *I want you. I think you're sexy, hot, smoking, banging.* I've complimented girls. I've encouraged them. I've made more than a few squeal with happiness, but I don't know that I've ever genuinely liked one.

But I like Hartley.

I stare at the screen and will her to respond. When the green balloon of text appears, I blow out a breath of relief.

> You have a weird way of showing it

Not quite the response I was going for, but at least she hasn't given up on me.

> So I love to fly, right? But my dad's grounded me. So sometimes I have to take the edge off. Fighting's the only thing that doesn't hurt anyone else. I mean, ppl r there bc they want to b-

I feel like I'm cracking open my chest and letting her see inside. It's not pretty there, but I don't want to let her go.

> Give me another chance

> Oh. OK. I don't get it, but I do at the same time. You're forgiven, but I can't this weekend

I scrunch my nose. I don't like that. That means she'll stew the whole weekend about the fight.

> What's up? I'm free to help out

> If you're genuinely sorry, then give me the weekend

Why? I can show u im sorry in person

Or you can show me you're sorry by
respecting my request

Is this adulting cuz I don't think
I like it much

You're welcome. This is followed by: Thank you for being real.

I send her a smiley face, but she doesn't respond. And after ten minutes of staring at my lonely little emoji, I get the message. She's done with me today.

Time slows to a crawl when you're bored. Each minute feels like an hour. Each hour feels like a day. By early afternoon, I'm convinced that a whole month has passed.

"What day is it?" I ask. Since my room is empty, no one answers.

I need to get out of this damn house. That's my problem. I'm a doer, not a thinker, and right now, I need to do something. So I text Pash. And then Dom. And then Babbage.

No one responds.

I guess that leaves the fam.

I hunt down Ella and find her outside near the pool with papers spread all around her. I grab two bottles of water from the fridge and then drop onto the lounge opposite hers, tucking one of the bottles against her leg.

"You looked thirsty," I announce.

She looks up from her work. "Oh really?"

"Really." I stretch out on the lounger. "And it also looks like you're due for a break."

Ella laughs. "Actually, I just sat down."

"Perfect. Then I'm not interrupting anything yet. Let's dish, girlfriend."

Her laughter becomes a wave of giggles. "Oh God, Easton, *please* don't ever say that again."

"Why not? I thought you'd appreciate my offer to gossip. That's all you and Val do."

"We do not!"

I kick my legs up and grin at the clear blue sky. It's a gorgeous day, and my spirits are rising. I'm still hungover, but my temples aren't throbbing as hard and my heart definitely feels lighter. Hartley isn't furious at me anymore—she's been downgraded to just "mad." I'll take mad.

"But fine. If you want to *dish*, girlfriend, let's dish. What do you want with Hartley Wright? Besides the obvious," she tacks on when I raise an eyebrow.

"I don't know. She's new. I'm bored."

"She's not a toy," Ella chastises.

"I know that." I twist the cap off the bottle and take a few swigs of water. "She's my friend, all right?"

"You don't have female friends, East."

"Sure I do. You and Val."

"Yeah, but only because neither of us would ever sleep with you. If we were interested but you knew going there would ruin our friendship, you'd still pick the sex in a heartbeat."

"If you and Val were interested in having a threesome with me? Um, *of course* I'd pick the sex."

"I didn't mean a threesome," Ella sputters. "Ugh. You're the worst." She leans over and whacks me across the arm with her water bottle. "Anyway, you know what I mean. You're only friends with Hartley because she doesn't want to hook up with you. If she wanted to hook up, you'd be more than friends."

I shrug again. "I don't know. Maybe."

"You should leave her alone."

"Why's that?"

"Because she made it clear she's not interested. And last night at the game, she was telling me and Val how she's looking for a second job because her current one doesn't pay enough. She said work and school are the only things she's concentrating on right now."

"Yeah, that's what she told me, too." I sit up. "Aren't you remotely curious why a kid from Astor Park is living in a run down studio apartment on Salem Street?"

"Of course, but she doesn't want our concern, and I get where she's coming from. I hated how everyone at Astor looked down at me. If she's going to school and she's feeding herself then we need to leave her alone. That's what I would want."

I decide not to point out that she's kidding herself. She was in our business from the moment she stepped into the house. Ella's a meddler. It sorta surprises me she won't admit it.

I change the subject instead. "What are you working on?" I flick a finger at her papers.

"Continuous functions. I'm not getting this."

"Basically it means that you could lay your pencil on the graph and continue it in negative and positive directions without lifting it off the paper." I draw a sinuous curve. "Right?"

She nods.

"Then to determine if the function is continuous, you have

to satisfy these three conditions." I make a few quick nota-
tions and hand the page back. While she studies it, I check
my phone. Pash texted me back. Finally.

> Sorry. Lunch w fam 2day. We've got
> family visiting from Atlanta

Dammit. I throw my phone down. "How many problems
do you have left?"

"Twenty."

"How long's that going to take you?"

"A while." She stands up. "I need a snack."

I trail her into the kitchen. "Great. Let's go over to The
French Twist. My treat."

"I can't go out with you, Easton. I've got to finish all my
homework today because Val and I are driving up to State
tomorrow. I'm surprising Reed to make up for not being able
to go to his game today."

Oh crap. I forgot that I'd planned to drive up for that—
Ella usually hauls my ass out of bed and drags me to the car.
But Reed won't care if I miss his home game. He'd way rather
see Ella than me, anyway, and I can always fly out to his game
against Louisiana State next Saturday.

"Wait," I say as something occurs to me, "why aren't you
going to the game?"

She keeps her back to me as she pokes her head into the
fridge. "Because Callum and I have a meeting with the DA
today. It was the only time that worked for both of them."

That sucks. "What time are you going?"

"Around four, I think."

"That's like hours away. We have tons of time to go out. How about this? I'll do your math problems and—"

"Four is in two hours and, no," she interrupts, "I need to do it myself. If I can't learn these concepts, it's only going to get harder."

I dig my feet against the tile. "Then I'll keep doing your homework. Come on, it's not like you're going to use half this shit in real life."

"Not everyone can do complex math problems in their head, Easton. You're too smart for your own good."

"Really? 'Cause you're always telling me how stupid I am," I tease.

"I mean you do stupid things, I know you're not stupid. You're very smart. You know that, right?"

"Some stuff comes easy," I admit. "But my grades suck."

"Because you don't like to take tests. Because concentrating on anything longer than ten minutes is boring for you."

"I like flying and that takes longer than ten minutes," I point out.

She places a platter of fruit on the counter. "There's something interesting up there that doesn't exist in class."

True. In a small plane, you have to be on the alert, but mostly you feel alive in the sky. I can get close to that feeling on a motorcycle going a hundred down an open highway, but it's just a dull copy. Not a substitution for the real thing.

"Fuck. I need to get up in the air again." I grab a piece of melon and shove it in my mouth.

"Have you talked to Callum about it?"

I answer with my mouth full. "No. I already know what he's going to say."

"Which is?"

"Get your grades up. Stop drinking. Be more responsible."

Ella slants her head. "Well. I guess you don't want to fly that bad, if all those things are too challenging."

I scowl at her. "That's a little harsh."

Unperturbed, she responds by raising an eyebrow.

"I don't want to fight, Ella Bella. Come on," I coax. "Let's go play."

"No."

I give up. I know from past experience she's not budging. Ella's more stubborn than a pack of mules. That leaves the twins, I guess. "Sawyer and Seb home?"

"They're in the media room with Lauren."

I don't stop my lip from curling. Lauren's been over more than ever lately, and I'm kinda getting tired of it. She's starting to act like she owns the twins, dictating where they can go and when. And they've been buying her stuff. Expensive shit that they can afford, but it strikes me as wrong.

"Have fun today. I'm sure you'll be able to find something to occupy your time." Ella pats me on the back before returning to the patio.

In the media room, I find Lauren sitting by herself, painting her nails.

"Where are the twins?"

The petite redhead lifts her head at my arrival. "Seb went to pick me up some ice cream at the store and Sawyer forgot something in his room."

"We've got ice cream here."

Lauren swipes a white line across her nail. "It wasn't the kind I liked." She lifts her hand and blows on it.

Jeez. Lauren has those boys wrapped around her finger. But I bite my tongue and go to find my brother.

I catch Sawyer carrying a shopping bag from Gucci. I squeeze the back of my neck. *Do not say a thing*, I advise myself. *This is none of your business.* "Want to go out?"

"And do what?"

"Dunno. Just get out of the house."

"Let me see what Lauren wants to do." He pushes the door open, but I know what the answer is going to be. Lauren doesn't like being seen hanging out with the twins outside of home. At school, she generally acts like she's only dating one of them. The twins think it's funny. At some point, though, it's going to start pissing one or both of them off.

Sawyer steps back out in less than a minute. "Lauren passes."

"What about Sawyer?" In other words, what do *you* want to do rather than what does Lauren want to do?

My brother makes a face. "I pass, too."

"Come on," I wheedle. "You can go out for one afternoon. Or you know what, fine, let's chill here for a while and plan something epic for tonight."

"Lauren doesn't want to go out tonight, either. Last time we went out, we got hassled and Lauren didn't like it."

"Maybe you need to date someone with thicker skin," I suggest.

Sawyer folds his arms across his chest and glares. "Why don't you go find someone who gives a crap what you think?"

"Why don't you find someone you can leave the house with?"

"Screw you." He backs up and slams the door in my face.

Good job, Easton. You've alienated everyone in your house.

Ella's choosing homework over me. The twins are choosing their spoiled brat girlfriend. Hartley made me promise not to bother her this weekend.

It's five o'clock somewhere so there's really only one thing left for me to do.

Pay a visit to the liquor cabinet.

Thirteen

I AM DRUNK, drunk, and drunk. And somehow, nobody in my dumb family has noticed. Ella and Dad left for their meeting with the DA without even sparing me a glass. I mean, a glance. They just waved and left. The twins, I don't know where they are. Maybe upstairs with Lauren. I'm sure one of them is fanning her while the other feeds her grapes.

I'm never gonna let a chick own my balls like that. Especially not Hartley Wright. Screw her. She's mad at me 'cause I like to fight? So what. Guys fight. We do stupid shit. She has no right to get all judgmental on me.

I can't believe she doesn't want to hang out this weekend. I thought we were friends.

She's the worst.

I hop off the couch and leave the media room. I meander down to Dad's study, where I grab the vodka off the liquor shelf. I already finished all his whiskey. I doubt he'll notice, though.

I take a swig straight from the bottle and sit in my father's worn leather chair. On the desk are some documents. I carelessly flip through them. It looks like an investigative report of Steve's movements from the past few months. Steve picking up his dry cleaning. Steve at a hotel bar. Steve, Steve, Steve. Lots of pictures of good ol' Uncle Steve, the murderer.

I know I should feel bad about Steve killing Brooke, but I don't. She was a toxic bitch. The thing I don't like is that he tried hurting Ella in the process. And he didn't come forward when my brother was arrested.

It wasn't Steve who tried to pin Brooke's mess on Reed—that was all on Dinah. She wanted revenge against the Royals, so she whispered in the prosecutor's ear and even hired some caterer to lie and say that Reed threatened Brooke before she died. Dinah did everything she could to ruin our family. And Steve let her. He just stood there when Reed got thrown in jail, and didn't confess that he was the real killer.

That's unforgivable.

And it pisses me off because I like Steve. *Liked*. I correct myself. Past tense. I can't like him anymore. I can't look up to him. I can't wish I was him when I grow up.

Which is easy because I plan to never grow up. Adulting sucks. Adulting requires you to pretend to care about someone other than yourself. And that means doing shit you don't want to do to make someone else happy.

What if I'm not happy? Who's gonna take care of that problem? No one. No one but me.

I pour some more vodka down my throat and dial Reed. His game's done by now. I wonder if he won. Probably. His team's good.

"What's up?" he answers.

"My dick," I joke.

"Jesus, East."

"Sorry. Being around Ella gets me going, you know?"

Reed breathes into the phone. I grin and suck down more liquor.

"When are you going to wise up?"

"Why would I want to?"

"Because your act's going to piss off everyone you love," he says bluntly. "Knock it off with the Ella shit. It's disrespectful to her."

"And we wouldn't want to do anything to upset the precious princess, right?"

"What is up with you? Why are you home on a Saturday night?"

"Nobody wants to play with me." Well, that's not true. There're two parties tonight and three girls sent nudes in the past hour, but I'm too drunk and lazy to move.

"And you're bored out of your mind," he guesses.

"Oh, look at how smart you are since you went away to college."

"You're in a mood tonight." There's a short beat. "How much have you had to drink?"

I hold the bottle up to the light. It's half-full. "Not enough. What's the plan for next weekend? Where's your game?"

"Louisiana. You and Ella were flying out for it, remember?"

"We are?"

There's a pause. "She's coming in on Saturday."

"Of course she is." I don't even try to keep the bitterness out of my voice. *Ella kissed me first*, I want to yell at him. *I stepped aside for you.*

"We're not trying to keep you out. I thought you were catching a flight on Saturday, too?"

I hate the gentleness of his tone. It's so fucking obvious he thinks I'm pathetic. "Sorry, bro. No can do. Change of plans."

I hang up and toss the phone onto the desk. It starts ringing two seconds later. Reed's name flashes on the screen. I ignore it.

The bottle calls my name. I take another huge swig and wait for the buzz to kick in. Lately, it's taken more and more drinks to get me to a place of comfortable numbness. The walls of Dad's study seem to be narrowing. The air in here is heavy. So I pick up the bottle and walk out to the patio.

It's dark outside, but our pool has lights that make the water look blue and eerie. I stare at it for a while before heading toward the path to the shore.

I wander down to the beach and toss a few pebbles back into the ocean. The vastness gets to me. It's too quiet and too big out here, and too suffocating in the house.

I start walking, drinking as I go.

Stupid Hartley. She wants me, I know she does. If she didn't, she wouldn't have stuck her tongue in my mouth when I kissed her. She would've just smacked me across the face and told me to never, ever kiss her again.

She's pretending she doesn't like me, and that bugs me. And now I have to pretend we're just friends, which is dumb as fuck. Ella's right—I'd totally give up Hartley's friendship if it meant getting together with her.

Not that I want us to be *together*. I think she'd be fun to fool around with, that's all.

But I'm tired of chasing after someone who keeps telling me to get lost. It ain't fun.

"Hi, Easton."

I jump, glancing up to see Felicity Worthington popping

up like an unwanted genie. I wonder how I can stuff her back into her diamond-encrusted lamp.

She gives me a finger wave. I suppress a shudder and ignore her. I tip the bottle back to my lips, but only a few drops come out.

"It's Saturday night and you're all alone?"

"Gold star for you," I mock. "You're very observant."

My sarcasm doesn't faze her. She steps closer and pries the empty bottle from my hand. Then she takes my wrist and leads me up the path to her pool house.

I follow because I'm curious what she wants. Felicity flirts with me, but she's never given off any vibes that she wants to get naked. Her ass is covered in a plain khaki skirt and she's wearing a prim, white-collared shirt and pink vest. The outfit isn't much different from her school uniform. Buttoned-up and boring is how I've always pegged her.

"Did you just come from a Model UN meeting or something?" I ask.

She furrows her brow. "No. My family and I were having a late dinner at the country club. Why?"

These folks put the stuffing in stuffy. "No reason."

"Sit here." She points to a blue, overstuffed chair. "Wait. Don't move. You look filthy."

She darts over to a cabinet and grabs a towel. After laying it on the chair, she waves for me to take a seat.

I look down at my T-shirt and jeans. I've probably had the shirt since I was fifteen. It's a little tight in places, worn in others, but it's comfortable and clean. We have a housekeeper, for Chrissake. My clothes get washed.

"What's wrong with my clothes?" I growl.

"It looks like you pulled those jeans out of the trash."

"The trash? Seriously? These things cost me a grand." Yeah, I'll drop a G on pants. Why not? I can fuckin' afford it.

"That doesn't make them any less ugly."

"Ripped jeans are in. Everybody wears them."

"Those aren't ripped. They're dirty and trashy. Seriously, you look like a hobo."

There isn't enough booze in the world to help me endure this, so I stand up and head for the door. "Thanks for your fashion critique that I didn't ask for."

"Wait," she says irritably. "You can't go yet. I have a proposition for you."

Since Felicity hasn't taken off her clothes yet, I don't think it's an offer I'm going to care about. "You're wearing too much for me to be interested."

"How about this?" She opens another cabinet and produces a fifth of vodka.

"Now *that's* what I'm talking about." I make a grab for it, but she whisks it out of my reach. "Tease," I accuse.

"Sit and I'll give you this bottle."

My options include going home and being bored to death or drinking Felicity's booze and possibly getting laid.

I sit down again.

With a triumphant smile, she hands me the bottle, which I quickly uncap and tip to my lips.

An expression of disgust sweeps over her face. "I can't believe you're a Royal."

"Believe it, baby."

"Are you ready to hear my proposition?"

"I'm not much of a listener." I flash a grin. "Why don't you just go ahead and show me what you've got and I'll let you know if I'm interested."

"I'm not doing a show-and-tell," she says coolly. "Here's the thing, Easton. I've been watching you all week—"

"Stalker much?"

"You're one to talk," she replies with a roll of her eyes. "You've been chasing after Hartley Wright even though it's obvious she's a big waste of your time."

"She is?" Hartley's a lot of things. Irritating. Prickly. Hot as shit. But I wouldn't call her a waste of time.

"Of course she is. She's pretty and comes from a moderately good family, but she isn't a Royal. If we were going to rate her on a scale of one to ten in importance, she'd fall somewhere between two and three."

"My rating scale for people is usually based on how much I want to bang them."

Felicity ignores me. "You know where *you* rank on the importance scale?"

"No, but I'm sure you're gonna tell me."

"Ten."

"No way!" I mock exclaim.

She ignores that, too. "Sure, you have a scandalous history, but you're attractive and you have money and your daddy's family has been around since this place was a colony, so your past is mostly forgivable."

"Thanks for the positive feedback."

"You're welcome."

She's not being sarcastic. Which means she didn't pick up on *my* sarcasm. This chick's weird.

I look around restlessly and wonder for the umpteenth time what in the hell Hartley's doing that I couldn't do, too. I think it's time to go. Even the solitude of Dad's study is more appealing than listening to Felicity drone on about social rankings.

Maybe I'll just cruise by Hartley's place. See if she's home and needs a hand.

"Appreciate your eval of me, Felicity, but I'm gonna head home."

"I'm not done yet."

"You've already spent way too much time assessing my status." I give her a mocking smile. "When do you have time to do your homework?"

She sniffs. "I don't need to do homework. Getting ahead in life has nothing to do with grades. You, of all people, should know this." Her tone is condescending as hell. "Getting ahead is about connections. The person with the best connections will go further than the person with the best grades."

Sadly, she's right.

I take another swig of vodka. I figure if I drink this whole bottle, doesn't matter what Felicity is saying. I won't be able to hear her. Besides, she seems to know more about Hartley than anyone I've run into, and that keeps my ass in the chair. "What else do you know about Hartley?"

Felicity's eyes gleam. If I was less drunk, I may have been able to read her expression, but her face is beginning to look blurry to me. And her voice sounds blurry, too. Can voices be blurry? They must, because hers totally is.

"She left school three years ago and just came back this summer. She doesn't really run in our circles."

"You mean she's not an entitled asshole like the rest of us?"

Again, my barb falls to the ground. Felicity doesn't give a shit about me or my opinion. She waves a manicured hand and says, "We'll come back to Hartley, okay? First, let me tell you what I want."

I'm starting to think what she wants is *not* me naked.

Damn. Total waste of a night, right here. "Whatever. Just make it fast."

"I want to sit at the top of Astor," she says bluntly. "There are a couple ways to do that. Option one—I can take Ella down."

I straighten up, my shoulders tensing. "Not happening."

"I could absolutely get it done, sweetie. Luckily, there's an easier way." She smiles, and this time, even in my drunken state, I correctly read it as a warning signal.

"Why do I feel like I'm about to be eaten alive?" I mutter.

"Option two—if you can't overthrow the Royals, then you join them. The easiest way for me to rise to the top is to be with you."

"I'm not the only Royal around," I tell her as I get to my feet. The thought of being with Felicity is making me nauseous.

"No, thank you. I'm not interested in the sick little games your brothers play."

"Hey, now," I say sharply. No one talks trash about my family. "They're not sick and they're not games."

Felicity wisely backs down. "I'm sorry. You're right. As part of the Royal family, I shouldn't insult my boyfriend's brothers."

I snort. "Boyfriend?"

"Yes. I want to date you."

"Why? What's wrong with you?" I laugh drunkenly at my own joke. But then I frown, because I think I just made fun of myself.

Her lips tighten. "This is our senior year and I want to have some of the benefits of dating a Royal. Like flying to D.C. to have dinner or being taken out on the yacht. I want those things. I want girls to look at me and envy me. I want to be on the cover of *Southern Woman* with a pictorial of you and me and your family gardens."

"Greedy girl. You want lots and lots of things." I drop the vodka bottle on the table. "Sorry. Not interested in helping you out."

"Wait!" She rushes in front of me and grabs my arm before I can reach the door. "You don't even want to know what I'll give you in return?"

I shake her off. "I don't want anything from you, baby."

"No, but you want something from Hartley Wright, don't you?"

That gets my attention. Kind of. My eyes are having trouble focusing on Felicity's face. Or on anything, really. "What's this got to do with Hartley?"

"It depends. Do you want to hook up with her, or do you want her to be your girlfriend?"

I snicker. "I don't do girlfriends."

No, wait, I've done girlfriends.

I had Claire, right?

But I didn't like Claire after a while.

Hartley's not Claire, though.

Maybe I *do* want a girlfriend?

Dammit, my head is spinning. I can't hold on to one single thought. They all pass through my head like wisps of smoke.

Looking a bit relieved, Felicity nods. "That's what I thought. All right, so you want to sleep with Hartley. But she doesn't want you."

"Hey," I protest. "That's a bitchy thing to say. You're a bitch."

Felicity rolls her eyes. "Sorry, but it's the truth. I told you, I've been watching you. That girl wants nothing to do with you. But . . ."

My ears perk up. *But*. I like buts.

"If you go out with me, you instantly become unavailable, and girls always want what they can't have. Hartley will be so jealous to see you with someone else that she'll start throwing herself at you. Trust me."

I'm not sure I can associate the word *trust* with Felicity, but she's not totally wrong. We all want the unattainable. The forbidden. Isn't that why I screwed around with Ms. Mann?

"Plus," Felicity continues, "there are other benefits. By dating me, you can go to prom and homecoming and events at the country club but without expectations. If you ask another girl, she'll think you like her. But I don't want to sleep with you, and you're free to sleep with anyone you want as long as they don't go to Astor." She sees my frown and quickly adds, "Except for Hartley. You can sleep with her, once or whatever— I mean, you said it'll just be a hookup. So you can do that, in secret, preferably. But if anyone finds out, I'll admit you cheated on me with Hartley but that I forgave you and we're stronger than ever."

"You're saying you want a fake relationship and I can make Hartley jealous and hook up with her but only if it's in secret." I think I'm too drunk for this conversation. But I like the idea of making Hartley jealous. Making her chase *me*.

"It's a business relationship. I do something for you and you do something for me. No one gets hurt."

No one gets hurt. I like that. It's pretty much my motto. Live your best life without hurting someone. I squint at her, because her face looks hazy again. "'Kay."

"Okay?" Her voice holds a note of surprise.

"Yeah, 'kay," I slur. "Let's make Hartley jealous." I love this idea.

Felicity sounds a bit frustrated. "That's not the only pur-pose of—"

"Night," I say as I open the door. Or, at least, as I *try* to open it. It takes three attempts before it swings forward. "Thanks for the vodka!" I call over my shoulder, and then I stumble out of the pool house.

Fourteen

DESPITE A MASSIVE hangover that knocked me on my ass my entire Sunday, I'm not late for practice on Monday morning. Go me. Most of the time is spent getting Bran up to speed on our spread offense. He's a quick learner and has good on-field instincts. I'm only able to tag him once during our end-of-practice full drill. Since I'm not allowed to tackle him without every coach on the sidelines drilling their foot up my ass, I give him a warning hug and then push him aside.

"Not bad, Mathis," I tell him.

"I'm just glad I don't have to face you this year," he says, patting his red pinnie that designates him as off-limits. Defensive players aren't allowed to touch the quarterback when he wears the red jersey.

"There's still Carson Dunn over at North and TJ Price at Gibson High," I warn.

"Nah, I know. But you're the best D-end in the league this year. You give quarterbacks nightmares, you know." He slaps me on the shoulder. "When I got hurt last year, the first thing my teammates said was that I did it on purpose so I wouldn't have to run from the Royal brothers."

The wistfulness in his voice when he speaks of his old school is obvious.

"Miss your boys, do you?" I say sympathetically.

"Yeah." He tips his head back as guys do when they try to hide their emotions. "There were some good guys there. But you make sacrifices for your future, right?"

"I don't," I say bluntly.

His chin drops and a rueful grin tips up the corners of his mouth. "Yeah, I've heard that about you. I figure once I'm in college, I can try to stop worrying about what my parents think."

He gives me another slap and then runs off to the locker room. I follow, but at a much slower pace. I'm in no hurry to get to class today. Mostly because I can't decide whose schedule to follow—mine or Hartley's. Maybe I'll do mine today. I have study hall first period, while Hartley has Feminist Thought. Study hall means I can sleep.

And, no, it doesn't escape me that I slept all day yesterday. I know if Ella hadn't driven up to State to see Reed, she would've spouted off some long, long lecture about how my drinking is getting out of control.

She'd be right. I can't remember a damn thing from Saturday night, other than pouring half a liquor store down my throat and then drunk-walking on the beach. I feel like I might've gotten laid, though? Maybe? It probably hadn't been too good if I don't remember it.

After showering, I head for study hall. Ahead of me, Bran is hurrying somewhere, drawing the hungry attention of more than one girl. The Astor chicks aren't much better than the Astor boys. They're eating up the newbie with their eyes. Bran might miss his old school, but there'll be plenty of ways he can find comfort here at Astor Park Prep.

Because he's hurrying, he ends up mowing down some poor bystander. She falls backward, her black hair flipping up.

Oh shit. It's Hartley.

I rush forward, but it's Bran who catches her before she hits the tiled floor. He helps her to her feet, and Hartley, the girl with the perpetual scowl on her face, actually smiles at him. Then they start talking.

Why's she always so nice to him?

"Hey, East, where you going?" Pash calls out to me from the classroom door.

"I'm going to class."

"This is your class," he points out. "We've got study hall."

"Nah." Change of plans.

By the time I reach Hartley's classroom, it's all full. I walk up to the guy sitting next to her and say, "Move."

He scrambles to his feet. Hartley pretends not to notice any of this. Her gaze is fixed on the front.

"What were you and Bran talking about?" I ask.

"How is that any of your business?" she replies without looking at me.

I clench my teeth. "What, you're a jock chaser now?"

"Seriously?" She sounds dumbfounded. "You've got issues, Easton."

Yeah, I do. Lots of them. And one of them is that I don't want to be her *friend*. "Are you still mad at me?" I blurt out.

Something in her body language relaxes. She glances over, sees my expression, and sighs quietly. "Argh. You're like a little kid, you know that?"

I'm about to make a smart-ass comment about how I'm all man, but she keeps going before I can.

"You get this guilty little-boy look on your face when you know you've pissed someone off."

"So you are still mad at me," I say glumly.

She doesn't answer.

"But you said we'd talk on Monday," I remind her.

Hartley raises one dark eyebrow. "Are we not talking?"

"We are. But . . ." I'm unusually flustered. "I just—"

Before I can say another word, Felicity Worthington appears in front of my desk. Then, to my utter amazement, she bends down and kisses me right on the lips.

"Good morning, sweetie."

I gape up at her. "What?" I say stupidly. Why's this girl kissing me?

"Good morning," Felicity repeats, then looks at Hartley. "Good morning. Hartley, right?"

Hartley looks as confused as I feel. "Morning," she says absently.

"Miss Worthington," the teacher calls from the front. "Is there a reason you're in my classroom? Because according to my list, you're not in this class. For that matter, neither are you, Mr. Royal."

"Sure I am," I call back, and she shuts up, because we both know I'm not leaving.

Felicity, meanwhile, beams at the older woman. "I know, Mrs. Ratcliff. I just popped in to say good morning to my boyfriend."

A collective gasp comes from the girls in the class.

"I'll be on my way now!" Felicity gives me another quick peck on the lips and then leaves.

Okay. What the hell is going on?

"You and Felicity are together?!" Nora Hernandez is practically salivating as she twists around in the chair in front of me.

I'm half a second away from saying *hell no* when I notice the slight frown on Hartley's lips. That makes me freeze. Is she jealous that I'm dating Felicity?

Wait. Jesus. I'm not dating Felicity. Even thinking it makes me want to hurl.

"Absolutely not," I tell Nora, and hide a smile when I notice Hartley's shoulders relax. The thought of me with Felicity *did* bother her. Ha.

During class, she pays attention only to the teacher, and afterward she walks out without saying a word. I race after her, but I'm brought up short when a hand grabs my blazer.

It's Felicity. "Let's go to Basil's tonight." Her commanding tone rubs me wrong.

I stare at her. "Why?"

"Because it's a good restaurant, and I want to go."

I keep staring. "Felicity."

"Yes, sweetie?"

"What do you think is going on right now?"

Confusion passes over her expression. "What do you mean?"

"I mean, why the *fuck* would I go out with you tonight, and why are you calling me your boyfriend—" I stop abruptly.

Memories from Saturday night crash into me like a tidal wave.

Me wandering along the sand, drunker than drunk can be. Felicity popping up in front of me and dragging me to her pool house. I was there for a while, and although I can't remember every last detail of the conversation, I remember the important ones.

Like agreeing to a fake relationship so I could make Hartley jealous.

Shit.

Shit, shit, *shit*.

"We made a deal," Felicity says in a low voice, oblivious to my growing panic. "And I specifically made sure to kiss you when Hartley was looking."

Christ. I need to stop drinking. I *need* to.

"Um." I gulp. "Look. Felicity."

Her blue eyes narrow.

"That deal . . ." Dammit, this is stupidly uncomfortable. I notice several kids eyeing us as I lead Felicity toward a row of lockers, away from the foot traffic in the hall. "I was drunk when I agreed to it."

"No, really?" Sarcasm oozes from her tone.

"Like, really, really drunk. Blackout drunk," I add, because it's true. I woke up on Sunday morning with no recollection of even seeing Felicity, let alone saying I'd be her boyfriend. "So, uh, yeah . . . whatever I said I'd do . . . I'm gonna have to back out."

She purses her lips, studying my contrite face. "No," she finally answers.

My shoulders jerk up. "What do you mean, no?"

"I mean no. You're not backing out." She curls her fingers over my forearm and gazes at me with fire in her eyes. "We made a deal, and I've already told my girls to spread the word that we're together. It's too late."

Anger creeps up my spine. "Then unspread the word," I order. "Because we're not together."

"Yes, we are," she argues like a five-year-old. Her fingernails dig into the sleeve of my shirt. "Don't make me mad, Easton. You *really* don't want to see me when I'm mad."

Why? Does she Hulk out and punch through walls? I don't get a chance to ask because Felicity flounces off, leaving me to stare after her in dismay.

◆　◆　◆

WORD SPREADS FAST. Felicity and her "girls" waste no time telling everyone at Astor Park that we're dating. Each time I try correcting some ignorant idiot who brings it up, they grin or slap me on the back and say, "Sure, Royal." I don't know what Felicity's saying, but nobody believes me when I insist we're not dating.

Luckily, the only people who matter are Ella, the twins, Val, and Hartley. The first four laugh it off when I join them for lunch. But Hartley? She disappears again. AWOL for all our afternoon classes. And I say *our* because I've given up on attending my own classes.

In fact, after the last bell, I pop into the office and make an official request to change my schedule. "I'll pass this along to the headmaster," Mr. Miller, my guidance counselor, tells me.

"Thanks."

He smiles dryly. "And if Headmaster Beringer denies the request?"

I shrug. "I'll keep going to these classes anyway. None of the teachers care that I'm there."

Mr. Miller shakes his head to himself as I head for the door. "This school," he mutters under his breath.

Yeah. This school. It's a screwed-up place where the students run the show and the teachers sit back and watch, completely powerless. Rich kids are assholes.

I text Hartley on my way outside. U missed afternoon classes. U get called into work

To my surprise, she texts back immediately. Ya. Do me a favor

I smile at the screen.

> Of course I'll have sex with u

There's a brief delay.

> Forget it

> Crap. Sry! Told u, comes naturally. What do u need, Har-Har

> Brit Lit notes, if you have any

Yup, took lots. I don't even flinch when I type out that lie, but I remember the lecture and will have a complete set ready for her when she's done. When u off work? I can come by ur place when ur done and drop em off

> Would you mind dropping them here? That way I can do homework on my breaks

A little map pops up—she sent me her location. Hungry Spoon Diner on East 14th Street.

Ya no prob, I type, and feel immensely proud of myself for being such a good, helpful friend. I can b there in hr-ish. Gotta drop Pash home first

> Thanks, e

Sweet. She called me "e." Progress!

I tuck my phone in my pocket and cross the parking lot toward my pickup, where Pash is already waiting. I've been playing chauffeur because his car's been in the shop for two weeks now—he totaled it racing on the twisty, scary-as-fuck road that follows the coastline. Lucky he didn't go over the cliff, but I'm not one to judge. Pash has one vice: illegal street racing. I've got like a million of them.

"Yo," he calls.

"Yo." I unlock the truck doors and we slide into our respective seats. I toss my phone in the cup holder and start the engine.

During the fifteen-minute drive, my cell dings at least ten times, prompting Pash to finally scoop it up.

"Dude. Felicity Worthington texted you like five billion times." He chuckles at something on the screen. "She wants you to wear a tie to dinner tonight. You're taking her to dinner?"

He says that in the way one would ask if his pal was going to sit down with a python.

"Hell. No." I grit my teeth and focus on the road ahead. "Can you text back for me?"

"Sure. Whatcha want me to say?"

"Say, *We're NOT going out*. Capital letters for *not*."

Pash snickers loudly. "Harsh, bro."

"Nice doesn't cut it with this chick." I flick the turn signal and steer the car left toward Pash's tree-lined street.

"Why does she think you're going out?" he asks, typing absently into my phone.

"Because she asked me, and I said yes when I was loaded."

He laughs again. "You're screwed."

"Thanks for the support."

"I'm just telling you the truth. There. Sent." The phone beeps in his hand before he can put it down. "She texted back, *A deal's a deal.*"

I groan in frustration. "Don't answer."

"So. How you going to get yourself out of this jam?"

Looking over, I see him fighting back more laughter. "No idea," I admit. Felicity's a force of nature. And, I'm starting to think, a bit psycho. "I'll figure something out."

I reach the end of his long driveway and stop the car in front of the Bhara mansion. "See you at practice tomorrow." I don't offer to pick him up, since I'm never on time. But his dad drops him off before work, so it's fine.

We knock fists and then Pash gets out of the car. "Later, East."

"Later."

I pull a quick turn and drive out the way I came, only instead of turning toward the road home, I take the one that leads to the city. I pull into an empty lot and park, and then I take out my pen, my phone, and a notebook and get to work. A year ago, I started recording class lectures on my phone. It helps at test time, if I can convince myself it's a class worth studying for. Admittedly, I only do the bare minimum. C's are a passing grade, as I've told my dad a million times.

But I take extra care with these notes. Because to Hartley, a C is probably a failed grade. Once I finish, I tuck everything away and go find my girl.

Hungry Spoon Diner is in a strip mall next to a Goodwill and a grocery store. The neon sign declares it's open.

I grab my notebook and head inside. The place has a few rows of fifties-style tables: the ones with the chrome sides and the shiny colorful tops. In the center is a big U-shaped counter.

There aren't many bodies, but that's unsurprising, seeing as how it's barely five o'clock on a weekday. I scan the room for Hartley, but I see only one waitress, wearing the same black-and-white uniform Hartley had on the night I brought her dinner.

Frowning, I look at the mostly empty booths, and that's when I spot her. Well, I spot the back of her head. She's sitting in the farthest booth, facing away from me. And she's not alone.

"You can seat yourself," the other waitress chirps after greeting me.

"Oh. Okay. Thanks."

"I'll be right over with a menu."

I nod and walk toward the back booths. I don't sit at the one right next to Hartley's, but two booths away. Far enough that her companion can't really see me, but close enough to hear what Hartley's saying.

And what she says sucks the breath from my lungs.

In a voice trembling with desperation, Hartley pleads, "I want to come home."

Fifteen

"YOU KNOW THAT'S not up to me."

I clamp my lips together to stop from interrupting. The woman is Hartley's sister, I think. I recognize her from the article, but I can't remember her name. She looks so much like Hartley, except her black hair is cut in a short bob with bangs while Hartley's hangs like a silk curtain down the middle of her back.

"No, but you're the oldest," Hartley says shakily. "You're their favorite, Parker. Dad actually listens to you."

"Not anymore," Parker answers. Her voice sounds tight. "Now he walks around like he's King Lear, waiting for all his daughters to betray him. God, I shouldn't even be here, Hart. I'm risking a lot."

"Is that so?" I can't see Hartley's face, but from the way her tone grows cold, I imagine her expression is equally chilly. "What exactly are you risking, Parker? You don't even live there anymore. You have a husband and two kids and—"

"—and a trust fund that pays for my children's private

school tuition and for the house my family lives in. If Dad finds out I saw you—"

Hartley makes a noise of distress in the back of her throat. "No one's going to find out."

"You don't know that. He's got spies everywhere."

I frown to myself. Hartley's dad is just an assistant district attorney, but Hartley's sister is making it seem like he's the head of a mafia family or some shit. Man. What happened between Hartley and her dad? It's sounding more and more like she got kicked out of her house, but why?

"Can I get you something to drink? Coffee? Water?"

The waitress interrupts my eavesdropping. "Uh, sure," I mumble, trying to keep my voice as low as possible. "Water's fine. Thanks."

"Have you had a chance to look at the menu?" she asks.

"I miss you guys so much," Hartley is saying, sounding heartbroken.

Frustration builds as I try to focus on both conversations at once. "Not yet. I need more time."

"All righty. I'll be back with your water and to take your order."

She flounces off and I'm able to catch the tail end of Parker's sentence.

"—could change your circumstance anytime. Just apologize to him and say you overreacted, beg for his forgiveness."

"I did *not* overreact," Hartley snaps. "What he does is wrong and it's going to come out someday. These sorts of things always do. All this covering it up will end up being worse for the rest of us."

"You think our family is the only one with dirt?" Parker

hisses. "Everyone's money is dirty. You should've kept your mouth shut."

"Then what about this?"

I have no idea what "this" is, because I can't see Hartley, but Parker's gray eyes fill with sorrow. "I don't know what to believe anymore."

"Are you kidding me? You *saw* what—" Hartley stops. Her head falls forward, and she draws a deep breath. "You know what? I don't care that I'm kicked out of the house or that I don't have money. I don't care about any of that. I care about our mom and sister. I want us to be together."

"Then you need to forgive and move on," Parker begs. "Dragging this out, making a spectacle of it, is only hurting the family. Do the right thing."

"I'm trying to!" Hartley cries, then quickly lowers her voice. "Why do you think I came back? I'm trying to make it all right, but you're not supposed to be seen with me. Mom won't talk to me. I haven't spoken to—" Her voice cracks and she breaks off.

My insides turn over. She's really upset.

Parker gets to her feet. "I'm sorry, Hart. I have to go."

Hartley's hand shoots out and grabs her sister's wrist. "Will you at least talk to Mom for me?"

"I already have, countless times. She doesn't listen to me," Parker says in frustration.

"Then, please, you *have* to talk to Dad."

"I can't."

"Why not?" Hartley sounds mad now. "Miles makes a good living. Do you really need the other money?"

Parker shakes her wrist free. "I thought you loved your

niece and nephew. Do you know how expensive they are? It costs two grand a month to keep Macy's pony stabled and it's five grand for Dawson's violin lessons. I can't sacrifice their future for you, Hartley. Don't ask that of me. Don't be selfish. If you don't care about your niece and nephew, then at least think about our baby sister. She wouldn't survive in a boarding school. She's too fragile."

Hartley makes a choked sound that rips at my gut, but Parker is unaffected by it. She walks out of the diner without a backward look.

I want to go to Hartley and put my arm around her, but I'm guessing that would be as welcome as pouring hot lava over her head. Plus, she'll totally bust my balls for eavesdropping. So I slouch in the booth and duck my head as low as possible. I hear her rise behind me.

"Jess, is it cool if I take another five minutes? I need some air."

"No prob, hon. It's dead in here. Take your time."

Footsteps sound, heading not for the door but the rear of the diner. I guess there's another exit back there.

"Here you are." My waitress returns with a glass of water. "Are you ready to order?"

"Actually, I've got to go." I hold up my phone and the notebook, as if the two items provide the answer to whatever mysterious problem is making me leave.

She just shrugs, probably because she gets paid whether she serves me or not. It's not like she's working on apple pie commission. "Suit yourself, hon."

I toss a twenty on the table and slide out of the booth. "Keep the change," I call over my shoulder.

Outside, I wait about twenty seconds, then walk around the side of the building toward what I'm assuming is a back alley.

That's where I find Hartley, sitting on a milk crate, dark head bent, shoulders shaking.

She's crying.

Fuck. What should I do?

Running away before she sees me doesn't sit right, but I'm not good at the whole comforting-people thing. Besides, Hartley won't let me comfort her. I annoy her too much.

Actually . . . that's the answer. I may not be able to put my arm around her and stroke her hair and promise her that everything's going to be okay—how the hell do I know how it's gonna be?—but there's one surefire way to make those tears disappear.

With a grin, I saunter forward, making sure my footsteps are extra loud so she hears me coming. "Have no fear, Easton's here!"

Her head whips in my direction.

I catch only a brief glimpse of her shiny eyes before her hands swiftly rise to wipe the tears. Then she juts her chin and sends back a tart reply. "No fear? That's the scariest thing I've ever heard."

I reach her and hold up my notebook. "Hey, now. Don't bite the hand that feeds you British Literature notes," I warn, all the while pretending I didn't see the tears.

She's pretty much recovered, though. Her eyes are rimmed red, but they're dry now.

"Thanks." Sincerity rings in her voice as she accepts the notebook from me.

I drag another milk crate over and flop down on it. "So,

you still have time left in your break? Because I've got the craziest shit to tell you."

She tucks a strand of hair behind her ear. "Yeah, we have time. There's nobody in the diner."

"Is that why you look so down?" I say lightly. "Because you're missing out on all those sweet tips?"

"I'm not down."

We both know she's lying, but I keep my mouth shut. I don't want to push her to tell me about that scene with her sister—I want her to confide in me because she wants to.

I pretend to mull it over. "Oh, shit. I know what it is. You were thinking about how you like me, and how it breaks your heart that you blew your shot with me."

A hoot of laughter flies out of her mouth. "I blew my shot with *you*? Um, I'm pretty sure it's the other way around."

"Babe, I didn't blow anything." I wink at her. "You're into me. All I got to do is snap my fingers and we'll be making out on your couch tonight."

"Ha. I'd rather make out with that light over there." She points to the streetlamp at the opening of the alley.

"Gross. Do you know how many dirty hands have touched that pole?"

"Probably as many as have touched yours." She grins broadly, proud of that comeback.

"Nice." Snickering, I hold my hand up for a high five.

After a long beat, she leans over and slaps her palm against mine.

Her eyes are no longer glistening and her shoulders are almost totally relaxed. I sneak a peek at her profile. The soft angle of her cheekbone, the pout of her bottom lip, her ear. It's a really cute ear.

"So what's this crazy story you have to tell me?" she asks.

I let out an exaggerated groan. "Oh Lord, you don't even want to know. It's brutal."

She looks amused. "Uh-oh. What'd you do?"

"Who says I did anything?" I protest.

"Um, I do." She raises one eyebrow in challenge. "So what'd you do?"

A huge sigh shudders out. "I got blackout drunk and told Felicity I'd be her fake boyfriend."

Silence crashes over us.

And then Hartley hoots with laughter. "What? *Why?*"

"Why did I agree, or why does she want a fake boyfriend?"

"Why any of that!"

"Well, she wants a Royal on her arm so she can climb the social ladder and show me off at parties."

"Of course," Hartley says, nodding as if that makes perfect sense. "And you agreed because . . . ?"

"Did you not hear the 'blackout drunk' part? I do stupid things when I'm wasted, Har-Har."

She crouches over, still busting a gut. "Oh God, Easton. You're priceless."

"I coulda told you that."

"So what are you going to do?" she asks between giggles, and I'm gratified to see that all traces of sorrow are gone from her pretty face. "You're not actually playing the part of her boyfriend, are you?"

"Hell no. I already told her it ain't happening." I chew on my lip. "She's not letting me back out, though. Said a deal's a deal."

Hartley snorts.

I wave a hand. "Whatevs. I'll figure out a way to ditch her. I mean, you can't *force* someone to date you, right?"

"You'd think not," Hartley says cheerfully. "But Felicity Worthington seems . . . tenacious."

"I think the word you're looking for is 'unhinged.'"

"Nah. Not unhinged. Just a rich bitch who knows what she wants."

And what she wants is me. Christ. "I'm scared, Har-Har. Hold me."

That gets me another snort.

We both go quiet for a moment. It's strangely comfortable—normally I hate silences. They make me itchy and anxious, and I fill them by babbling incessantly. But right now, I simply sit there next to Hartley and admire her profile again.

I'm dying to ask her about her sister, but I can't. Just because I'm really fucking curious about that conversation in the diner doesn't mean I need to stick my nose where it doesn't belong. I have more willpower than—

"I saw you with your sister," I blurt out.

So much for willpower.

Hartley's body language goes right back to stiff and unwelcoming. "What?"

"I came in when you guys were in the booth," I confess. "I sat nearby and listened."

"You . . . listened?" Very slowly, outrage creeps into those two words. Then she explodes. "What the hell, Easton!"

"I'm sorry. It's not like I did it on purpose," I say defensively. "I just didn't want to interrupt you."

Hartley's jaw tightens. "You should've let me know you were there."

"I'm sorry," I say again.

This time, the silence that falls is *swimming* with awkwardness.

"So your folks kicked you out?"

She swivels her head toward me, glaring hard enough to make me shiver.

"At least, that's the impression I got from what I heard. So what happened? Did they catch you snorting coke or something? Try to send you to rehab?" Holy fuck, why am I still talking? She obviously doesn't want to speak to me about this. But my brain-to-mouth filter isn't working. It rarely ever does.

"None of the above," she mutters.

"Okay. So . . . what, then?"

"My dad and I had a disagreement" is her cryptic response.

I want to know more. I *need* to. But Hartley's too prickly. I can't ask her anything else without completely spooking her.

Actually, she sort of reminds me of Ella. When Ella first came to town, getting details out of her was damn near impossible. Eventually she dropped her defenses, once she realized we didn't want anything from her. Or rather, that *I* didn't.

That's another thing I got before Reed—Ella spoke to me about her stripping before she ever spoke to Reed about it. I wonder why she did that. Maybe . . . Is it because Ella never saw me as a threat?

I drum my fingers on my knees as the realization sinks in. I barely have time to analyze it before another one comes.

Hartley sees me as a threat. That's why her back is always up.

I suddenly think about the way she talked to Bran Mathis, all smiles and no hostility. Why? I guess because . . . because he hadn't mocked her about getting in her pants the way I'd done? No, the way I'm still *doing*. I promised her I'd stop hitting on her, that I'd be a good, platonic friend to her, but— story of my life—I didn't follow through on that promise.

I'm an asshole.

"Hey, if you want, I can come inside and chill in a booth while you work, quiz you on Brit Lit whenever it gets dead," I offer.

Hartley looks startled. "Wait, what?"

"I asked if you want me to quiz you—"

"No, I heard you," she cuts in. "I just don't get it . . . You're not going to ask me about my father?"

"No."

Her eyes widen and then almost immediately narrow. "Why not?"

"Because it's none of my business. If you want to tell me about the disagreement with your dad, or whatever it was, then you'll tell me." I shrug. "Friends don't force each other to talk." There isn't one false note in those seven words, because I've come to some more conclusions during this brief exchange.

Hartley's not going to sleep with me. She's attracted to me—I know she is—but she's not going to act on it. She's got something everyone says I should acquire: self-control. She's not going to climb into bed with me or in the back of my truck or under the bleachers, and I think it's time I accepted that.

But I like her. I don't want to stop talking to her. I don't want her to be threatened by me.

So . . . if Hartley is going to stop viewing me as a threat, then I've got to start treating her as something other than a hookup.

I need to treat her as a *friend*. A real, *give a shit about each other, don't need to be naked to care about you* friend.

"I mean it," I say gruffly. "I'm here if and when you're ready to talk about it. 'Til then, we can talk about other stuff. Deal?"

Her thoughtful expression stays with her for several moments. Finally, she opens her mouth and murmurs, "Deal."

Sixteen

"DID YOU SERIOUSLY switch up your *entire* schedule?" Ella demands the next morning.

I slam my locker door shut and turn to grin at her. "Nope. I'm still in calculus."

She gapes at me. "But all your other classes are different?"

"Pretty much."

"And Beringer *approved* this?"

"Yup."

"Was he on crack?"

"Probably?"

She snatches my new schedule out of my hand. Mrs. G printed it out for me when I popped into the office after practice.

"This is ridiculous!" Ella huffs. "You need to take certain classes in order to graduate, Easton. There's only one language class on here—you need two this semester. And you're taking Government! You took that last year! Why are they letting you take it again?"

"I'm going with your crack theory."

She shoves the paper against my chest. "This is Hartley Wright's schedule, right?"

"Yeah, so?" It's not a big secret—I already told everyone last week why I was attending all different classes.

"So, don't you think you should leave her alone?"

"That'd be a negative."

"But . . . she's made it pretty clear she doesn't want to go out with you."

"I know, and I'm cool with that. We're best friends now, Ella. Don't you worry about a thing."

Ella's not buying what I'm selling. "What are you up to?"

"Only very good things, baby sis." I sling an arm around her shoulder.

She sighs. "I have a bad feeling about this."

Her skepticism begins to annoy me. "Why? Is it so hard to believe that I could be good for Hartley?"

"Yes, it is. You know I love you to death, but come on, Easton. You make decisions based on how people make you feel, not the other way around."

"Come on. I'm not that bad," I joke.

But Ella's on a roll. "Are you denying it? Denying that you screwed around with your brothers' girlfriends? That you told me once that—"

Stung, I drop my arm and slow down. "Did I piss in your cereal this morning? Why are you throwing this shit in my face?"

"Because I care about you. When you hurt people, it ends up scarring your own heart." Her expression softens. "I want you to be happy. I don't think this is going to make you happy."

"How about you stay in your own lane and worry about

whether Reed's being faithful all the way up at State without you?" I snap.

As hurt floods her face, regret replaces my anger.

"Fuck, I'm sorry. That was a crappy thing to say. Reed worships the ground your little feet walk on." I ruffle the top of her head. "But, look, I'm being serious, okay? Hartley and I've come to an agreement. She needs a friend, and for some reason, I want to be that friend. I'm not going to hurt her and she's not going to hurt me."

Ella doesn't look convinced. "If you say so."

"I do. We good?"

She gives me a short nod and then throws her arms around my waist. "I want you to be happy," she whispers against my chest.

"I am," I say and then escape to my classroom.

I don't like spending a lot of time in my head. Reed and Gideon are broody McBroodersons. I take action and don't give much thought to how it's all going to turn out. Probably because most of the time, it's turned out okay. The times that it hasn't? Well . . .

If I spend too much time dwelling on the shit that's gone wrong, then I'm bound to end up pouring pills down my throat like I did when I was fifteen and my mom's depression caught her by the tail and wouldn't let go.

If hanging with Hartley made me deep dive into an emotional pit that would swallow me whole, I'd get off that ride. But being with her makes me feel good. She's funny, doesn't take much shit from me, and . . . I feel like she needs me.

No one has ever really needed me. Ella needed Reed. My mom needed pills and booze. The twins have each other.

Hartley is alone. And there's something about her loneliness that strikes a chord in me.

But I don't want to dwell on it, so—very uncharacteristically— I pour myself into my next four periods. I answer questions. I volunteer theories. I participate, leaving my classmates and my teachers shocked as hell.

"Are you drunk?" Hartley whispers to me during Government.

I roll my eyes. "No. Are you?"

She just wrinkles her forehead, still looking confused.

And she's not the only one. "What's gotten into you?" Pash demands as we leave class for lunch. "Is your dad riding your ass?"

"Nah, I bet he has some big thing planned and you want cover, right?" guesses Owen, another teammate.

"Can't a guy answer a question in class without something being up?"

Both Pash and Owen shake their heads.

"Whatever you've got planned, count me in," Pash announces. The two guys slap each other's hands in agreement and then run off, presumably to spread the word that I'm going to execute some huge stunt.

I let them speculate, because the answer inside my head— that I'm trying to forget the way a girl makes me feel—would sound even worse if I gave voice to it.

Naturally, the first person I run into when I reach the cafeteria is Hartley. She walks by with a tray piled so high that I wonder if she's getting food for another person in addition to herself. I scan the room suspiciously but see no one lurking around. Except for me. I'm the only Hartley Wright stalker. Which is how it should be.

"Need some help there?"

Her head shoots up and the tray tips dangerously in her hands. I grab it before the pasta, sandwich, and three bananas fall to the floor.

"It's fine, I can take it." She moves to snatch the tray back, but I swing it out of her reach.

I spot Pash in line and yell to him. "Grab me the curry dish, would you?"

He gives me a thumbs-up. That task taken care of, I look for a place to sit. Usually, I sit with Ella, Val, and a few others, but I'm trying to avoid Ella and her prying eyes and nosy questions.

I spot an empty table near the corner that everyone avoids because the administration had this bright idea to plant trees in hopes of brightening up the place. Thing is, there was a bug infestation last semester, and the corner was filled with them. Now, everyone's afraid to sit there. Hartley wasn't here last year, so she won't know this.

"Really, I can carry that," she insists.

"I know." I don't stop until I reach the table. I set the tray down and pull a chair out for her. "But we're best friends now and besties eat together. It's the law. Look around." I wave a hand around the room where all our classmates are grouped together in twos, threes, and more. "We're herd animals. We like to be together."

She scratches some spot on her neck and eyes me warily. "I think I'm more of a loner."

"Great. We'll be alone together." I tug my tie loose. I don't mind the pants or even the blazer, but the tie we have to wear pisses me off.

"Here's your lunch." Pash appears at Hartley's side and

sets the tray on the table. "Why aren't we sitting down? Is something wrong?" He gives me an alarmed look. "Wait, are the bugs back?"

"What bugs?" Hartley asks.

I slice my hand in front of my neck for Pash to ixnay the bug shit, but he's not paying attention. "I hated those freaking things. If whatever you're planning deals with bugs, you're on your own."

He runs off before I can correct whatever misconceptions he's cooked up. It's better this way.

"What's this about bugs?" Hartley repeats.

"Are you scared of them? I'll kill them for you."

"I can kill my own bugs, thank you very much."

"Good. I hate them. I appoint you as the official bug killer. But don't worry, this is a bug-free zone." Or at least I hope it is.

Our asses barely hit our respective chairs when a cheery voice calls my name from across the dining hall.

"There you are, Easton!"

Every head in the vicinity swivels to watch Felicity sway over to my side.

"Thank you for saving me a seat," she gushes.

When she leans down and kisses my cheek, a collective gasp silences the room, followed by a huge boom of chatter as the gossip machines crank into high gear. Dammit. Not this again. She texted me like a dozen more times last night, but I ignored every message. I'd hoped that if I kept ignoring her, she'd go away.

Obviously that was hoping for too much.

Across the table, Hartley's mouth quivers as if she's trying not to laugh. I'm suddenly glad I told her about Felicity's crazy fake relationship idea, otherwise this grand entrance might've freaked her out.

"I didn't save you a seat." I cross my arms and try to look as foreboding as possible.

Felicity's hide is tougher than an armadillo's. She trills an annoying laugh and drops next to me. "Of course you did." She turns to Hartley. "We haven't officially met. I'm Felicity Worthington."

Hartley nods. "Hartley Wright." She sticks out her hand and offers it to Felicity, who, like the bitch she is, proceeds to ignore it.

"I'm Easton's girlfriend. We just started going out this weekend, isn't that right?"

"Felicity," I growl.

"What?" She blinks innocently. "I didn't realize we were keeping it a secret."

Biting my lower lip, I send a pleading look to Hartley. *For the love of God, help me! Get me out of this!*

Instead, the little witch does the opposite.

"Oh wow, I'm so happy for you guys!" Hartley exclaims. "New relationships are so much fun, aren't they? Like, those first few weeks where everything is so shiny and perfect and you're just all over each other? Isn't that the best?"

It's the most bubbly I've ever seen her. Too bad it's fake.

She beams at me. I try to convey with my eyes that I am going to murder her after lunch.

"The best," Felicity agrees, and to punctuate that, she scoots closer and rests her head on my shoulder.

I unceremoniously shift three inches to the right. Felicity topples over, nearly smacking her head on the side of the table before managing to regain her balance.

"You two look precious together. You should be in an ad. Oh, wait, I have an idea." Hartley twists around and pretends to look for someone. "Who does the pictures for the yearbook? Your first lunch together should be commemorated."

No one answers her. She shrugs and pulls out her phone. "How about I take a picture and when I come across the person in charge, I'll send it to her?"

She aims the camera at us.

If it was acceptable to strangle a girl in the lunchroom, my hands would be around Hartley's throat. Instead, Felicity decides to drop into my lap and I have to use my hands to push her aside.

"No pictures," I growl.

Hartley pretends to think it over. "You're right. You should have a professional photographer for your first picture. You can only have one first time."

"You wanna die, don't you?" I warn.

Felicity gives Hartley a patronizing smile. "I appreciate how you're trying to cover your jealousy with this fake happiness, but be warned. Easton and I are a couple now. You'll learn to accept it. In the meantime, if you want to feel sorry for someone, go console Claire."

We all turn to see Claire two tables over, wearing an expression of utter despair. I grimace and shift away. Hartley's glee slides off her face, too.

Felicity, on the other hand, can't stop beaming. "Oh, there's our new quarterback." She waves a hand. "Bran! Bran. Over here."

Bran waves back and wanders over to us. "Hey, thanks for the invite," he says as he sets his tray opposite mine. "I wasn't sure where to sit today."

"There's a football table." I point my fork toward the two large groups of guys near the window.

"I see them every morning," Bran says. "I think that's enough togetherness, don't you?"

It's hard to say no since I hardly ever sit with them, either.

"This is nice," Felicity announces. "What's your family do, Bran?"

A confused expression crosses his face. "Ah, I'm not sure what you mean."

"She wants to know where you fall on the ladder of capital success. In other words, whether you're important enough to talk to," I explain.

Felicity clucks her tongue. "That's not true at all, Easton." But she ruins her fake humility by repeating herself. "So what is it that your parents do?"

"My dad's an accountant and my mom is a teacher at Bellfield Elementary."

"Oh, well, that's . . ." She flounders for an appropriate adjective, because in her mind, she's appalled.

"Arthur Fleming's got a seat available next to him." I gesture to the slender senior with the dark brown hair and round hipster eyeglasses. The Flemings own a major frozen food company. "And I hear he's single."

"Thanks, but I'm good," Bran says dryly.

"He meant me, sweetie." Felicity pats Bran on the hand before addressing me. "Why would I care about that when I have you, Easton Royal?"

Hartley laughs out loud, then quickly covers up the sound with a cough. "So," she says to Bran, "how were your classes this morning?"

With a grateful smile, he answers, "Not bad, although I'm

surprised at the amount of homework I have. My teachers at Bellfield didn't assign this much shit."

"I know, right?" Hartley groans. "I've got a paper due in three weeks and I need to plan for the chem project. I don't want to be doing that last minute."

Bran clucks his tongue in sympathy. "I did my science lab last year. I can give you my notes—"

"Ella! Val!" I wave the two girls over.

Bran breaks off at my glare. I can see where this is going and I need to nip it in the bud. Bran will give his notes to Hartley and then it will lead to Bran at Hartley's tiny apartment, sitting on the sofa. Their heads will be close together. Then his mouth will be on hers, followed by me busting the door down and breaking the arm of our new quarterback.

Just because I've resigned myself to the fact that Hartley and I won't be banging doesn't mean I want Bran Mathis anywhere near her.

Luckily, Ella and Val make their way over, bringing with them a change of subject.

"Why are we sitting here today?" Val asks. "Don't we always sit by the windows?"

"There wasn't enough room," I reply, kicking out a chair for her to take a seat.

"But our table has plenty of—"

"It's quieter here," Ella interrupts. "I think that's why Easton chose it. Right, East?"

I roll my eyes. Since when do I have to explain myself? "Right."

"How nice of you to join us," Felicity says, but her tight smile reveals that she doesn't like this development at all.

I remember her insinuation that she could easily take Ella down, and a frown creases my forehead. If she messes with my family, I'll mess right back.

Bran and Ella know each other from Spanish and start chatting right away. Val and Hartley start talking about Val's eye makeup.

Leaving me stuck with Felicity, who tugs on my sleeve. "Let's go out tonight."

"Nope."

"Why not?"

"Because I don't want to."

"We're supposed to be a couple," she hisses.

"No, we're not," I hiss back.

"You said yes."

"You can't hold me to something I said when I was drunk!"

Hartley glances over. "You lovebirds okay?"

Val snickers softly, while Ella just sighs. I already gave both of them the heads-up that Felicity thinks we're going out.

"We're fine," Felicity assures the table, as if anyone actually cares how "we're" doing. "We're just having trouble figuring out where to go on our date tonight."

I grit my teeth so hard that my molars ache.

"You know where you should go?" Val pipes up.

I give her the evil eye for daring to play along with this insanity. "Nowhere," I grind out. "We're going nowhere."

Val ignores me. "The pier," she says.

"What's on the pier?" Bran asks curiously.

"A carnival, games, some restaurants," Val tells him. "It's fun."

"I heard there's a haunted house that's pretty cool there," Ella ventures.

I pin her with a murderous look. Why is *she* entertaining this? She hates Felicity!

"What are you doing tonight, Hartley?" Felicity asks, surprising me.

Hartley appears just as taken aback. "Studying, probably."

"Ah, studying's boring." Felicity smiles sweetly. "Apparently Easton and I are planning a get-together at the pier. You and Bran should come."

"That doesn't sound half-bad," Bran says. He knocks his shoulder against Hartley. "What do you say? Want to ride the Ferris wheel?"

Oh hell no.

Seventeen

"THIS IS FUN, isn't it?" Val chirps later in the evening. "We've eaten at the pier, but I haven't been to the ride part in ages."

"If by 'fun,' you mean it's better than the seventh circle of hell, then yeah, sure, it's fun." I glower at the backs of Hartley and Bran, who are at the ticket counter. Bran's trying to pay for Hartley, and she keeps shaking her head no.

It gives me a tiny amount of satisfaction that Hartley is giving Bran the brush-off over the money thing. If she was interested, she'd let him pay, right? That's how it works. Girls want you to buy them things. If they don't accept gifts from you, then they're not interested.

Hartley wins and pays for herself.

I hustle up to the counter and lay down my card. "I've got these two." I gesture to Ella and Val.

"What about me?" my fake girlfriend squawks.

I spare her a glance over my shoulder. "Your dad owns an auto plant. You can pay your own way."

"Easton!" Ella says in shock.

"What? It wasn't my idea to come here." I take the card and tickets and move on through the turnstile. Maybe Felicity will decide that I'm too much of an asshole to deal with and break up our fake relationship.

I could only be so lucky.

That's the only reason I agreed to this "date," though. I plan to talk some sense into Felicity and convince her to leave me the hell alone.

"I expect more out of you, Easton!" Felicity huffs when she joins us inside the park. Her platinum-blond hair is tied in a long braid down her back, and she's wearing a beige shift dress and nude three-inch heels that are in no way suitable for a carnival.

"Don't. That way you won't be disappointed."

Her mouth flattens, as it tends to do when she's pissed off. "We're going to talk after tonight."

"Pass." I'd rather be pummeled for an hour straight by the bouncer at the Salem Street poker game.

"Nice shirt," Ella says to Hartley when we join her and Bran.

I notice that they're both wearing the same cropped white sweatshirt with a stripe down each belled-out sleeve. Hartley has hers paired with a pair of skinny jeans that show off her great ass while Ella's wearing a blue miniskirt.

Hartley grins. "Got it on sale."

"Me too." And, like that, they're best friends. If I'd known that was all it took, I'd have sported a white crop top a long time ago. I'm not afraid to show off my abs.

"Want something to drink?" I ask the group.

"I'll have a Diet Coke," Felicity announces. "And a frozen banana with no chocolate or nuts."

"So a banana," I say.

"But frozen."

I don't even argue. "Bran?"

"I'll have whatever. Coke is good."

He, like me, probably needs a beer, but we're underage and they're pretty strict at the pier. Then I remember he's a straight-edge who doesn't drink. I turn to Hartley.

"How about you, Har-Har?"

Felicity scowls at the nickname.

"I'm good." Hartley shakes her head.

"You sure? I'm not going to offer to pay every day," I tease. The only reason I made the suggestion in the first place was to have an excuse to buy something for Hartley.

"I'm getting an orange cream float," Ella pipes up. "Val?"

"Root beer float for me. And funnel cake with strawberries."

"I wouldn't mind a funnel cake," Bran admits.

"Lend me a hand, Bran?" This order has gotten bigger than I anticipated. Besides, I'm not about to leave him alone with Hartley.

"Sure."

We go up to the concession stand and I order three funnel cakes, a frozen banana—they don't have any non chocolate covered ones—and six foot-long corn dogs.

"Are we feeding an army?" Bran jokes.

He might be sweet on Hartley, but he's not very observant. Hartley was licking her lips when Ella was ordering food. When her tongue darted out, my knees got weak. Sadly, I know that look of hunger wasn't for me but for food.

"You can never have enough carnival food."

"True."

As we wait at the counter, Bran shoves his hands in his pockets and gives me an awkward look. "Be honest, Royal—is it cool that I'm here with Hartley?"

I stiffen. The way he says that, it's like he thinks they're on a date or some shit. Are they? They showed up separately, I know that for a fact. Hartley came on the bus, and Bran drove up in his Dodge. But that doesn't mean much. They could've still talked about it being a date sometime between when school ended and we all arrived here.

Does he have her phone number?

Jealousy burns at my insides. He fucking better not.

"Why wouldn't it be?" Somehow I manage to put on the most casual of tones.

He shrugs. "I dunno. You just seem really protective of her."

"We're friends. I'm protective of all my friends."

"Same." He smiles and invites me to smile with him, but all my humor's in my shoes at this moment.

"You really interested in Hartley?" Bran seems like a decent guy and he's the only player on our team who can throw the ball, but that doesn't mean he should be sniffing around my girl.

"Maybe? She seems like a cool girl."

"You shouldn't date anyone your senior year, because that relationship won't last," I inform him.

Bran arches an eyebrow. "You write an advice column on the side, Royal?"

It's hard to hold back a blush, but I manage it. Years of not caring what anyone thinks helps.

"Yeah, it's called Dear Man Who Knows Better Than Me. I'm here to help you not make a fool of yourself."

"And you're saying that pursuing Hartley is going to make a fool out of me?" He looks amused.

"I'm saying she's not interested."

"I'll take my chances." He grabs a funnel cake. "But thanks for the advice."

I've got no good response, so I keep my mouth shut as we return to the girls. By the time we reach them, the crowd has swelled to more than a dozen—most of them friends of Felicity's.

"It looks like half the senior class came," Val observes as I start handing out food.

Felicity pats her hair. "I guess word got out that I'm here."

I stare at her, wondering if she's being at all ironic, but apparently not. She's serious. I glance around to see if anyone else is amused by her delusions, but Ella and Hartley are busy scarfing their food. Felicity's crew is nodding as if her declaration was delivered by an oracle.

Once we're done eating, Bran suggests going on rides.

"I love the Ferris wheel," Hartley admits. "I haven't ridden on one since I was twelve, I think."

"Rides are for children," Felicity interjects. "Why don't you win something for me?"

"And games aren't for children?" I counter.

"How about a shooting contest?" Tiffany, one of her friends, suggests. "The guys can win us all prizes."

Felicity claps her hands. "Yes! Come on, Easton. You can win me something to make up for not paying my admission." She loops her hand around my elbow and tugs me toward the games.

"How about you?" Bran says to Hartley. "Should I win you something?"

"Oh no. I don't need anything," she protests.

Damn right. If anyone is going to win Hartley a prize, it's me. She's *my* friend.

"How about we win our own prizes," Ella suggests dryly.

As Felicity and the other girls chorus their dismay, Hartley gives a thumbs-up. She, Ella, and Val separate from the group, wandering off toward a booth where some jackass is offering to guess everyone's weight. Kinda rude, if you ask me.

I try to follow them, but Felicity grabs my arm again.

"I'm getting real tired of that." I stare pointedly at her hand.

"Of what?"

Gently, but firmly, I extract myself from her grip. "How far are you going to take this?"

She plants her hands on her hips. "I don't know what you mean."

I stifle a shout of frustration. "Felicity. Listen to me. I was drunk when I agreed to your proposition. I didn't even re-member seeing you when I woke up the next morning."

"Well, you did see me, and you said you'd be my boyfriend, so tough cookies, Easton Royal. This is happening."

"Look, you're a nice girl." I choke on the lie. "You don't want me as your boyfriend, fake or otherwise, okay? I'm a terrible person, and on top of that, I'm pretty damn lazy. You need to find someone else to hitch your wagon to."

Her hands slide up from her hips to cross tightly across her rack. Huh. I never noticed her chest before. Probably be-cause I never cared enough to check her out.

"No," she says.

"No?"

"No. I've already announced we're a couple and so we're a couple. I don't care if you're rude or insulting. Your bad behav-ior will only result in sympathy for me."

Holy mother of God. She's clearly not right in her head. "I'm not doing this. Period. Like, honestly, I don't know what else to say or how many other ways to put it. I'm not playing along."

"Yes, you are."

I take a few steps away. I'm done with this conversation.

"Because if you don't," she adds, "I'm going to make Hartley's life miserable."

I stick my tongue in the side of my cheek and pray for a little patience. After all, I did agree to this stupid charade in the first place, even if I don't have the clearest memory of doing so.

I walk back to her, trying to appeal to her rational side. "Let's be reasonable. Why don't you dump me? You can say I cheated on you or that I'm just too stupid to waste your time on or that I'm bad in the sack. Tell whatever lie you want and I'll back you up."

"No."

Arghhhhhhh. I'm seconds away from slamming my fist into the nearest wall. This girl is absurd.

And if she's going to be an asshole over this, I can be even worse in return. "Try coming after Hartley and you'll be crying for mercy within a day," I say tightly.

Instead of being scared off, Felicity gives me a smug smile. "After I'm done with Hartley, I'll go after Ella."

I scoff. This again? No way Felicity takes Ella down. Ella already fought and tamed the meanest girl Astor Park Prep has seen—Jordan Carrington. "I'm not interested in the games you want to play, babe. And Ella's strong enough to stand up to you."

"We'll see, won't we?" With the same sick grin plastered to her face, she saunters off to join her friends.

Swallowing a groan, I stick my hands in my pockets and

watch my classmates play a bunch of games. Bran's playing the basketball game and draining shot after shot. There are several girls gathered around him, cheering him on.

Hmmm.

The sight of their obvious adoration for Astor Park's newest athlete gives me an idea.

If Felicity wants to be on the top of the social chain, then it makes sense for her to hook up with Bran. Despite his lack of money, he's good-looking and, most importantly, he's our quarterback. Everybody loves a quarterback. Hell, even Hartley thinks he's all that and a bag of chips. I just need to convince Felicity that Bran's a better catch than me.

And, fine, if Bran getting with Felicity also keeps him away from Hartley, that's just a silver lining.

I totally don't have an ulterior motive or anything.

I hurry over to the arcade game. I shove money into the machine next to Bran and start shooting. It's pretty easy. Soon, I have my own little crowd of admirers. When Bran pauses to watch me, I make my move.

"Want to make a bet, Mathis?" I ask, casting out the lure.

He bites, just like I knew he would. He's an athlete, which means he's got plenty of competitive juice in him. "Sure. What are the stakes?"

"If I win, you buy ride tickets for everyone here. If I lose, I buy them."

"There are twenty-three of us," Ella says quietly. "That's nearly a thousand dollars."

I didn't even see her come up beside me. Val and Hartley are back, too, and when I look over, there's no missing the worry in their eyes. "I know," I reply. "Pocket change, right?"

The Astor kids nod, but Bran, the son of a teacher and an

accountant, isn't a regular Astor kid. He doesn't have a trust account and an allowance of thousands of dollars a month.

When he pales underneath his tan, I know I'm right. "Um, sure. I guess." His pride won't allow him to back down.

I squeeze his shoulder, because he's not in any danger of having to pay up. I'm going to lose big. "Awesome."

Felicity claps her hands in glee. "I want the big panda." She points to one of the giant stuffed animals that we could probably pick up for five bucks at a place that Felicity would die before stepping foot into. She doesn't want the panda. She wants what the panda represents in her dippy mind.

Too bad she's going to be disappointed.

We start shooting. For the first round, I drain as many baskets as I can. I need to make my loss look realistic. Bran, however, isn't cooperating. The thought of buying all those tickets is getting to him, which is weird because on the foot ball field he's never ruffled. He starts bricking his shots, and the lead I built up doesn't go away. Not even after I pretend to go cold.

In the third round, he picks up steam, but it's too little, too late. When the buzzer goes off, I'm the winner.

Fuck.

"Double or nothing," I blurt out.

"No, I'm good," Bran says, but his complexion has taken on a greenish cast.

"I knew you'd win, Easton!" Felicity gushes. "Good breeding always prevails."

I know Ella's disappointed, but it's the disgust in Hartley's eyes that kills me. Ella will believe my explanation—how I tried to rig it so Bran would win and I'd buy the tickets. But Hartley won't. She already thinks I'm an asshole.

I swallow hard and pull out my wallet. "It was a dumb bet. I'll get the tickets."

"No, man. A bet's a bet. Gotta be a man of my word." Gulping visibly, Bran staggers off to go buy the tickets.

Some of our teammates slap him on the back as he passes. "That's our QB!"

"Shit," I mutter.

Ella grabs my arm and pulls me aside. "Go stop him," she pleads.

"I can't. If I try to buy the tickets, he'll lose the respect of his teammates."

"You guys are idiots." She looks like she wants to slap me. Frankly, I could use a blow to my face.

Bran returns with the tickets and hands them out. I stand off to the side and wait for everyone else to get them first. When Bran reaches me, I renew my offer to pay.

"I've played this game so many times with my brothers that I could make these shots with my eyes shut. Let me pay, okay?"

Bran snorts. "So you set me up?"

"Not exactly." But I don't sound convincing, because I *did* set him up, just not in the way that it turned out.

"I guess I thought we were playing on the same team," he mumbles, "but thanks for showing me your true colors early on. I know what the rules are now." He slaps a ride card in my hand and then walks off.

"You're a real jerk."

I look up to see Hartley approaching me. Her gray eyes look like two storm clouds.

Misery jams in my throat. I swallow hard, then gesture for her to follow me to a spot out of earshot of our classmates. Miraculously, she comes with me.

"It's not what it looked like," I tell her, lowering my voice. "I was going to lose so I could pay for the tickets."

She shakes her head in disgust. "Yeah. Sure, Easton."

"It's true."

"Uh-huh. Then why'd you play the stupid game anyway? Why not just pay for the tickets outright?"

"I wanted Bran to look good in front of Felicity."

"What?" Hartley's brow crinkles.

"I thought maybe if she got hot for someone else, she'd forget this stupid idea that she and I are dating." Jeez. The whole thing sounds ridiculous now that I'm trying to explain it to someone else. "Look, I made a mistake. I didn't mean for Bran to be out that money."

Hartley searches my expression for what feels like forever. "You really weren't trying to be an ass to him, were you?"

I unhappily shake my head. I realize that I'm the male version of Felicity. I won't leave Hartley alone, even though she keeps demanding it. I'm self-centered. I make other people miserable with my stupid, impulsive decisions.

Actually, that's not very Felicity-like. She's a cunning planner. I just want to have a good time.

But not at the expense of others.

"Oh, Easton." There's a wealth of disappointment in those two words.

"I know." I straighten my shoulders. "I'm going to fix it."

"How?"

"I have no idea. You're my best friend, though. Can you help me out?" I throw her a pleading glance.

She surprises me by moving closer to squeeze my arm. "We'll figure something out," she assures me.

And then she proceeds to shock me again—this time by

planting a quick kiss on my cheek. Maybe I'm not the male Felicity, after all. Hartley likes me and she's as decent as they come.

My entire body soars from that one second of physical contact. *Down, boy,* I order. *We're friends with Hartley and that means no getting excited in inappropriate places.*

"Coming?" she asks, a few steps ahead of me.

A perverted comeback pops into my head, but this time my brain beats out my mouth. It's a close call, though.

Eighteen

THE NEXT DAY, I'm on damage control. First order of business? Make things right with my quarterback, whose only crime yesterday was being the unwilling pawn in my mission to rid myself of Felicity.

I wait until the locker room clears out before I approach Bran. "Got a sec?"

He scowls at my approach. "What do you want, Royal?"

I offer a rueful smile. "I come with a peace offering."

"That so?" He doesn't look at me as he shuts the locker door harder than necessary. He's already dressed for practice and looks impatient to get going.

I glance around to make sure we're alone, then hold out the ten crisp hundred-dollar bills in my palm.

His green eyes flash. "What the hell?"

"Look, I'm sorry about last night, man. You were right, okay? I *was* trying to set you up, but not in the way you think." I try to press the bills into his clenched fist. "Take it."

He shoves my hand away. "Keep your money, Royal. I'm not a charity case."

"This isn't charity. It's reparations."

Bran snorts.

"I'm serious. I wasn't trying to embarrass you or diss you about not being loaded like the rest of us."

"No?" His voice is tight. "Then what were you trying to do?"

I heave out a sigh. "I was hoping you'd shoot the hell out of those targets and get Felicity so hot and bothered that she'd ditch me for you."

His eyebrows shoot up to his hairline. "Um. What?"

"I made a huge mistake agreeing to go out with that girl," I admit. "She was on my case at the carnival, and I figured, hell, maybe I could get her off my back and onto your dick. Win-win."

A reluctant smile creeps onto his face. "Win-win? As in, you win and Felicity wins? Because I don't see how I'm a winner in that scenario."

"Hey, she's not a bad chick." I'm lying through my teeth. She's awful. But I already screwed up and cost Bran probably all of his savings—I'll look like a total dick if I admit I tried to saddle him with the demon spawn.

"She's hot," I add, and this time I'm not lying. Felicity *is* hot. "She's popular. She comes from old-school money." I shrug. "She wouldn't be the worst choice of girlfriends if you're looking to date someone at Astor."

He bends down to lace up his shoes. "Uh-huh. If she's such a great choice, why don't you want her?"

"Because I don't do girlfriends," I answer truthfully. "I suck at that shit. I was wasted when I said I'd go out with her, wasn't thinking about what I was saying."

"Okay." Bran straightens and runs a hand through his close-cropped hair. "Let me get this straight—you conned me into a shooting match so that you could lose and I'd look good in front of Felicity?"

I give a sheepish nod.

"Because you want me to date her." He pauses. "So that *you* don't have to date her."

I nod again, biting my lip to keep from laughing. But then Bran barks out a laugh, and I can't help but chuckle in return.

"That's some messed-up logic."

"I'm a Royal. 'Messed-up' is my middle name." I shake my head in exasperation. "I just didn't count on you getting stage fright and blowing the match."

"Hey," he protests. "A thousand bucks was on the line. I choked."

I reach out and smack him on his arm—his non-throwing one. "Don't let Coach hear you say that. Choking ain't allowed."

"There's no money on our games," he replies. "Which means no money pressure. Just the pressure Coach puts on us to win."

"Money pressure?"

"Yeah, that kind of shit stresses me out. Probably because cash has been tight in my house ever since I was a kid."

Once again, guilt lodges in my throat, making my voice come out hoarse. "Seriously, dude. I did a crappy thing last night. And it's not that I think you can't pay your debts. It's just that I shouldn't have made that bet in the first place." I forcibly grab his hand and smack the bills into his palm. "Take it. It's not charity. It's me promising to never again throw you under the bus to save my own hide. I'll deal with Felicity another way. If you don't take it, I'm going to follow your ass around and shove the cash in your pocket at inconvenient times. I might even buy you a car and park it in the lot outside with a big-ass bow on top. I can be real annoying."

"I never would've guessed," he drawls.

"So you'll take it?"

After a long moment, he nods. "All right." Gratitude and a tinge of respect line his voice. "I'm glad you told me the truth. I really didn't want to have to hate you."

I laugh. "You wouldn't have been able to hate me anyway. Nobody can."

Bran and I bump fists and then head out to the practice field.

✦ ✦ ✦

NEXT UP IS Hartley. As I make my way to first period, I finger the chain in my pocket. There's a fancy velvet box that goes with it, but I figured that would be overkill.

"Hey, bestie." I catch up to Hartley before she can enter the classroom.

She steps away from the doorway to let a few other students in. "What's up?"

"I made up with Bran."

"Did you?" She brushes a strand of hair away from her face. My fingers itch to do it for her.

"He can't resist my charm," I tease.

"No one can," she replies with a grin. "Not even me, obviously."

A broad smile breaks across my own face. I reach into my pocket and pull out the necklace. "Anyway, since I'm apologizing, I want to give you this."

Her eyes widen as I dangle the necklace in front of her.

She stares at it for a moment and then reluctantly brushes a finger across the delicate chain. "I can't accept this."

"I got it from Candy Machine," I tell her. "So either you take it or I'm going to throw it away."

"A candy machine?" she asks. Her fingertips linger on the chain, tracing it down to cradle one of the three little gold charms. She wants it, but for once in my life, I don't press her. She likes to make her own decision and in her own time.

"Yup." I grab her palm and drop the chain in it. "Here. It's yours to do whatever you want with. If you don't want it, toss it."

And then I make myself walk into the classroom without another word.

❖ ❖ ❖

THE REST OF the day flies by. Much to my relief, Felicity steers clear of me, even at lunch. She sits with her headband-wearing girlfriends, looking like a fifties girl group, while I joke around with my own friends.

In calc, I sit between Ella and Hartley, but we don't get a chance to talk much because Ms. Mann springs a pop quiz on us. To my uneasiness, she watches me for most of the period with an unhappy look.

I'm not the only one who notices. At one point, Hartley pokes me in the ribs and whispers, "What'd you do now?"

"Nothing," I whisper back. I haven't had any contact with Ms. Mann since I, well, had *contact* with Ms. Mann.

"Mr. Royal, Ms. Wright," comes the sharp voice of our teacher. "Less talking and more solving, please." She's just asked everyone to solve questions one through five in the textbook.

Hartley immediately bends her head to resume the task. I've already solved all five equations, so I scribble something else in my notebook. I tear off the corner of the page, wait until Ms. Mann is looking away, and slide the note onto Hartley's desk. I'd written: *Coming to the game Friday night?*

She stiffens for a beat, looks to the front of the room, and then unfolds the note.

After she reads it, she picks up her pencil, writes something, and slides the paper back.

Maybe is her response.

I scribble again and pass the note. *Maybe?? We're best friends! I need support. Best friends support each other.*

She passes it back. *I might have to work Friday. I told one of the other waitresses I can cover for her if she needs me.*

The note passes between us several more times.

OK. But you don't know for sure if you're working?

Not yet. I'll find out the day of.

OK. Let me know. If you're not working, you're coming to the game! OR ELSE.

Hartley snickers softly, but not softly enough. Ms. Mann's sharp gaze once again lands in our vicinity.

"Eyes on your own work, Ms. Wright."

Hartley flushes at the implication that she's been cheating. She discreetly tucks our note under her notebook and gets back to work.

The moment the bell rings, I shove my books into my backpack and get to my feet.

"Mr. Royal, a moment, please."

Crap. "See you at later?" I say to the girls.

Ella nods and pats me on the arm while Hartley shoots a wary look between me and Ms. Mann. Right. Hartley was outside the door that day, which frickin' blows, because the last thing I want is to remind her of that. She already thinks I'm a dog.

"Mr. Royal," Ms. Mann commands.

Gritting my teeth, I approach her desk. "Ms. Mann," I mock.

She glances toward the doorway to make sure it's empty but doesn't make a move to get up and close the door. I guess she wants to eliminate temptation.

When her gaze returns to mine, her expression is cloudy with frustration and her voice is barely above a whisper. "Whatever you're saying to people, you need to stop."

I wrinkle my forehead. "What are you talking about?"

"Dammit, Easton!" She gasps at her own raised voice, swallows nervously, and looks at the door again. Then she's back to whispering. "You told someone about what happened between us."

That gives me pause. I didn't tell a damn soul about— No, wait. Ella knows. So do Hartley and Reed. And Pash definitely suspects.

"Another teacher insinuated it in the faculty lounge this morning." Panic creeps into her eyes. "If this gets back to Headmaster Beringer, I'll be fired!"

I can't stop a sarcastic retort. "Don't you think you shoulda thought of that before you fooled around with me in this classroom?" I wave my hand around the empty space.

Her pretty face collapses. She looks like I just slapped her, and even though a rush of guilt floods my stomach, I try to tamp it down. Why can't people take responsibility for their actions? I knew what we were doing was wrong when we did it. I own that. She needs to own it, too. The woman made it clear from the first minute I stepped into her classroom that she wanted to take me for a ride.

We didn't even do *that* much.

I try to reassure her. "Look, relax. Nobody saw us, and there's absolutely no proof that anything happened. If Beringer questions us, we just deny it."

Ms. Mann bites her lip. "We deny it . . ."

"Yes." My tone is firm. "It never happened, okay?"

A weak smile lifts the corners of her mouth. "What never happened?"

I grin wryly. "Exactly."

✦   ✦   ✦

AFTER THE LAST bell, Felicity corners me at my locker before I can escape. With quick, determined strides, she marches up and plants a loud, sloppy kiss on my cheek.

"Awww," someone sighs from behind us, but I can't tell if it's with appreciation or jealousy.

I turn briefly and notice the covetous stares of the girls standing at the end of the locker bank. They take one look at me and Felicity and start whispering to each other.

There's a tug on my hand. I peer down in time to see her lace our fingers together. I try to snatch my hand back, but she holds on tight. Man, she's got a lethal grip for such a tiny thing.

"What are you doing?" I growl.

"Holding my boyfriend's hand," she chirps.

I take a deep breath. Then, slowly and methodically, I bring my mouth close to her ear and hiss, "Swear to God, woman, I'm about to lose my shit. I told you a million times, *I was drunk*. I'm not fucking doing this."

She stares up at me. "Yes, you are."

"This is over, Felicity. Do you hear me?"

I don't bother to lower my voice, and Felicity whirls around to make sure nobody heard what I said. When she's satisfied her cover hasn't been blown, she speaks in a tone you'd normally use on a bratty toddler.

"Easton. We had an arrangement, and it doesn't end unless *I* want it to end."

"That's not how this works."

"That's exactly how it works."

I can feel the anger surging in my veins. I hate Felicity's kind. I'd pick girls like Ella and Val and Hartley over girls like Felicity and Lauren and Jordan any day. Their sense of entitlement makes my blood boil. Which is all sorts of ironic, because I'm as entitled as they are. I get whatever I want, whenever I want it. That's what it means to be a Royal.

But for some reason, it's really unattractive when I see that quality in other people.

Does Hartley view me with the same scorn and disgust I feel toward Felicity? I hope not.

"Look, can't we just walk away like normal people?" I ask politely. "Having a girlfriend, even a fake one, cramps my style."

She makes an annoyed noise. "I told you, as long as you're discreet, you can hook up with whoever."

"Discreet? Baby, I don't know the meaning of that word. I screwed my brother's ex-girlfriend in his *bed*. I hooked up with Niall O'Malley's mom during an after-party at his house. I took on two of the Pastels a year ago in the Carringtons' pool. If we keep this up, I'm just gonna embarrass you and make you look bad."

Her nostrils flare.

"Not on purpose," I add hastily. "But because that's who I am. I don't think about shit before I do it. Do you really want to be the girlfriend of the guy who broke it off with his girl-friend over a text message?" That's what Claire likes to tell people, even though I conveyed the message in person. For once, that lie is going to work in my favor.

Felicity goes quiet. When her haughty expression eventu-ally falters, I know I've gotten through to her.

Girls like her are all about image. And, yes, having a Royal on her arm is a massive image booster, but we both know she'd be better off if that Royal was Gideon, my upstanding older brother. Or Reed, who might be a broody bastard but doesn't usually fuck up in public. Me, I'm the Royal mess and everyone knows it.

Her hands drop to her sides. I can see the wheels in her head turning and turning. "Last night at the pier . . ." she starts. "You said I could tell everyone I broke up with you."

I eagerly grasp on to the lifesaver she throws me. "Yes," I answer quickly. "You can say I did some terrible thing to you and that you dumped my ass."

"No. Telling them is not enough."

For fuck's sake. "So what do you want, then?"

"A public breakup," she says decisively. "I want to tell you off in front of everyone and make it clear that you are *so* far beneath me and I want nothing to do with you anymore."

It takes some effort not to roll my eyes. "Sure. Whatever."

"My beach bonfire is on Friday," she reminds me. "After the game. You said you would come."

Did I? I don't remember agreeing to it, but I probably would've ended up there anyway. "Okay."

"We'll hang out for a bit before I break up with you. And you'll just stand there and take whatever I give you."

Hey, if the end result is being free of this wacko, I'll run through the bonfire buck naked and let her throw tomatoes at me. I nod at her. "Fine."

Pleased, Felicity rises on her tiptoes and gives me another kiss on the cheek, probably for the benefit of a passing trio of pretty sophomores. My skin crawls, but I manage to fake a smile. Also for the benefit of the sophomores.

"So I'll see you at the party?" she says cheerfully.

Unfortunately. "Absolutely."

Nineteen

BRAN'S FIRST PLAY of the game on Friday night is a fifty-yard pass directly into the hands of his receiver, who runs it in for the TD.

That badass play sets the tone for the rest of the game—we score on nearly every other drive, if not touchdowns then field goals, and we have a twenty-seven-point lead going into the half.

Hartley didn't end up having to work, so she's in the stands with Ella and Val again. So are Seb and Sawyer. Lauren, surprisingly, is nowhere to be seen.

I can't miss Coach's halftime speech, so I'm not able to stop and chat, but I grin and wave at my crew before disappearing into the tunnel. I'm pumped that Hartley came. I hope this means she's going to chill with us after the game.

The second half is as high-scoring as the first. Saint Lawrence Academy manages to get on the board with two TDs, but Astor Park's lead is commanding and SLA can't make up for the huge shit they took on the field before halftime.

We win. Obviously. And Bran gets the game ball. Coach Lewis tosses it into his new quarterback's hand, smacks Mathis on the shoulder, and says, "You played some damn good football tonight, son."

The rest of our teammates, myself included, cheer in agreement. I jog over to Bran and slap his ass. "Dude. That was brilliant. You've been holding back on us in practice." No joke—he threw for over four hundred yards tonight.

He shrugs modestly. "Hey, I can't reveal all my secrets right out of the gate."

I grin. "A man of mystery. I dig it."

Bran chokes out another laugh.

Dom wanders over to us. "We're hitting the Worthington place, right? Felicity's been telling the whole school that's where the after-party is."

I nod. "Yeah, that's the plan. I need to stop off at home first, though." I plan on raiding Dad's liquor cabinet because I don't trust Felicity to serve the hard stuff. Last time I partied there, it was mostly wine and pre-mixed drinks.

The guys and I charge into the locker room, and I'm one of the first ones out of the showers.

"See you on the beach," I call to Pash and Dom. Then I turn to Bran. "You coming, too?" When he hesitates, I give him a stern look. "Come, man. You're the star tonight—gotta show up and accept your reward in the form of free booze and hot girls who're dying to ride your dick."

Bran smiles slowly. He really is a decent guy. I'm relieved he not only took the money the other morning, but also forgave me for being such a jackass at the pier. "Fine. I'll make an appearance," he agrees.

"You do that, Superstar." I'm snickering as I leave the locker room.

At home, I'm not the only one who decided to make a pit stop. The twins beat me there, only they're not raiding the liquor cabinet like I am. In fact, they're changing out of their ripped jeans and T-shirts into the sweatpants and tanks they usually wear at home.

"What are you guys doing?" I ask from Sawyer's doorway. "Aren't you coming to the Worthingtons'?"

"No." Sebastian sounds reluctant to admit it.

"Oh. What are you doing tonight, then?"

"Lauren wants to chill here," he mumbles. "She's on her way over now."

Christ. Of course she does, and of course she is. Honestly, I thought Lauren was pretty cool last year, but that was before she started hanging around for more than just the occasional visit. The more I get to know her, the more I dislike her. She treats my brothers like they're interchangeable. Like they're just two little toys designed to amuse her.

But Seb and Sawyer seem to be okay with that, so I guess I have to be, too.

I follow my brothers downstairs. We reach the foyer just as the front doors open and Ella, Val, and Hartley appear.

"Hey, sexy ladies," I say, whistling at my girls.

Ella and Val roll their eyes, but Hartley is too busy looking around the grand entrance. Her apprehension is obvious as she examines the twin staircases, the endless ceiling, and the smooth marble beneath her feet. I use her moment of distraction to examine *her*.

She looks cute tonight. She's wearing jeans with rips on

both knees, a dark purple tank top, and an unzipped black hoodie. Her hair is down, and she even put on a bit of makeup — mascara, and shiny lip gloss that makes her mouth look wet and sexy.

The best thing on her, though, is my necklace.

She's wearing it. Like, actually wearing it. And it looks great around her throat. I want to lay a kiss right at the bump of her collarbone.

"I forgot my phone," Ella explains before darting upstairs to her bedroom.

"And I gotta hit the loo before we pay a visit to the Wicked Bitch of the East Coast," Val declares, and then disappears into the hall.

I snicker, but the humor dies once Hartley and I are alone. I'm dying to comment on the necklace but am afraid she'll take it off, so I pretend not to notice. She continues to take in her fancy surroundings, but I don't get the feeling she's judging me. If anything, she looks sad.

"Everything okay?" I ask.

She nods, but she's biting her bottom lip, an action I'm starting to associate with her nerves. Then her lips part and she releases a quick, shallow breath. "It's just . . ." Her tone grows wistful. "Your house is really beautiful, Easton. All the glass . . ."

She's referring to the enormous windows that make up most of my coastal mansion. "My mom loved the sunshine," I admit. "She wanted the whole house to be full of natural light." Except in the end. By then, there was no light in Mom's life. Only darkness and depression that eventually pushed her over the edge.

Silence falls over the massive entryway. I hear Ella's soft murmurs coming from upstairs, and the sound of running water from the hall bathroom.

"You know what?" Hartley says suddenly. "I think I'm just going to take off."

Disappointment shoots through me. "What about the party?"

She shrugs. "I'm not in the mood."

"Aw, come on. You can't bail now."

Obviously she's made up her mind, because she pulls her phone out of her pocket. "I'll get an Uber."

"That sucks," I complain.

Her gray eyes slowly meet mine. "I really don't feel like going to a party tonight, Easton."

Something in her tone, that weird chord of sadness, has me dropping the issue. "Okay, fine. Then we'll stay in." I grab the phone from her hand and close the Uber app.

"What are you doing?" she protests.

"Listen up, Hartley Davidson. We played a ridiculously awesome game tonight and won the hell out of it. I want to celebrate." I raise one eyebrow. "With my best friend."

Hartley laughs out loud. "You're really milking this best friend crap, aren't you?"

"It's not crap. I like chilling with you. And if you don't want to go to the party, then we'll chill here." Felicity will lose her mind if I bail on our big performance, but she can fake break up with me anytime. It doesn't *have* to be tonight. "The twins and Lauren are staying home, too. We'll all hit the game room and shoot some pool, or watch a movie in the media room. Or we can take a swim—the pool's heated."

She shifts awkwardly in her feet. "I don't know . . ."

"It's not even ten o'clock on a Friday. Live a little." When she doesn't answer, I challenge, "Are you working in the morning?"

"No," she admits.

"Good. Then we're hanging out here tonight. Forget the party."

"That sounds like the best idea ever," comes Ella's voice.

She descends the stairs, but Val, who appears in the doorway behind us at the same time, immediately nixes that idea. "No," she says to Ella. "I told you, we're making a show of force tonight."

"I think you're totally giving Felicity too much credit," Ella argues. "She's harmless."

"No, she's not," I say grimly. "I have to agree with Val on this, baby sis."

Ella glowers at me. "Seriously?"

"Seriously. She's already told me a bunch of times that she wants to run the school and how she has no problem taking you down."

Ella's eyes blaze with anger. "She really said that?"

"Yup."

Val pins Ella with a stern look. "See? We need to show the bitch that Ella Harper O'Halloran Royal isn't afraid of her."

"Just Royal will do. And fine, I'll go. But I still think you guys are making a big deal out of nothing." Ella glances at me and Hartley. "So you guys are staying here?"

A tiny thrill shoots up my spine when Hartley responds with a quick nod. Those big gray eyes briefly lock with mine as she says, "I guess we are."

Twenty

"MOVIE? GAME? FOOD?" I offer after Val and Ella leave. I turn to the twins. "What are you all up for?"

The twins shrug and look to Lauren.

"Game is fine." She eyes Hartley speculatively. "Unless you guys need alone time."

"No, but I'm not good at games," Hartley answers. "Unless we're playing Pokémon. I can do that."

God, she's sweet. I chuckle. "I was thinking board game."

"A board game?"

"Yeah, we have a ton of them. My . . ." I trail off as I remember Mom playing Chutes and Ladders with the twins and me when we were little. We'd sit in the nook in the kitchen. Her dark hair would come alive in the sunlight. I remember getting distracted trying to count all the colors.

"Your what?"

I shake it off. Not gonna get sappy tonight. "My mom used to love them. Remember when we played Chutes and Ladders with her?" I ask the twins.

"When we were five," Sawyer says.

I hurry to change the subject. "How about Monopoly?"

The twins defer to Lauren. Again.

She smiles. "I'm good with Monopoly."

"We're good with Monopoly," the twins echo.

I swallow a sigh of frustration.

"Great. The games are in the media room."

I direct Sawyer and Sebastian to grab us sodas and bags of popcorn. Lauren immediately throws herself on the floor and prepares to be waited on, while Hartley follows me over to the game cabinet.

"Original and old-school," she comments as I take the white box off the shelf.

"Of course. I'm a purist."

"He's also a shark," Sawyer warns as he walks into the room, arms full with food. Behind him, Sebastian's carrying a tub with a bunch of bottles in it.

"Didn't know what you were feeling like tonight, baby," he says to Lauren, carrying the drinks over to her.

She haughtily peruses the offerings and then wordlessly points to a diet lemonade. Sebastian plucks it out, twists the top off, and then pours the damn drink into a glass before handing it to his girlfriend.

"What do you want?" I ask Hartley, my tone a little sharp.

"I can help myself," she replies, looking a bit amused. "Why don't you set up the game board?"

I carry the box over to the twins and Lauren.

"I'll be the dog," Lauren announces.

I thumb through the remaining pieces. "What do you want to be, Har-Har?"

"The iron." She plucks it out of the pile and sets it on the board.

Sawyer chooses the ship and Sebastian the old shoe.

I choose the car.

After the first four rounds, Sawyer and Hartley are domi-nating.

"Hey, I'm older than you. Respect your elders," Hartley teases when Sawyer escapes one of her properties by one space.

"Sorry, I'm at the whim of the dice and they say I should buy St. James."

He hands me the money and I give him the property card.

"Well, the gods of Chance are telling me to pass Go and collect another two hundred." Hartley waves the card in Saw-yer's face. "And with my newfound riches, I think I'll buy an apartment so that you have someplace to stay the next time you visit."

"He's not staying at your place," Lauren gripes.

I roll my eyes at her. "Chill. It's just a game."

"I'm bored," she says and then gets to her feet. "Let's go watch a movie in your room."

Before I can protest, the twins are following Lauren out the door.

"Was it something I said?" Hartley asks.

"No. Lauren's just . . ." I pause, not wanting to run down a girl I barely know. "She's Lauren," I finish. "Still want to play?"

"Heck yeah. I'm kicking butt." She pushes the dice in my direction. "Your turn."

I roll and land on Chance. The card I pick from the pile sends me directly to jail. Hartley smirks at my bad luck. She hops around the board, buys another property, and then sits back and watches me flail.

I roll and get a five, which lands me on the property Hart-ley just bought. "Damn. Already you're bleeding me dry."

She rubs her hands together like an evil villain. I fork over my payment and watch as she irons her way to the Community Chest.

My next roll lands me on Tennessee Avenue. "Finally." I wipe fake sweat off my brow. "I thought I was going to be landless."

"It's still early."

"I didn't take you for the ruthless type."

"Watch and learn, pretty boy."

She proceeds to prove me wrong. After the next trip around the board, she owns five properties to my one. This game is going to be a massacre.

"How long are you going to torture me?"

"Do you have money left?"

I look down at my meager pile. "Some."

"Are you giving up?"

"Nope."

"Mmmhmmm." She hands me some cash. "I'm going to buy a house for Indiana Avenue."

I pass her the house with a big sigh. "This materialistic side is a new one," I comment.

"How so?" She nudges the dice toward me.

"Dunno. You seemed so nice and easygoing before. You play the violin. That seems really . . ." I trail off, unsure of the point I was trying to make.

"Soft?" she supplies. Then she scowls. "Playing an instrument is as hard as playing football. Do you think sitting for hours with a piece of wood stuck between your shoulder and neck is comfortable and easy?"

"Um, no?"

"No. Do you know how many times my fingers bled after practicing?" She shoves her pretty hand in my face.

"A lot?" I guess.

"That's right. A lot. And when your fingers hurt, you can't do anything. Not even button your own shirt."

"I'd button your shirt for you," I say thoughtlessly.

She throws the house at me. "Easton!"

I catch the house and set it on her property. "Sorry. It's an old habit."

"Why?"

"Why what?"

"Why is it an old habit?"

"Dunno. Just is," I mumble. I roll the dice and move my piece. It's another railroad, but I can't afford it, so I push the dice over to her.

"Come on. Tell me."

"Why?"

"Because friends tell each other stuff."

I raise both my eyebrows at her. "And you've confided *so* much in me."

She shrugs. "You know about my home situation."

"Not because you told me anything," I object. My blood is at a low simmer. "I overheard it."

"You still know," she pushes.

Irritated, I blurt out, "I do it because that's my role."

I immediately regret my outburst and pretend to study my car like it's a detailed miniature of the million-dollar Bugatti that Steve owns. I love that damn car.

"I'm not going to pretend to know what that means, but I do understand what it's like being the middle child. You can't measure up to your perfect older siblings and you aren't the sweet baby anymore."

"It's not like that," I protest, but the truth of her words strikes me in the gut. Reed and Gideon are extraordinarily focused. They have self-discipline that I lack, and that's why they're playing college sports and I won't. The twins are connected on a deep level that I don't think even Lauren appreciates. I've always been in the middle. Surrounded by my brothers but somehow still alone. The one thing that stood out was how much my mother doted on me, and in retrospect, even that makes me feel uncomfortable.

"I like being Easton Royal. There's not a thing in this world that I can't have," I declare to show her that I'm not the sad sack she's trying to paint me as. "I said 'habit' because so many people are in love with me and I try to pay them back with compliments to make them feel better."

"Okay," she says.

Her mild tone grates on my nerves more than an argument, but I mash my lips together. Instead, I focus on the game, rolling the dice, and moving my car along the board, but I can't stop thinking about the past.

How Mom always told me I was her favorite, her special boy who could always be counted on to be with her when she needed me. Which meant only that I was the person who couldn't tell her no.

"Sometimes when you're the focus of one person's attention, it can be bad," I say roughly. "For both you and the other person, so giving a compliment shifts the focus, you know?"

I feel like I've said too much and duck my head. I wait for the inevitable question of what I meant and who I was referring to. Surprisingly, the only sound I hear is the dice hitting the board. She lands on the last railroad, which essentially means I'm screwed.

"I'm hungry," I announce. "Let's get some food and then watch a movie or something."

"But we're not done with the game."

"I concede." I get to my feet. "Food?"

"Sure." She takes out her phone.

"What are you doing?"

Grinning, she snaps a pic of the game board and my pathetically small money stack. "I'm commemorating this event. I may never beat you at anything again."

I latch on to the one word: *again*. Hartley wants to keep spending time with me. That's enough to wash away those bad memories.

I direct her toward the kitchen and gesture for her to sit down. "We probably have some leftover ravioli. Yea or nay?"

"Yay. I love ravioli. Can I help?"

"Nope. Sit and entertain me."

She slides onto a stool. "How exactly do you want me to entertain you?" When I open my mouth, she holds up her hand in a stop sign. "Forget I said that. You want me to read you the news?"

"Do you want to drive an ice pick through my forehead?"

"So that's a no."

I pull the dish out of the refrigerator and read the instructions Sandra taped to the top on how to reheat it. *Convection oven, 3 minutes*. After I pop it in, I turn and lean against the counter.

"I'm surprised there aren't more people living here," she says, looking around the large empty space. "I stayed with a family in New York over one of my breaks. Their place is about an eighth of this one, and they had three full-time staff."

"We used to have a lot. But after my mom died, the staff wouldn't stop giving interviews to the gossip rags about how sad our family was. Dad fired everyone except Sandra, our housekeeper." I jerk a thumb toward the stove. "And she only works a few days a week now because she's got a grandbaby she helps take care of. I like it better this way. How'd you like the north?"

"It was cold in the winters. Really cold. I don't miss that at all. I loved the seasons, though. Spring and fall were my favorite."

"How long were you away?"

"Three years." She hesitates, and I know she wants to ask me questions about my mother's death and probably the scandal that happened earlier this year. But instead of launching into a gossip hunt, she tosses me a towel. "Use this so you don't burn your hands."

"Good call." I gingerly remove the glass dish. "Can we share? Or do I need to get some plates?"

"We can share. Do you want water or something else?"

I really want a beer, but I figure Hartley might not like that. She didn't seem thrilled that I was drunk the night she found me after the poker game.

"Water's fine."

After we demolish the bowl of pasta, Hartley asks to use the bathroom. I show her the one off the kitchen and then go down the hall to use the other first-floor bathroom.

When I get back, I hear Hartley's and Lauren's voices. I guess Lauren came downstairs to get something, although I'm shocked she didn't just order one of her servants to do it.

I don't mean to eavesdrop on them. I really don't. But before I can step into the kitchen, Lauren says something that glues my feet to the floor.

"Nice to see you're making use of the Royal name."

"What do you mean?" Hartley sounds confused.

"I mean, there are serious perks to dating a Royal. It's awesome, isn't it?" Lauren's smug, flippant tone makes my shoulders stiffen. This chick is the worst.

"I'm not dating a Royal. Easton and I are just friends."

Lauren snickers. "Girl, come on. Friends don't buy each other expensive jewelry."

"What? Oh, you mean this thing? Easton got it from a candy machine."

"Right. The Candy Machine."

"I don't get it."

"That's a custom jewelry place over on Sixth. The charms start at five grand and go up from there." There's a moment of silence as Lauren mentally adds up the baubles inside the clear glass heart on Hartley's necklace. "You've got three charms in there. Mostly diamonds, rubies, and emeralds. I'm guessing that set Easton back about fifteen grand. Not that he can't afford it. Like I said, it's a good start."

"But . . . I don't want him buying me expensive stuff," Hartley protests, and I curse Lauren for bringing up the subject. It was hard enough getting Hartley to agree to accept the gift in the first place.

"Oh, please, don't act all innocent. Dating the Royals means dealing with their messed-up family. Might as well be compensated for it, right?"

I back up a little and then stomp on the floor so the girls will hear me coming. Sure enough, they both fall silent. Lauren smiles broadly when I walk into the kitchen. Hartley has a stormy look on her face.

She holds up the necklace the moment she sees me. "I can't keep this."

I fight the urge to glare at Lauren. "Why not?"

"It's too expensive. I can't go around wearing a necklace that costs this much."

At the counter, Lauren heaves an irritated sigh, as if Hartley has let her down. She grabs her water glass and leaves the kitchen without a backward glance.

"Why not?" I repeat, focusing on Hartley again. "It's not like you're poor. You've got a trust fund."

"The only trust fund I have is for academic purposes. It's from my grandma and I can only use it for lessons, tuition, stuff like that. That's how I'm able to go to Astor."

I watch as she fumbles with the clasp, tugging and pulling like the gold chain is burning her skin.

"Help me," she orders.

"No." I back away. Taking the necklace off would be a loss, and I don't want to feel that.

"I'm serious, Easton. I don't feel comfortable keeping it. I'd never be able to afford something like this. Why do you think my dad—" She cuts herself off. "I can't take this."

"What were you going to say about your dad?" I press.

"Nothing."

I let out an annoyed groan. "Why do you always have to be so difficult? Why is your life such a secret?"

She stops fiddling with the clasp for a moment. "What does it matter?"

"Because we're friends. Because I want to get to know you better." And because I'm tired of being the one who's doing all the sharing. I've told her things I haven't told anyone else. Meanwhile, she continues to be all mysterious, acting like she'd rather shave her head than confide in me.

There's a tiny flicker of scorn in her eyes. "Yeah, you keep throwing around the *friend* word. You keep saying you're cool with just being friends. But a part of me feels like it's a long con or something. Like you're doing all this because you want to get in my pants."

I curl my fists against my sides. "If you believe that, why are you even here?"

She goes silent again.

"You're lucky I decided to keep my hands off you."

Her mouth falls open. "Lucky?"

"Yeah. Because if I wanted us to be naked, we'd be naked. I'm just playing the game the way you want right now."

"Wow. Real nice, Easton." She jerks hard on the chain, and the fragile clasp gives way. "Thanks for the game, movie, and food."

Fuck.

"Wait. Don't go. I was joking."

She drops the necklace on the counter without meeting my eyes. "Uh-huh. I've got to take off now."

I tamp down a burst of anxiety. The night's barely begun and I definitely don't want to be home alone. "Come on, Hartley. I stayed in for you tonight and you're leaving already? Over what? Because I jokingly hit on you?"

"No, because I'm tired and I want to go home. You didn't have to stay in. It was your choice." She strides out to the front hall.

I snatch the necklace off the counter and chase after her,

the gold chain dangling between my fingers. "I made that choice because it's what friends do, remember? Make sacrifices."

"Don't do me any favors," she replies coolly.

I can feel my temper boiling. "I won't. In fact, you can find your own ride home."

She jerks the heavy oak doors open. "I will."

And then she leaves.

She just . . . walks out the door, down the steps, and keeps going. I watch her from the foyer window, her slender frame getting tinier and tinier as she makes her way down the driveway.

Not once does she look back.

I'm glad she's gone, I tell myself. I've been dying for a drink, and now that I don't have to worry about making her uncomfortable, I can get that drink. I stare at the necklace in my hand, tempted to whip it against the wall. In the end, I shove it in my pocket, because Lauren was right. Damn thing *did* cost fifteen grand. Might as well save it for the next girl. This time I'll pick someone who's grateful and actually appreciates me.

I stomp off to Dad's study and raid the liquor cabinet. The only stuff that's left is his disgusting port. I guzzle the sweet shit down anyway. Booze is booze. This'll get me the buzz that I need.

I can't believe her. I've been nice to her. I've stood up for her. I've protected her. She should be glad. She should be on her little knees thanking me for throwing the mantle of the Royals over her.

The mantle of the Royals?

I nearly puke in my mouth. Is that the kind of person I've

turned into? No wonder she didn't want to spend more time with me.

I fumble around and look for another bottle. Somewhere in the back of my mind, I hear the warnings of my brothers, telling me not to flush my life down the tube.

"No pills. No drugs," I tell my imaginary brothers. "Just a little booze. Nothing wrong with that."

As I tip the bottle against my lips, I catch a glimpse of myself in the mirror on the wall. My mom's picture used to be up there. Now it's a reflective monstrosity. How can the old man stand to look at himself? Wait, he's never here, so that's why.

I'm the only one here, drinking crap I can't stand because I don't want to spend a minute of my life alone. My head's a bad, bad place.

I clench the bottle tighter in my fist. Drinking alone is for losers. I, Easton Royal, am not a loser. I finish off the bottle and grab a second one and stumble toward the beach.

Twenty-One

THE WALK TO Felicity's is a blur, but I find myself at the right spot. Or at least what appears to be the right spot, judging by the number of bodies smashed on one patch of sand.

"Easton Royal!"

I hear my name called out by a number of kids. Felicity must've invited non-Astor peeps, because I recognize the faces of some folks who've started college already.

"Hey, Felicity's been looking all over for you," someone says. "She's pretty pissed. You may want to hide."

"Stu brought girls from college down. They're so fine." Another guy bites his fist. "I can't wait to graduate."

"Where's the booze?" I mutter.

"Pool house. But . . . man, you look lit already. Sure you need any more?"

"If I want your input, I'll ask for it."

I shove past him, not even registering who it was. Up the small incline, I spot the pool, pool house, and a small dance floor set off to the side. Ella's on it with Val. They love to shake their booties.

I grab a glass out of some dude's hand and make my way

over. Behind me, there's a scuffle and some protests, but I flip the guy off and then ignore him. He can get another drink easily. I muscle over to the girls, spilling half my drink along the way.

"God, who's the drunk—" Lindsey from Government breaks off mid-rant. "Oh, it's you."

"Got a problem with me?" I drawl.

"No," she replies, but her eyes say a different thing.

I give her a cool smile and step to the side. "Good call."

"Asshole," she mutters under her breath.

"Bitch."

A meaty hand grabs my shoulder. "I heard that, Royal. You're the one spilling shit all over people."

Blearily, I peer into the new face. It's Zeke, Lindsey's thick-necked boyfriend.

"I know you don't get enough attention at home, Zeke, but you're barking up the wrong tree," I inform him. "Either get your hands off my Tom Ford original or fork over the grand for a replacement."

A red-faced Zeke hauls back to deliver a punch. If it landed, it would've hurt like hell, but he moves slower than a snail. I duck under his grip, grab his wrist, and pull it up behind his back. He falls to his knees.

Lindsey cries out. Then another voice yells my name.

"Easton! Easton!" A pair of small hands ineffectually pushes at me. It's Ella. She looks worried.

"What's up, baby sis?"

"What're you doing?"

I whip my free hand wide and the remaining liquid in my glass splashes over the rest of the dance floor. "I'm here to party."

"You're drunk." She claws at my fist—the one that's gripping Zeke tight.

"Two gold stars for you! I'd clap for you but my hands are full." I lift the glass high. If I bring it down at the right angle, I could knock Zeke out. That might be fun.

Lindsey's screaming has turned into sad little cries. I start humming to drown her out.

"Where's Hartley?" Ella demands.

"Who cares?" My throat seizes up on the lie. I care. I care too fucking much.

"Easton, please."

"You beg like that when you're with Reed?" I wink at her. Or try to, at least. "That must be why you carry his balls in your purse."

Her worried face turns ice cold. "You're drunk," she repeats. "Go home."

Another set of hands join Ella's. These are big and strong and almost manage to get Zeke out of my grip.

Bran's face swims into view. "Hey, dude. We're going to play Frisbee football and could use another body."

"It's too dark," I grumble.

"Nah, Bran stuck some LED lights on it," Pash says at my side. "Come on."

Reluctantly, I let go of Zeke. Lindsey collapses on his back, which doesn't look comfortable at all. I start to say something, but Bran and Pash drag me away. Last thing I see is Ella's stormy face.

I guess I hurt her feelings again. I'll have to apologize in the morning. She's so sensitive.

Someone tosses a lighted disc in the air.

"Got a joint?" I ask.

"Let's just play," Bran says with a sigh. "We don't need anyone smoking pot tonight."

I turn on Bran. "Are you monitoring my recreational habits now?"

"Just trying to keep the captain of our defense healthy and suspension free."

The disc comes hurtling in our direction. Bran leaps up and catches it before it hits me between the eyes. "Maybe Frisbee is the wrong plan tonight," he says wryly.

Pash nods. "Maybe we should chill at my house? We could watch a movie."

"Movie? The last thing I want to do is a movie." I slap one fist against my palm. "How about we fight?"

"There will be no fighting at my party!" Felicity's shrill voice says.

I pivot to see her standing a few feet away. Her eyes are spitting fire. I wonder why she's so mad. Then I remember. She wanted to break up with me here, where everyone could see.

Well, I'm happy to oblige.

"Felicity. There you are." I walk over and wrap an arm around her shoulder. "My pretend girlfriend. Hey, everyone," I call out. "We've got something to share with you. Felicity has an announcement. She's going to break off our fake relationship."

There's a hushed silence, broken by a few female titters.

I back off and spread my arms wide. "I'm here. Have at it. Whatever you want to say to break it off, say it. Make it look good."

"Easton, let's go home." Ella shoves her way to the front of the crowd.

"No can do, baby sis. I promised my pretend girlfriend she can humiliate me in front of all our friends." I wave at Felicity again. "Stage is all yours."

Her mouth's screwed up into a tiny circle of disapproval, as if someone stitched around the edges and then pulled the threads tight.

"You're an evil, cruel bastard, Easton Royal," she hisses.

"That's all you got? This from one of the bitchiest girls at Astor Park Prep? Come on. Don't let me down." I gesture with both hands to bring it, but it's not her who delivers the blow.

"Sorry about this, but I think you'll thank me in the morning." Bran leans back and then lets his fist fly. It's the last thing I see.

✦　✦　✦

I WAKE UP to blinding light and a marching band traipsing around in my head. An agonized groan slides out, which only causes the marching band to play louder. The pounding drumbeat throbs in my temples and pulsates in my gut until the waves of nausea it produces have me lurching out of bed and racing to my private bath.

I puke until there's nothing left to puke, and I kneel there dry-heaving for a few minutes. Eventually I find the strength to stand up. I brush my teeth and chug two glasses of water. I shower. I shave. By the time I step back into the bedroom and put on a pair of sweatpants, I feel halfway normal.

Hangovers blow. Mine aren't usually this bad, though. I can't remember the last time I woke up feeling so shitty after a night of boozing. Granted, I did drink quite a lot last night. Enough to act like a total ass, piss off Felicity, and take a fist in the face courtesy of Bran Mathis.

"How much did you have to drink last night?" My frowning father appears in the open doorway of my bedroom. "You're never getting back in that cockpit if you don't straighten up."

"Who says I had anything to drink?" I challenge.

"It's eight in the morning and you just spent the past ten minutes retching loud enough for the entire neighborhood to hear. So I repeat—how much did you have to drink?"

He's using that commanding boardroom voice that scares the pants off of his business associates. But I'm not one of his associates—I'm his kid, which means I know firsthand that Callum Royal is a total pussy outside the office. He's let me and my brothers run wild for years, even before Mom died.

"Maybe I'm sick with the stomach flu—did you ever think of that, Dad?" I shoot him a defiant look. "I love how you immediately think the worst of me." Muttering under my breath, I stalk over to my walk-in closet and yank open the double doors.

Across the room, Dad's face takes on a stricken expression. "I'm sorry, son. Are you ill?"

"Nah." I glance over with a grin. "Hungover."

"Easton." He runs a frazzled hand through his hair. It's the same dark brown as mine and my older brothers'. The twins' hair is a few shades lighter. "Of all my kids, you're the one who's going to give me gray hair, you know that, right?"

"Obvs. Gid's too much of a prude. So's Reed." I cock my head thoughtfully. "Actually, the twins might be worse than I am. You know they're dating the same girl—"

"I can't hear you!" Dad grumbles, covering his ears as he quickly backs out of my bedroom.

I snort to myself because, damn, my dad's gotten kinda cool ever since Ella moved in with us. Before that, he never made time to check in on us or lecture us about our crazy behavior.

Speaking of Ella, she strides into my room less than a minute after Dad departs it. Her blond hair is up in a high ponytail and she's wearing yoga pants and a State football jersey with Reed's number on the front.

Oh crap. I forgot we're flying out to Reed's away game today. His team's playing Louisiana State.

"What the hell is the matter with you?" Ella's ponytail swings rapidly as she advances on me.

"That question's too vague, baby sis. There's tons of shit wrong with me."

"You acted like a jackass last night," she accuses.

"So you mean I acted the way I always do?"

Dismay fills her blue eyes. "No, that's not how you act, at least not toward me."

I scan my brain, trying to remember what I'd done or said to Ella yesterday. When I got to Felicity's, Ella and Val had been dancing. I'd gotten into it with that jackass Zeke, and Ella had interfered. And I . . . Oh right. I made some juvenile comment about how she has Reed whipped and mocked her about whether she begged my brother when they were in bed together.

I swallow a sigh. Damn. I really am an asshole.

"Why do you do this stuff?" she asks.

Aw hell, her bottom lip is trembling. Swear to God, if she starts to cry—

But Ella recovers quickly. Her mouth flattens and her chin sticks out. The girl has steel in her blood. Nothing keeps her down. Ever. It's no wonder my brother fell for her the moment she walked through our front door.

"You have addiction issues, Easton."

"No, really?"

Her eyes flash. "It's not something to joke about."

No, it isn't. The last person in our family who had addiction issues fucking killed herself. But I'm not like my mom. I love life too much to off myself.

"So I like to drink," I say with a shrug. "Big deal. It's not like I'm popping pills anymore." I search my closet for my own State jersey. "When does the jet leave?" I ask over my shoulder.

"In an hour." From the corner of my eye, I see her crossing her arms. "But you're not going to be on it."

I spin around. "Fuck that. Reed has a game."

"I don't want you there," she returns with a scowl.

I can't help but laugh. "Gee, little sis, well, if *you* don't want me there, I guess I'll just stay home." I pull the jersey off its hanger. "Not."

"I mean it," she says in a haughty voice that gets my back up. "You were such a jerk last night, not just to me, but to Val and Bran and—I can't even believe I'm saying this—Felicity. You don't deserve to come to New Orleans with us and watch Reed play and then eat yummy beignets and enjoy dinner on Bourbon Street. That's like inviting the raccoon who just threw your trash all over the lawn to come inside and do the same thing in your kitchen."

"Luckily, you don't have a say in whether or not I come," I say snidely. Did she just compare me to a fucking raccoon?

"You sure about that?" Smirking, she takes her phone out of her pocket and types something.

Less than ten seconds later, my own phone buzzes on the nightstand. With suspicious eyes fixed on Ella, I back up toward the bed and grab the phone. I read the incoming text message. It's from Reed.

Stay home today. Don't want you here

A jolt of outrage sizzles up my spine. Are they fucking kidding me?

"So that's how it's gonna be, huh?" I mutter angrily. And I love how she's mad at me because I said she's got my brother whipped. She just proved my case!

"Until you get your shit together?" Ella says. "Yes."

She spins on her heel and flounces out of the room, a golden tornado of self-righteousness.

❖ ❖ ❖

ELLA AND REED weren't joking around. I'm legit barred from flying to Louisiana with Dad and my traitorous stepsister, forced to watch them saunter out the door without a backward look. Damn childish, if you ask me.

But whatever. That just means I get to spend the day lounging around the house and being lazy by the pool. I can handle one afternoon alone. Lazy's fun, I lie to myself.

I sprawl out on a lounger, a bottle of water and one of beer on the little table next to me. I alternate taking sips from each bottle so I can stay both hydrated and buzzed. And luckily, there's nobody around to lecture me about day-drinking.

Between naps, my mind drifts to Hartley. I try calling her,

but she doesn't answer. I know she's not working today, so that means she's ignoring me.

What's her problem? I don't get why she won't talk to me about *anything*. I told her stuff about my mom, didn't I? She can't trust me to reveal a single detail in return? And that necklace was a *gift*. Who returns gifts? Why is everything about her so difficult? She should've just stayed in boarding school. Then she wouldn't fucking be here driving me fucking nuts.

And why *did* she come back? Who wouldn't want to go to boarding school? Think of all the freedom. I mean . . . I'd miss my family, but I wouldn't mind being sent away from home. Would I?

It bothered Hartley. It bothered her enough that she returned to Bayview against her parents' wishes. How would I feel if I couldn't see my brothers at all?

It would suck. I can barely tolerate being banished for a day without having to drown my sorrows.

I check myself. Why the hell am I being so pathetic? I can handle being by myself for a day. Or a week. Or a year, if necessary. Hartley's a big baby if she can't hack it at a boarding school. Running back home where she's not even wanted? Why do that? Make a new life for yourself.

I take a long swig of beer. I don't know why I care, anyway. I don't need Hartley, not even as a friend. I can call up any chick and she'd race over here to chill with me. I can have anyone I want. Chicks can't resist me—and that includes the dark-haired girl who suddenly appears on the patio holding hands with my brother.

The moment Savannah Montgomery and I lock eyes, a thread of tension stretches between us.

I shift awkwardly and take another sip of my beer. "Hey," I mumble at the newcomers.

They're both wearing swimsuits, and Gideon has a couple towels draped over one muscular arm. He's been coming home nearly every weekend since he and Savannah got back together. Sav's at college with him because she graduated a year early, but I guess there's more privacy for them here in Bayview. They both have roommates at school.

"Hey. You mind if we swim?" Gid asks.

"No. Go nuts." I gesture to the pool and stretch out on my lounger again. "I'm taking a nap. Hey, Sav—how's life as a college woman?"

"Hi," she says tightly. "Life's good."

I feel a sliver of irritation, the same chagrin I felt toward Ms. Mann when she acted as if it was all my fault that we hooked up.

Savannah and I slept together last year, way before she and Gid got back together. At that point she was still out to hurt him, and I was out to hurt . . . myself, I guess.

Reed had just run Ella out of town, and I'd been pissed. Any attraction I felt for Ella was gone by then, but our connection wasn't. Truth is, although I have a lot of friends, I don't actually have many friends. It's all surface-level shit.

With Ella, it was more than a surface friendship. I trusted her. Still do, even though she acted like a total bitch this morning.

I lost it when Reed's idiotic actions drove her away. I spiraled. Spiraled hard, like one of Atlantic Aviation's test planes that doesn't make the grade and crashes in the desert, sending Dad's engineers back to the drawing board to figure out what design flaw led to the crash. I'm the design flaw in the

Royal family, the one who isn't quite like the others, the one who crashes and burns more often than not.

That said, nobody forced Savannah to be with me. And yeah, I felt guilty after it happened, but not guilty enough to shoulder all the blame. There'd been two people in that bed. Gideon knows this, and he doesn't condemn us for that. Honestly, I think he's so happy to be back with his girl that he's willing to forgive all her sins. Considering his own list of sins, he'd be a hypocrite not to.

"Decided not to go to Reed's game?" Gid asks as he drops the towels on the lounger next to mine. I guess nobody told him I've been banished from Louisiana.

"Wasn't feeling up to it," I lie. "I've got a hangover."

"I heard," he says dryly.

Savannah drifts toward the shallow end and dips a toe in. "Water's nice," she calls to Gideon. "Let's swim, Gid."

"Be there in a sec." He looks to me again. "Sawyer said your new quarterback carried your drunken ass home last night and tucked you into bed."

I make a mental note to beat Sawyer's ass later. Or Sebastian's. Either twin will do, since those fuckers are pretty much one person. Just ask their girlfriend.

"You need to slow down with the drinking," Gideon advises me. "You're getting too old for this shit, East. I thought you wanted to fly again."

The words grate. Gid can be such a judgmental ass sometimes. "I will fly again. I'm just waiting until I'm out of the house and away from the parental unit. Besides, just because college turned you into an old man doesn't mean I'm going to follow in your footsteps, dude. I wanna enjoy being a teenager for as long as I can."

The disappointment on his face grates even more. "Sure, East. Go ahead and enjoy it, then."

He walks over to Savannah, I sit back on the lounger, the two of them jump into the pool, and we all pretend that I haven't seen my older brother's girlfriend naked.

Twenty-Two

THE REST OF the weekend goes by fast. I think about Hartley more than I should, but no matter how bad I want to track her down, I manage to find some restraint. I decide I'll just wait and talk to her at school. Apologize for being an ass to her and hope she's not too stubborn to forgive me.

On Sunday night, Ella decides she's talking to me again. She joins me in the media room, turning her nose up at the TV screen. I'm watching a Tarantino movie, and it's gory as hell.

"Someone's in a bloody mood," she remarks with a wince.

I shrug and keep looking at the screen. "Oh, we're suddenly speaking to each other?"

"Yes." Remorse colors her voice.

I hide a smile. Thing about Ella is she's not as tough as she makes herself out to be. She's got the kindest heart of anyone I've ever met, and she cares fiercely about people. If she believes you're worth her time and effort, she'll move heaven and earth to make you feel loved and appreciated.

"I know I've been a jerk to you this weekend," she admits. "I was doing it on purpose."

I smirk. "No, really?"

She wanders over and flops down beside me. "I was trying to prove a point."

"What, that you're really awesome at giving the silent treatment?"

"No. That your actions drive people away." She shakes her head in disappointment. "So many people care about you, East. Your dad, your brothers, me, Val, your teammates—we *love* you."

My spine feels itchy, like a hundred porcupine quills are pricking it. I instinctively lean forward to grab my glass and then remember it's soda water. Dammit, I need something stronger.

I start to get up, but Ella clamps her hand around my arm. "No," she says gently, reading my mind. "You don't need a drink."

"Yeah, I kinda do."

"Every time things get emotional, or a conversation gets a little too serious, you try to distance yourself from it. Numb yourself—"

"I don't need another lecture."

"It's not a lecture." Frustration shadows her eyes. "I just don't like seeing you get so drunk that you talk to your own friends like they're pieces of garbage—"

Sawyer's voice on the intercom interrupts Ella. "Yo, East. Hartley's here."

Equal parts surprise and joy shoot through me. She's here? For real?

Without delay, I get up and hurry to the door.

Ella's voice stops me before I can exit the room. "I love you, Easton, but I'm worried."

The genuine concern in her voice makes me hesitate. I don't like making Ella feel bad. She's one of my favorite people on earth.

I slowly turn to face her. "I'm sorry I said that stuff to you at the party," I mumble. "I didn't mean to hurt you."

"I know." She pauses. "It's just that I want you around for a long time, so . . . take care of yourself."

I give her a careless, one-finger salute. "On it."

When I reach the front hall, I find Hartley peering into the sitting room, where Mom's portrait hangs over the fireplace.

"That's my mom," I tell Hartley.

"She's beautiful."

"Want to go in?"

"Sure."

I push the door open wider. The sitting room was one of Mom's favorite places. It's a huge room with two floor-to-ceiling windows at one end and a fireplace at the other. The last time I was in here, Dad announced his engagement with Brooke.

"You look like her," Hartley remarks, her silver gaze still fixed on the portrait.

I stare up at my mother's oval face. "We've all got her eyes."

Hartley shakes her head. "No, it's the shape of the face. And your eyebrows. Your mother had perfect eyebrows and you do, too."

"I guess?" I've never given it much thought. "Who do you look more like—your mom or dad?" I instantly wish I could take the words back. I know she hates talking about her parents. "Forget I asked."

"No, it's fine." Hartley shrugs. "I look more like my dad. Parker, my sister, takes after our mother. Delicate. Sweet."

I snort. "She didn't seem delicate or sweet at the diner."

Again, I want to bite my tongue off. Why do I keep saying dumb things?

But Hartley surprises me. She leans an arm against the mantel, her fingertips rubbing along the lower part of the mahogany frame. "Sweet and delicate are her weapons. You don't want to make her angry because she's such an angel. You want her approval. Her love and affection."

Wow. She could be talking about my mom. "But you'll never get it because she's too self-absorbed."

My turn to surprise Hartley. Her eyebrows raise a notch. "Know someone like that?"

I point to the painting.

Hartley's pretty lips turn down at the corners. "That sucks." She twists around to face me. Her hands are clasped. It looks like she's holding something between them but I can't tell what it is. "I'm sorry about the other night. I flew off the handle and got mad at you for no reason."

I exhale as if a giant balloon inside me just popped. "No, hell. I'm sorry. I've been pushing you."

She raises a hand for me to shush. "How about I apologize first and then you go?"

"Okay." I make a zipping motion across my mouth.

Her lips twitch. "I'm very sorry for being a brat the other

night. I'm sorry for yelling at you. I'm sorry for ripping off the necklace. That was terrible." She reaches for my hand and places something in my palm.

Curiously, and with a lot of excitement, I gaze down at the gift. It's a thin leather bracelet with a silver buckle.

"I know it's not much—"

"It's awesome," I interrupt. I hold it out. "Put it on for me."

When she does, her fingers tremble. I want to pull her into my arms and hug her, but I'll wait until she's done fixing the clasp.

The walnut-brown leather looks good against my tanned skin, and I like the silver accent. "Love it," I tell her.

"I know you don't wear anything but the watch but—"

"It's perfect. Don't say anything else, because I love this and I won't stand for anyone insulting it, not even you." I hold my wrist in the air. "Looks sick."

She grins. "I don't know how sick it is, but I'm glad you like it. Oh. I have one other gift."

"Yeah?" I ask cautiously. I don't want to scare her off with my eagerness.

"My other gift is this—I did something to piss off my parents and now they've banished me." Her fingers absently trace the frame of the painting. "I have another sister. Did I tell you about her?"

I shake my head. "No, but I saw her picture in the newspaper article I found online."

"Her name's Dylan. She's thirteen. I've only been able to talk to her eight times in three years."

Hartley stops talking. I can tell she's on the verge of tears.

I take a step toward her, but she puts up a hand. "No. I

can't take any sympathy at the moment. I'll break down and I don't want to do that."

"I talk to Reed at least once a week," I find myself admitting. "I'd probably be an emotional mess if I couldn't see or talk to my brothers more than a couple times a year."

"Yeah . . . It hasn't been easy." She twists away and ducks her head. I suspect she's wiping away a few tears, but I pretend not to notice.

"We should kidnap her," I suggest.

"My sister?"

"Yup. We'll go to her school, sneak her out during the day, and go to the pier. Whaddya say?"

"I wish."

"I'm serious. I'm good at shenanigans. I could pull this off without a hitch. We'd buy funnel cakes, which I know from past experience you love. Headbands with animal ears. Bunnies for you and Dylan. A tiger for me."

Hartley's smiling. "Why not a tiger for me and bunny ears for you? You'd look cute in pink."

"I'd be so cute that the whole midway would grind to a halt and then Dylan wouldn't get to go on any rides." I wink.

Hartley's smile grows bigger, and the anxious, itchy, crabby feeling that ate at me for the past twenty-four hours fades away.

"I want to see her!" someone shouts from the front hall.

The familiar male voice freezes me in my tracks.

"Ella's not home," comes my father's icy reply.

"Bullshit. I know she's here," Steve snaps. "Get out of my way, Callum. She's my daughter and I need to speak to her."

Hartley taps me on my shoulder. "I should probably leave," she murmurs.

Her discomfort at hearing this matches mine, only for different reasons. She thinks I'm embarrassed, but I'm worried about Ella. "No. Stay here," I whisper.

"What you need to do is stay far away from her," Dad snaps back. "The only reason we haven't filed a restraining order against you is because we didn't think you were stupid enough to show up here."

"You're the one who opened the gate," Steve says snidely.

I inch the door forward, and Dad's and Steve's voices immediately get louder. I'm perplexed why Dad would let Steve in. Hopefully, Ella is far away and doesn't know her dad's here.

I grab my phone from my pocket and text Reed.

> Steve's here

> I kno. Ella texted me

Damn.
Where r u? Reed asks.

> In the sitting rm. Where's Ella?

> Top of stairs

"Shit," I mutter.

Hartley comes up beside me. "What's wrong?"

"Ella's bio dad is out there causing problems." I jerk my thumb toward the foyer, where the argument's still going strong.

"What choice did I have?" Dad says. "You were waking up the entire neighborhood, parked out there and laying on your horn like a maniac. You're lucky I didn't call the cops."

"Why didn't you?" Steve mocks.

"Because Ella's already been through enough. The last thing that girl needs is to see her father once again carted away in handcuffs. But I mean it, Steve. You're not to come near her. You're no longer her guardian—*I* am. The court—"

"Screw the court!"

Hartley flinches. I lay a reassuring hand on her shoulder.

"She's *my* daughter, Callum. And I don't know what horse-shit your lawyers have been feeding you, but Ella is going to be a witness for the defense, not the prosecution. My daughter is *not* going to testify against me."

Hartley gasps and then slaps a hand over her mouth.

I bring my lips close to her ear. "And you think *you've* got skeletons in your closet, huh? Trust me, no secrets you have are dirtier than the ones we Royals have."

"You Royals always have to be the best at everything," she jokes weakly. Her face is pale and her eyes are wide.

"Welcome to my life." I take her hand and grip it tightly in mine. She squeezes back.

Out in the hall, the two dads are still arguing. In here, we're comforting each other.

"You're no longer part of this family," Dad says coldly. "You're not Ella's father. You're not my boys' godfather. You're not my friend or my business partner. The next time we see each other, it will be in court, when your daughter testifies against you."

"We'll see about that," Steve retorts.

The front doors slam. I wait until Dad's footsteps no longer echo against the marble floor before I peek out into the hall. It's empty. "Come on," I tell Hartley, pulling her behind me.

"Where're we going?"

"To find Ella."

Hartley shakes her head. "You go. I feel weird talking to her about this."

"She won't mind—"

"It's none of my business," Hartley says firmly. "Besides, I really do have to go. I've got homework to finish up for tomorrow. I came straight here after work."

I grab her hand before she passes through the doorway. "Wait." My forehead creases. "I want to know more about your sister and what's going on with your family. Will you tell me more about it tomorrow? Maybe at lunch?" When she stays silent, I swallow my disappointment. "Or you can keep holding back on me, I guess."

Her cheeks take on a pink blush. "I'm sorry. You're right. I do hold back. It's not on purpose, though. I've never really liked talking about myself. Even before boarding school, I was kind of a loner. I mean, I've had boyfriends—"

"Names and addresses," I order. "I need to know who I'm beating up."

That gets me a snicker. "Oh, relax. They're ancient history. But, yeah, aside from them, I haven't confided in a lot of people. I don't think I'm too good at it."

"Obvs."

Hartley smiles faintly. "I'm young—still learning and growing and all that crap, right?" She shrugs. "I'm going to try to be a better friend. That's basically what I came here to say."

She holds out her hand for a shake, and my first instinct is to bypass that and go straight for a hug. Then I realize that I need to meet her gesture of friendship with one of my own.

I take her hand in mine. I probably hold it longer than

friends normally do, but I'm young, too. Still learning and growing and all that crap.

It feels right to be doing that with someone holding my hand, though. Especially with her gift wrapped around my wrist.

Twenty-Three

I'M DRAGGING MY feet at practice the next morning. Not because I'm hungover, but because I stayed up late last night watching movies with Ella. She was upset about Steve showing up at the house, so I tried to distract her. But now I'm operating on about four hours of sleep. Coach tells me that if I don't fucking wake up he's gonna make me do fucking suicides until I'm fucking puking all over the fucking turf.

Coach Lewis has a bit of a potty mouth.

I chug some Gatorade hoping it'll give me a boost of energy. It doesn't, but Coach doesn't pay much attention to me for the rest of practice. He's too busy talking to Bran about a couple of new plays we'll be running on Friday.

The school day flies by, and before I know it, it's last period. The first thing I notice when I walk into the classroom is that Ms. Mann isn't at her desk. A substitute sits there instead. Normally I'd be psyched about that. A sub means I could talk to Ella and Hartley and do absolutely nothing productive without the fear of consequences. But I'm too damn tired for that.

I heave myself into my chair and sigh loudly.

"Well, aren't we chipper," Ella says with a wry smile.

"I'm too sleepy," I grumble. "I went to bed at two and woke up at five thirty."

"Me too," Ella chirps. She gets up at the crack of dawn to work at a bakery called The French Twist. "And I'm doing just fine."

"Goodie for you," I mutter.

She smirks. "Nice accessory, by the way."

I lift my wrist to show off the leather band. "This thing? Got it from my bestie." I nudge Hartley, who gives a little embarrassed laugh.

"Where were you at lunch?" she asks.

"Team meeting. We've got a lot of new plays to learn and review before Friday. Coach is riding us hard."

She opens her mouth to respond, but the substitute teacher cuts her off.

"Easton Royal?" he calls, searching the classroom from behind his black-rimmed hipster glasses. He's holding the iPad that every teacher at the school carries around; the tablet is their main form of communication.

I raise a hand and point to my chest. "That's me, Teach. What's up?"

"You're wanted in the headmaster's office. Please gather your things and report to the main office without delay."

"Uh-oh," Hartley murmurs from beside me.

Ella, meanwhile, wears a resigned expression. "What have you done now, East?"

Resentment burns a path up my throat. Everyone in my life has such a low-ass opinion of me. They always think I've done something wrong, even when I haven't.

Unfortunately, Ella had every right to ask, because apparently I did do something.

Or, rather, I did *someone*.

When I enter the headmaster's office five minutes later, the first person I see is Ms. Mann.

Beringer is behind his desk, and my father is in the second visitors' chair opposite Ms. Mann.

Shit.

"Have a seat, Easton," Beringer orders in a voice that brooks no argument.

There's a deadly glint in his beady eyes that I've never seen before. Normally he wears a defeated expression, like a death row inmate who's finally accepted that he's getting the chair. Beringer knows he doesn't have any control over the school—the gazillionaire parents who sign his paychecks do. But this morning, judging by his expression, it's like he's got some actual influence over something.

Over me?

My gaze slides to Ms. Mann. No, *she's* the one he has power over. My dad will get me out of whatever this is—and I have a good feeling I know why we're all here—but Beringer is the furthest thing from powerless right now. He's the one holding the axe at the guillotine, and it's Ms. Mann's head on the chopping block.

"What's this all about?" I demand. To Beringer, I flash an annoyed look. To my dad, an aggrieved one. I'm a good liar when I need to be.

"Yes," my father says, "what's this about, Francois?"

I love that my dad pulls out the first-name power play.

Beringer wrings his hands together on the shiny mahogany desktop. "Some very serious allegations have been brought to my attention. Allegations that I'm afraid I simply cannot ignore . . ." He trails off ominously, like some lame-ass detective in a cop show. All he needs is the menacing music. *Du-dum-dum.*

"Just spit it out," Dad snaps, also irritated by the theatrics. "I was called out of a board meeting for this." He spares a quick glance at Ms. Mann. "You're my son's calculus teacher?"

She nods weakly. If she grows any paler, she's gonna look like a piece of notebook paper.

"So what kind of trouble did my son cause in your class?" Dad asks her. "Cheating? Did he get ahold of test answers and sell them to his classmates?" He's listing transgressions I've actually committed in the past.

"No, Callum. The situation is far more dire than that," Beringer says grimly.

That's when it clicks for my dad. Concern fills his face as he studies Ms. Mann again, as if he's seeing her for the first time now. Her beautiful features, her youth.

Visible disappointment clouds his eyes as he glances over at me.

"Thanks to an anonymous source, it's come to the school's attention that your son and Ms. Mann might have been engaging in inappropriate . . ." He pauses tactfully. ". . . *relations.*"

Ms. Mann releases a sound of distress. Her gaze locks with mine, just briefly, and I know we're both thinking about the pact we made in her classroom the other day. Deny, deny, deny.

I'm the first one to follow the plan. "That's bullshit!" I stare at Beringer with pure astonishment, as if a teenage boy hooking up with his hot teacher is the craziest thing I've ever heard. "I never touched her."

Beringer looks startled by my denial. What, did he think I'd own up to it? Moron.

"I see," he says. He pauses, then addresses Ms. Mann. "And what do you have to say about this, Caroline?"

Her name's Caroline? I had no idea.

"What do I have to say?" she repeats, and damn, I'm impressed by her calm, even tone. "What I have to *say*, Francois, is that I'm shocked and disgusted and, frankly, insulted that you would bring me into this office and accuse me of fraternizing with a *student*."

"Is that a denial?" the headmaster asks.

"Of course it's a denial!"

I hide a smile. Forget math—she should be teaching drama.

"It's one hundred percent a denial," I chime in, matching her level of outrage. "I'd never hook up with some old lady—" I quickly look over and say, "No offense."

"None taken," she says tightly.

"Trust me, I get plenty of action from girls my own age."

There's a short silence.

Dad studies Ms. Mann again. "How old are you, Caroline?" he inquires.

"I'm twenty-four, sir."

Dad turns toward Beringer. "Easton is eighteen. Even if something untoward did happen, there's no crime here."

"You're right, this isn't a criminal concern. Unfortunately, it's an ethical one. If this is true—"

"It's not," Ms. Mann and I say. Angrily, and in unison.

We're putting on the performance of a lifetime. I'm tempted to high-five her.

"Actually," I say as an afterthought, "I'd really like to know who made these allegations, because *that's* the person you should be talking to." I raise my eyebrows at Beringer. "You know, for spreading lies and trying to hurt the reputation of an Astor Park faculty member."

I gesture toward Ms. Mann in a dramatic fashion. I'm starting to really get into this.

"Ms. Mann is an awesome teacher," I declare. "She actually makes math fun, if you can believe it. You know how hard it is to capture my attention—"

Dad snorts softly.

"But she's able to engage me in the classroom, so much that I actually look forward to going to calc every day." When Beringer's eyes narrow, I quickly hold up my hand. "To *learn*, sir. And nothing more."

"There," my father says briskly. "I believe my son and this young woman have both said their piece. Other than this anonymous informant of yours, what other evidence do you possess that suggests they're involved in an inappropriate relationship?"

The headmaster hesitates. Then his shoulders sag, just slightly. He has no evidence, and we all know it.

"Eyewitnesses?" Dad prompts. "Anyone who can swear to seeing them together?"

Beringer shakes his head. "No, we have only the word of the student—"

Student?

That gets my attention. What asshole ratted me out to Beringer?

It wouldn't have been Ella or Val. Not Hartley or any of my teammates. One of the guys might've blabbed to someone, though. And that someone could've told Beringer.

So. Who's cruel enough to want to get Ms. Mann fired, and catty enough to try to get me in trouble . . .

Uh-huh. I have a good idea about who that could be.

Luckily, this stupid little meeting breaks up not long after Beringer admits to his lack of evidence. Before he dismisses us, however, he lets it be known that he's keeping an eye on the situation. Ms. Mann huffs and makes suitably angry and affronted noises, demanding to speak to him in private.

Dad and I leave the office without a word. He places a hand on my shoulder and we both nod pleasantly at Beringer's secretary. Only when we're in the lobby and out of earshot of anyone, Dad curses under his breath.

"Jesus, Easton. A *teacher*?"

I blink innocently. "I don't know what you're talking about."

"Contrary to what you may believe, you are not that good a liar, son." He shakes his head in frustration. "At least assure me that it's over?"

"What's over?"

"Easton." He draws a calming breath. "All right. You know what? Don't say a word. Just nod if this irresponsible insanity is no longer going on."

I don't play dumb this time. I jerk my head in a quick nod.

Dad looks relieved. "Good. Make sure it stays that way." After a quick goodbye, he strides out the front doors.

Through the glass windows of the lobby, I watch him descend the steps and duck into the waiting Town Car out front. His driver, Durand, closes the back door and hops into the driver's seat. The Town Car speeds off, probably to whisk Callum Royal away to Atlantic Aviation's corporate headquarters.

The click of heels on the polished floor has me turning around. I scowl when I see who it is.

"Is everything okay?" Felicity asks, and there's no mistaking the note of glee in her voice. "I heard you were called into

Beringer's office. And someone told me one of your teachers was summoned, too. What a coincidence!"

"Drop the act," I order in a low voice. "I know you were behind it."

"Behind what?"

I ignore her batting eyelashes. "That woman could've lost her job, Felicity."

She is totally unruffled. Indifferent, actually, as she rolls her eyes at me. "Hey, she made her own bed. She fooled around with a student and now she gets to be held accountable for her actions."

It's exactly the same thought I had not so long ago. Now, I can't stop thinking about the fear in Ms. Mann's eyes when she'd faced the possibility of losing her job. *My* stupid, horny actions almost ruined that woman's career, and I feel sick about it.

I meet Felicity's victorious expression. She seems to be enjoying herself.

"Congratulations, you got back at me for ruining your party on Friday night," I say through gritted teeth. "Can we call a truce now?"

"Oh, sweetie. A truce?" She laughs loudly, a peal of sound that echoes in the huge, empty lobby. "Sorry, but the war's just begun."

Twenty-Four

TO MY SURPRISE, I find Hartley lingering by my locker, a worried expression on her face. "Is everything okay?" she asks, clutching her math book to her chest.

"All good." I throw my stuff in the locker and take her arm. "Want to grab something to eat?"

I expect her to say no, but she follows me without argument.

"Easton, what happened?" Ella accosts me when we exit the main building. "Someone said they saw Callum on campus."

"I'll tell you later. Hartley and I have somewhere to be." I tug on Hartley's arm. "Come on."

We climb into my truck. Hartley doesn't say a word. I'm afraid of telling her what happened in the headmaster's office. She'll hate me.

But my mouth, which has never had a good barrier, opens and starts spilling.

"Someone found out about Ms. Mann and me and told Beringer."

Hartley winces. "Oh no."

"Oh yeah."

"I never once bragged about this."

"I didn't think you would. But how could it have gotten out? I was the only one who opened the door." She goes quiet for a moment, as if she's thinking back to that day. "I guess there were other people in the hall that could've seen something, but why wait until now?"

"I don't think anyone saw anything."

"Then how did it get out?"

I focus straight ahead. I don't want to see her expression when I admit this. "I might've inadvertently said something. It was stupid. Pash was hassling me about hooking up with an Astor girl and when I said no, I might've implied that I liked a bit more of a challenge."

"So Pash told?"

"Well, I don't think Ella or Val would."

"Easton Royal! How many people did you blab to?"

"Too many," I say miserably.

"Why? Why on earth would you do that? Are you proud of what went on with you and Ms. Mann? Are you happy that she's going to get fired?"

"She's not going to get fired. We both denied anything happened. And no, I'm not proud, and no, I wouldn't be happy if she got fired. I just . . . I wanted to have a good time."

My response sounds terrible, because I have no justification other than I'm Easton Royal and my goal in life is to do what makes me happy. So long as no one else gets hurt, it's all good. The problem is, someone is always getting hurt.

I wait for Hartley to lay into me, rightfully so, but she surprises me.

"All right. Well. It's done and there's no point in dwelling on it, right?"

Right. I throw her a grateful look and start the engine. "Where should we go?" I ask as we leave the school behind.

"Will you go by my house?"

She sounds so uncertain that it summons a smile. What's she so worried about, that I'll make digs at her house? I've already been there twice. "Sure. So should we stop for food and eat at your place?"

"Not my apartment." She sighs. "My house . . . my old house."

"Oh." I want to slap myself on the forehead for being so dense. "Sure."

We make the ten-minute drive in silence. I'm itching to ask a thousand and one questions but miraculously manage to keep my mouth shut.

"Watch the curve," she murmurs as we get close.

"Yeah, I know. I almost ran into my brothers the first time I was here."

"Lauren lives down the road." Hartley points off to the distance.

"I figured."

I go past her driveway and then swing a U-turn, bringing the truck to a stop across the street from the front door. "It's a good thing I have a pickup instead of a van. Someone might think we're kidnappers. We aren't doing that, right?"

I slide a glance toward her, half-teasing, half-serious. She's not paying a lick of attention to me. Her eyes are glued to the house.

Two cars sit to the left of the house, close to a side door. One's the Mercedes SUV that was parked in front of the Hungry Spoon Diner. I'm guessing those are Parker's wheels. There are filmy curtains drawn closed in the front window, so we can't make out exactly what's happening inside.

Out of nowhere, Hartley says, "I'd tell you about what went down in there, but I can't."

I frown. "Why not?"

"Because I'm trying to win my way back into my family. I'm hoping I can get my mom to meet me. But if I blab about the past, then I'll keep being punished."

Even though I'm dying of curiosity, I don't push for more details. "Do you want me to go up and check if your dad is home? Maybe he ran out for milk."

She snorts. "Even if he was dying and needed to drink it to save his life, he'd make Mom do it. But no, he's not home." She gestures to the cars. "His Beemer's not there. Parker's here, though—"

She breaks off as people start pouring out of the house. I recognize Parker, who's carrying a dark-haired boy. Next are Joanie Wright and a tall man with shiny black hair. Behind them, a little girl dressed in patent leather shoes and a pretty dress holds hands with a sullen teen wearing ripped skinny jeans and a tight midriff top.

Hartley slaps a hand on the window and whimpers. I swear the brooding teen hears her. The girl stops in her tracks and stares in our direction.

Not wanting Hartley to get caught, I lunge across the console and push her down. Under my chest, I can feel her body shake with silent sobs.

I brush a hand over the side of her face and quietly narrate the scene. "They're getting into the cars. Dylan and some guy—"

"Parker's husband."

"—Parker's husband and Dylan are getting into Parker's car. Parker is in the passenger seat. The little girl is going with your mother."

"Macy is my mom's favorite," Hartley mumbles.

The car doors slam shut and the red taillights turn on. "Those girls safe in there?"

She hesitates. "I think so." And then, more forcefully, "Yes. The thing between me and my dad was a one-time deal."

I didn't like the moment of indecision, but I don't say anything. I slide down lower as the cars pull out. The engines rumble and then grow distant as they get farther away.

Now that it's safe to sit up, I ease off Hartley's back. "Want me to follow them?"

"No."

"Okay. So what are we doing?"

Hartley meets my gaze. "How do you feel about breaking and entering?"

I ignore the tear-glistening eyes and grin. "One of my top ten activities."

"Of course it is."

We both hop out and run toward the side door that Hartley's family just exited. She passes it by. I catch up with her at the back of the house.

Every good Southern home has a veranda, and this one is no different. The wide, covered deck runs the length of the house. Two French doors, one leading to a kitchen and another to a family room, are framed by floor-to-ceiling windows.

She tries the first one. It's locked, but the second one is open. I hear a beep when the door opens and notice a red light above the frame. The security system marks when the doors are open and closed.

"Ignore it," Hartley tells me. "It's just for show. Dad had it installed when I was a kid, but he got into a fight with the security company over them not showing up fast enough when he called, so he canceled the service."

I nod and examine my surroundings. It's a nice house as houses go. Smells like cleaner. Looks immaculate.

Hartley passes through the family room and makes for the stairs. I follow her up, stopping at the top as she pauses.

"Which room is yours?"

She points to the last room on the left.

"Do you mind?" I ask, because I'm bursting with curiosity.

She gives me a half smile. "Knock yourself out."

Strangely, she chooses to go into the second room on the right. I keep going to the end of the hall. Hartley's bedroom. Damn, I'm excited. I'm finally going to get some insight into her.

Or not.

When I open the door, a big wall of nothingness greets me.

There are a few boxes in the middle of the floor. The walls are a stark white. There's no bed or furniture.

It's as if no one has ever slept in this room.

Disheartened, I back out and retrace my steps to the landing. As I pass through the hall a second time, I notice the family pictures on the wall, but it's as if this family only has two daughters instead of three. It's like they erased her. Man, that's brutal.

I wonder if she knows. She must.

I knock on the open door, pushing it wider to see Hartley sitting on the side of the bed, a purple pillow clutched in her arms. The walls are purple, too. The bed is littered with stuffed bears and dogs. The posters on the wall feature boys with hair dyed the color of Easter eggs. This room obviously belongs to her younger sister, the one she hasn't seen in three years.

I tug on the collar of my shirt. It's getting hard to breathe in here. "Let's get out of here," I say gruffly.

Hartley glances up at me and gives a weak nod.

I don't wait for her to change her mind. I pull her to her feet and hustle her down the stairs.

◆ ◆ ◆

WE END UP at the pier. The lights are on, and twilight is giving way to evening. I park and jog around to Hartley's side of the truck. She lets me help her down. She lets me take her hand. She lets me lead her over to a food stand, where I order a hot chocolate and a funnel cake.

After she's downed the drink and eaten half the cake, her zombielike expression softens. "Thanks for dinner."

"My pleasure. Want to ride the Ferris wheel?" I suggest. "You haven't been on one since you were twelve."

"You remember that?"

"Of course." I don't give her any time to think about it. I pop over to the ride counter, buy our tickets, and then lead her toward the giant buckets of rust. The things I do for this girl.

"Know why I love the Ferris wheel?" she asks as she steps into the shaky metal basket and takes a seat.

"Because you have a death wish?" I climb in after her and wait for the safety bar to lower.

"Because you can see the whole world from the top."

"You should try flying," I suggest. "It's a thousand times better—and safer—than this."

The tin can starts to sway. A bead of sweat breaks across my forehead and my stomach turns over. I lean my head against the thin metal post and start counting backward from a thousand. Maybe this is a mistake. I should get off. I push at the bar, but it doesn't move.

"You okay?" I hear Hartley say. Her hand touches the back of mine.

Okay. Mind changed. I can handle this. "Yup."

"You're sweating."

"It's hot out."

"It's sub sixty and you have a T-shirt on."

"Anything above freezing is hot for me."

"You have goose bumps."

The basket sways and the creak of metal against metal makes my heart pound.

"Because I'm sitting next to you," I push out through gritted teeth.

A soft body presses against mine. "I think I stepped in a pile of poop in the funhouse the last time we were here."

"That place needs to be condemned. Val got someone's chewing tobacco stuck on the bottom of her shoe."

Ugh. And if they can't maintain the funhouse, then what about this piece of terror? I start timing my breaths with my counting.

"Are you afraid of heights?" Hartley's voice is gentle. So is her hand as she lightly strokes my knuckles. "I thought you loved flying."

"I do love flying. I hate incompetence. In the air, I'm in control. I know who built the plane. I know the instruments. I control it. This thing could be held together with wire and gum." The basket rocks again. "And that's probably giving them too much credit."

"Why'd you come on this thing with me, then?"

"Because you wanted to."

She's silent for what seems like an endless moment. I close my eyes. Maybe if I can't see anything, I'll stop picturing this rickety car plummeting from the sky.

"Are we at the top yet?" I ask.   .

"Almost."

"I'm not kissing you at the top," I tell her. "Even though it's probably expected, I'm not easy like that."

She snickers. "I never thought you were easy."

"That's a lie. You think I'm a slut."

Her body shakes as she laughs again. "I think the term is 'partner-inclusive.'"

And that makes me laugh. "Okay. I take it back. I am kissing you at the top."

"Uh-uh. Best friends don't kiss."

"Since when?" I counter. "You're *only* supposed to kiss your best friends. It's one of the best-friend privileges."

"So you've kissed all your best friends?"

The car jerks to a stop. "No. I think you're my only best friend."

Maybe even the only real friend I've had outside my family. I don't say that to her, though. I already feel way too pathetic.

There's a featherlight touch against the side of my cheek. I hold my breath. The touch becomes firmer. It moves from the side of my cheek to my lips.

I turn to face her. Her eyes are open and she smiles. I can feel the curve of her lips against mine.

"Don't worry. You're not kissing me," she whispers. "I'm kissing you."

My mouth parts. Her tongue slips in. Up here, time stops. It's a freeze frame. Me, her, the endless sky.

In the vast void, her kiss tells me I'm not alone. She touches her tongue to mine, and a groan slips out. I think it comes from me. I'm dizzy and breathless and full of strange emotions that I can't make sense of and don't want to. I know the gist. I'm happy. This is a high I've never been able to achieve through pills or booze or other people.

Hartley makes a soft, breathy noise that drives me crazy. My fingers curl around her hip, pulling her closer. Our tongues meet again and I swear my heart nearly explodes from my rib cage, it's pounding so hard.

This kiss is goddamn amazing. I want to grab on to her, hold her close, and keep this moment going endlessly.

But then the gears of the spinning wheel of death start again and the bucket begins its downward rotation.

Hartley releases me and slides away. Not far, but enough to let me know that the barrier she likes to place between us is back in place.

"Thanks for distracting me up there," I blurt out before she can get out anything cutting.

"Of course," she replies, but the sound is flat. Did I piss her off?

When the ride comes to a halt and the safety belt lifts, Hartley hops off. I take my time. Hell, I kind of want to buy the entire ride and take it home so I can have the car bronzed. It was that kind of moment. The kind you want to etch in permanent ink so you can relive it again and again.

I join her on the ground. "Hartley," I start.

"Yes?"

A light breeze blows and ruffles her dark hair. I press it

down, shaping her scalp against my hand. She reaches up and grabs my wrist right above the leather band, not to draw me away, though. To hold me in place. Or to pull me closer.

I swallow hard. "I want—"

"You two look so sweet together! Smile!"

Hartley and I both look up in surprise. A flash blinds me, and by the time the white dots in my vision clear up, the culprit is hurrying away. Two of them, actually. They've got blond hair and high-pitched squeals and they're not even trying to lower their voices as they dash off.

"Felicity is gonna freak when she sees this!"

"Post it on Instagram, and then do a Snap story!"

Shit.

I scowl at their retreating backs. Figures that the one time Hartley lowers her guard around me, a bunch of Astor Park gossips capture the moment.

"Should I be worried?" Her dry voice jerks me from my thoughts.

I glance over and manage a careless smile. "Nah. I doubt it."

Her eyes tell me she isn't convinced of that.

Neither am I.

Twenty-Five

"HERE ARE YOUR notes," Hartley says when I approach her desk the next afternoon. "I forgot I had them."

"I didn't need them back."

"I know."

"You do?"

"Of course. You probably have the textbook memorized. Your whole 'I'm a bad boy who hates school' act is easy to see through." She swivels to face the front, but not before I see a hint of a blush on her cheeks.

Is she thinking about how she kissed me last night? I am. It's *all* I've been thinking about since I opened my eyes this morning. And all I thought about when I got home from the pier yesterday. It's really hard to sleep with a hard-on that won't go away, so once again I had a crappy night and once again I was a zombie at practice.

I tuck the pages away in my notebook. "It's not an act. I don't test well."

"Or you have a hard time focusing," she guesses.

"That, too."

I decided to sit behind her today, flopping down and stretching my legs out on either side of her desk. I like watching her from behind. I can see her shoulders tense and relax. The curve of her neck sometimes appears when she bends over. The little knots of her spine have somehow become the cutest thing. I'd like to take a big ol' bite there.

I shift as my uniform trousers grow tight.

"Where's Ella?" Hartley twists around to look at me, gesturing to Ella's empty desk.

"She's got the day off. She and my dad are meeting our lawyers in the city."

Hartley's expression fills with sympathy. "Will she really have to testify at her father's trial?"

I nod. I'm grateful to focus on something other than Hartley's way-too-pretty neck. And really? Necks? That's what I'm hot for these days?

"Yeah. She was there when Steve confessed to everything."

"That sucks."

I don't particularly want to rehash Steve's actions, so I change the subject. "Better question is—where's Ms. Mann?"

Two rows over, Tonya Harrison pipes up. "She was down in Beringer's office. That's twice this week."

"Someone's in trouble," my teammate Owen sings.

A bunch of kids turn and look in my direction. I glare at Owen, but either he really is confused or he's a far better actor than I knew. I make a tiny slicing motion across my throat to indicate he better keep his lips shut tight. His response is to wrinkle his forehead.

Suddenly the door bursts open.

"Oh my God. Someone's getting busted today!" exclaims Glory Burke, the captain of the girls' field hockey team.

A chorus of questions arises from my classmates.

"What do you mean?" Tonya asks.

"Beringer and Officer Neff are looking through someone's locker," Glory answers.

"Can they do that?"

"What about student rights?"

"The honor code says that if there's a reasonable suspicion a crime has been committed, the lockers can be searched," Rebecca Lockhart explains. She would know. She's our class president.

Worried whispers spread as the debates begin over who's in trouble. There are few angels here. Some kids are taking uppers. Some are sleeping around. Some are drinking. Some are doing all of the above.

Only one has screwed around with his teacher.

This time it's my blazer that feels tight and itchy, as guilt starts pouring through my veins. Dammit. Why'd I ever give in to the temptation of Ms. Mann in the first place? It was stupid. So stupid. And for what? So I could have a five-minute feel-good experience? I'm such an idiot.

I cross my arms and slide lower in my chair. Over her shoulder, Hartley casts a sympathetic glance, which I avoid by staring at my desk.

I know what she's thinking. *Easton Royal's the dumbest ass I know. Why am I even with him?*

But she's not really *with* me, is she? She kissed me at the top of the Ferris wheel. What does that even mean? Probably nothing.

Halfway into my fit of self-pity, I straighten up. Because

screw this. What do I care what Hartley, an outcast that her family doesn't even talk to, thinks about me? What do I care what anybody here at Astor thinks? I didn't even bone Ms. Mann. If I'm going to be crucified for having sex with a teacher, I should actually get to have sex with her.

I give myself a fierce shake and drawl, "What? There's someone being naughty besides me? Stand up and show yourself. There's only room for one asshole here at Astor, and I'm currently occupying that slot."

A nervous laugh spreads among the gossipy whispers.

"Actually, I think it's her locker they're searching." Glory awkwardly points to Hartley.

"Me?" Hartley blurts out.

"You're four sixty-five, right?"

Hartley nods warily.

"Pretty sure it was yours."

The whispers rise to a dull roar as everyone starts speculating what Hartley could've done. She's a mystery to most of the students here, having appeared out of nowhere after three years of absence. She's not involved in any activities. Her Astor Park–mandated elective is music and she spends her study periods in the private music rooms, away from the rest of the student body.

Except for the couple of football games she attended where she sat with Ella and Val, Hartley's been mostly absent from the Astor scene.

I hear snatches of conversation.

". . . she's been hanging around Ella. Bet she's one of her stripper friends."

". . . didn't her father have to drop out of the mayor race because of a scandal?"

". . . rumor is she and Royal were having sex in the music room."

If I can hear them, Hartley can, too. I reach over and give her shoulder a reassuring squeeze. She freezes when I touch her and then I feel a tiny flinch, a shrug of sorts, a silent brush-off.

Stung, I let my hand drop to the desk.

The door opens again. Everyone's heads swivel toward it.

When Ms. Mann enters, I brace myself for another pitiful expression. But her chin is up and she's surveying all of us as if she's the queen and we're her worthless minions. Then she moves aside and Headmaster Beringer appears.

The entire room falls silent.

"Ms. Wright," the headmaster barks, "if you would gather your materials and follow us." He crooks his hand in Hartley's direction.

She doesn't move immediately.

Beringer clears his throat.

With a soft sound of dismay, Hartley pops to her feet, grabs her stuff, and walks to the door, books clutched to her chest, spine as stiff and straight as a steel pole. Beringer holds the door open until Hartley passes him. The two exit, leaving Ms. Mann inside the room.

"Open your books to chapter four and read the Chain Rule," she announces. "I want you to do problems one through twenty-two."

"Twenty-two?" Owen balks. "It'll take ten minutes to do one of these equations."

"Then you best get started or you'll get to do fifty problems before tomorrow," Ms. Mann snaps.

"Yes, ma'am."

We all apply ourselves, because clearly Ms. Mann isn't messing around today.

I barely get all the problems done before the bell rings. My attention kept straying to the door, wondering when Hartley would return. She never does.

Pash pounces on me the minute I step into the hall. He'd been waiting outside the classroom. "Dude, Owen just texted and said Hartley Wright got arrested."

I sigh. "She didn't get arrested. Her locker was searched."

"Seriously? Why?"

"No clue." I stalk over to my locker and shove my books in.

"She doing something illegal?"

"Not that I know of." When a few papers spill out, I bend down to pick them up. They're my calc notes, I realize.

The toe of a navy-blue pump presses down on the papers.

"What are these, Mr. Royal?"

I peer up at Ms. Mann. "Notes."

"They look like notes to my class. In fact, they look like answers to my last two pop quizzes." She extends her hand, palm up.

I shuffle the papers together, rise, and stick them back into my locker. "First, they aren't answers to your pop quizzes, and second, even if they were, what would it matter? Those quizzes are over."

"Why should I believe you?"

"Because it's the truth." I slam my locker shut.

"Did you share these notes with Ms. Wright?"

A big red light goes off in my head. I can't lie, not with Hartley possibly being in trouble, but I can't tell the truth, because I don't know how it will affect her.

"First, I get Cs, so a student using me to cheat off would be dumb. Second, I didn't realize sharing notes from class was inappropriate. Good to know." I signal for Pash. "Ready to spot me? I want to work on my guns today."

He flicks a glance toward Ms. Mann and then back to me. "It's leg day for me," he says promptly.

"Isn't it too cold for shorts, Mr. Bhara?" Ms. Mann snipes. Technically, we're only allowed to wear shorts when it's warm out. Warm is a relative term in Pash's mind. He wears shorts and Timbs year-round. Doesn't matter if it's forty degrees out. He's sporting shorts.

"No, ma'am. Sky's out, thighs out." He thrusts a leg out, model-style, toward our teacher.

"It's too bad the administration doesn't do something about kids who break school rules," a sickly sweet voice says.

I whirl around to find Felicity sauntering up to us. Great.

Glaring at Pash, she adds, "Our reputation as the best in the country is being ruined and no one seems to care. Shameful."

Ms. Mann nods regally. "I agree, Miss Worthington. It is shameful."

Instead of giving Felicity the trashy response she deserves, I hustle Pash down the hall.

"What's going on?" he asks, a little bewildered.

"Thanks for having my back."

"Always."

I chew on the inside of my cheek. "I think Hartley might be in real trouble."

"What?"

"Dunno. Like I said, her locker was searched, and Beringer came to get her before class started." I give him a sideways glance. "You didn't say anything about Ms. Mann and me, did you?"

He frowns. "Course not. Why would I?"

"Right." I stop just short of the Admin office. "It's out there, though."

"You weren't very discreet about it," he points out.

"I know." I rub my forehead. I'm starting to feel a dull ache at my temples, but before I can start banging my head against the wall, the office door opens and Hartley appears.

"What happened?"

"I . . ." She has a dazed look on her face. "I can't even . . ."

I immediately take her arm and direct her toward the back exit. Pash hurries after us, but Hartley doesn't seem to notice him. She keeps shaking her head in astonishment.

"I'm being suspended for the rest of the week, and a letter is being put in my permanent record."

Behind us, Pash whistles.

"For what?" I demand.

She gulps. "For cheating. I got a really good score on the last quiz because I used your notes to study. I didn't realize that was cheating."

"It's not cheating. Is that what they accused you of?" I say angrily. "That's bullshit. My dad will take care of this." I whip out my phone and start one-hand texting.

"No," Hartley protests. "Please don't do that."

Reluctantly, I slide the phone back in my pocket. My jaw remains tense as I ask, "What exactly did Beringer say?"

"That my scores were statistically so much better than how I performed before that it must be because of some type of outside help. He asked if I had tutoring. I said no. He asked if someone helped me. I said no. I forgot about your notes, because when they asked if someone helped me, I imagined someone sitting beside me, like a tutor, you know?"

Pash and I both nod.

"Easy mistake," Pash says gently.

"But then my guidance counselor—he was there, too—pulled out an answer sheet."

"To the quiz?" I ask.

She nods miserably. "They found it in my locker folded and taped into the back of *All About the Girl*," she mumbles, referring to the book we're reading in Feminist Thought.

My mind's whirling. The pieces are starting to fall into place. Ms. Mann looking smug instead of scared. Felicity blabbering on about Astor's declining reputation.

Oh hell no.

"Let's go," I growl, taking Hartley's wrist.

"Where?" she squeaks.

"Yeah, where?" Pash echoes.

"To clear Hartley's name."

It's easy to find Felicity. She hasn't moved from her locker—it's as if she was waiting for me. A couple of frenemies flank either side of her. One of them happens to be Claire.

I raise my eyebrows and Claire responds by jutting her chin. Is this show of defiance something I should care about? Resisting the urge to roll my eyes, I dismiss her and turn to Felicity.

"Felicity." I bare my teeth in a cheerless smile.

"Easton." Her smile is equally icy.

"I don't know what the hell you think you're doing, but you need to stop."

"Why should I?" she says.

I'm momentarily stunned into silence. I thought for sure she'd deny that she did anything wrong.

"Wait a minute." Hartley shoves me out of the way, as if it's just dawned on her why I made a beeline for Felicity. "You planted those notes in my locker?" Her head swivels to me. "She planted the notes?"

I nod grimly. Felicity smiles again.

Shock and anger flood Hartley's gray eyes, darkening them to metallic silver. "Why!" she growls at Felicity. "Why the hell would you do that! I could've been kicked out of school!"

"So?"

Hartley lunges forward, and it takes both me and Pash to yank her away from Felicity. Catfights are hot as hell, but not when Felicity Worthington is one of the fighters. And not when Hartley is so obviously close to tears.

"Enough!" I jab a finger in front of Felicity. "You're gonna pay for this, you hear me? You can't just go around destroying people's reputations—"

Felicity interrupts with a loud, genuinely amused laugh. "Oh my God! You are such a hypocrite!" Her continued laughter makes my blood boil. "You and Reed destroyed Ella's reputation before she even got to Astor! And you tried to destroy *mine* with that stunt you pulled at my party!"

Fuck, that drunken mistake is going to haunt me forever. I am never allowed to drink again. Ever.

"So, no, I couldn't care less if you"—Felicity sneers at Hartley—"get kicked out of school. Actually, I'm disappointed Beringer went so easy on you." She pushes away from the lockers and brushes by us. Over her shoulder she says, "By the way, I'm just getting started."

Her friends follow, including Claire, who smirks as she passes Hartley. "Your ass looks huge in that picture," she snarks. "You might want to look into a gym membership."

Claire flounces off before Hartley can respond. She joins up with Felicity and the other girls, and their laughter echoes through the hall. I can still hear it even as they all turn the corner.

Twenty-Six

HARTLEY'S FACE IS beet red. Pash, meanwhile, gapes in the direction where Felicity and her posse headed off. "What is wrong with her?" he marvels.

I let out a ragged breath. "No clue."

"She probably needs a good—"

I sense more than see Hartley about to explode and so I slap a hand over Pash's mouth before he gets us both in trouble.

"Don't say it," I warn.

"What?" he mumbles and shoves me off. "I was going to say she needs a good kick in the ass."

I give him a *sure you were* look before straightening my jacket. He responds by pulling his phone from his pocket, and starts swiping.

"You humiliated her," Hartley says finally. "Or we did. She said she was dating you and you kept denying it. Then you told her she could break up with you but instead you went to her house, her *party*, and embarrassed her in front of all her friends."

"And I guess this was the icing on the cake," Pash remarks.

We look over at him for clarification. He holds up his phone.

Dammit. The picture that girl took at the pier last night stares back at me. She used the Astor hashtag, and although she posted the picture just this morning, there are already tons of likes. More than a thousand people have enjoyed the sight of Hartley and me staring moodily into each other's eyes with the Ferris wheel in the background.

Hartley groans. "Oh God, it's the top post on the feed. If that's not rubbing salt in Felicity's wound, I don't know what is. I'd want revenge, too."

"It's a nice shot," Pash comments.

"A nice shot?" I say incredulously.

"Yeah. Nice shot. Whoever took it used high speed and caught the lights. It looks professional." He scowls at me. "So it's the top post because it's a good photo, not because you two are in it. Sorry to burst your giant ego."

I return his glare. "She's targeting Hartley because of me. That's not my giant ego talking. That's the truth."

"Can you two stop fighting?" Hartley interrupts. "Does it really matter why the picture is popular?"

"She's right," Pash says. "The question is, how do we get Felicity to calm the eff down?"

I arch an eyebrow. "We?"

"Well, sure. I don't want to see Hart here"— he knocks her lightly on the shoulder—"take the fall for something she didn't do. So let's appease Felicity."

Hartley musters up a smile. "Thanks."

"Why are we appeasing her?" I ask.

"Because you can't beat her up."

"There are other things."

"Like what?" Hartley says suspiciously.

I open my mouth, but nothing comes out because I don't have a clue what to do. The last time a mean girl tried to take my family down, violence *was* the answer.

"Remember when Jordan Carrington taped that girl to the side of the school?" I finally say. "Ella beat her up."

Pash and Hartley look at me like I've lost my mind.

"I think you've been hit in the head too many times," Hartley says. She nudges Pash. "You don't have to get involved. This is messy. *I* don't even want to be involved."

He shrugs. "It's our senior year. I got nothing better to do. Besides, who's to say I won't be next? I'm Easton's second-favorite person at Astor."

This draws a glimmer of a smile from Hartley. "Yeah? Who's first?"

"You are, of course. Then there's Ella. But me and her are tied. I'd appreciate it if you'd keep that between us, though, because she's got a mean right." He playfully rubs a hand down his arm.

"Having been punched by Ella more than once, I can say he's not wrong," I volunteer, appreciating the lightheartedness that Pash is trying to inject.

As some of the stress lines in Hartley's face smooth away, I decide that Pash is going in the right direction. We need more jokes. More laughter. Life's been a downer lately. What happened to having fun?

"Let's throw a party," I announce.

Hartley's jaw drops. "A what?"

"A party. You know, an 'I don't have to go to school anymore' party."

"I'm in." Pash holds up his hand, and we exchange a high five.

Hartley, however, starts walking away.

"Wait up," I call, abandoning Pash to run after her. He comes, too. "You don't like the idea of a party?"

"I have to work." Her voice is flat and her expression is shuttered.

"We can party after you're done with work."

She stops abruptly. "A party? Really, Easton? I just got suspended. That's nothing to celebrate."

Beside me, Pash sobers up. "Are your parents going to kill you? Because mine would kill me," he admits.

Hartley turns ghost white.

Damn.

"I guess a party is a bad idea," I mumble, feeling stupid as hell.

I didn't consider the ramifications of her suspension, and I don't think she fully did, either, until Pash brought up family. First thing the headmaster is going to do is call her parents. And since she's currently not allowed to see anyone in her family for some mysterious reason, this isn't going to go over well for her.

"Want me to talk to your folks?" I offer. "I can explain—"

"No." If possible, she grows paler. "Don't say a word to them. Not one word." She grabs my blazer, digging her fingers into my arm. "Please."

"Okay. I won't," I assure her.

She drops my arm. "I've got to go."

Before I can blink, she's hurrying away. When I start to follow, Pash holds me back.

"Give her some time alone with her family, man."

"She doesn't . . ." I stop myself before I spill shit I'm not supposed to talk about. But watching Hartley run away isn't a good idea, either. "I can't just stand around doing nothing, dude. I need to do something."

"Fine. Then go home," he advises. "Talk to Ella. Who knows, maybe she's got an idea about how to solve this."

✦   ✦   ✦

AS BADLY AS I want to go after Hartley, I decide to take Pash's advice. When I get home, I hunt my stepsister down and find her in her room, studying.

"Got a minute?" I ask, knocking on her open door.

Ella glances up from her book. "Yeah, come in. What's up?"

I give it to her straight. "Felicity framed Hartley for cheating in calc. Hartley got suspended."

"Oh my God," Ella gasps. "Why would Felicity do that to Hartley?"

"To get back at me. I'm the one she's actually pissed at."

"Of course she's pissed. You were an ass to her at the party. But why go after Hartley and not one of your closer friends, like me or Val or Pash?"

"I guess you haven't checked your Insta or Snap today."

"No. I was with Callum and the lawyers all day." Ella sets down her book and snatches her phone off the thick duvet.

I drop down on the bed and lean back against the padded headboard. I know the moment she finds the picture because she gasps again.

"Are you guys kissing in this pic?" she exclaims.

"Almost. We kissed on the Ferris wheel, though."

Ella looks startled. "What happened to the rules? Hartley said you weren't allowed to hit on her."

"I didn't," I protest. "*She* kissed *me*, for your information."

That shuts her up for almost thirty seconds. Her gaze bores a hole in my face. It's like she's trying to burrow her way into my mind and . . . and what? I'm not sure why she's looking at me, but it's starting to make me antsy.

"Anyway," I start.

"Uh-uh, no. Don't 'anyway' me. We're not done with this kiss thing." Ella runs a hand through her golden hair. "So are you guys a thing now?"

"Maybe? I don't know."

Her jaw drops. "Do you want to be? You don't do girl-friends, remember?"

"I do lots of girls," I drawl, dragging my tongue over my lower lip. Maybe if I turn this into something sexual, Ella will be so disgusted, she'll drop the subject.

Sure enough, it works. "Gross," she says. "But, okay, it makes sense now. If Felicity thinks you and Hartley are together, then she'd definitely go after Hartley to get revenge on you." Ella pauses. "You kinda deserve her vengeance, if I'm being honest."

"Thanks a lot." I frown. "Why're you bringing me down?"

"Oh, are you annoyed by the truth? I'm sorry. Maybe you shouldn't have gotten drunk, gone over to Felicity's, and humiliated her in front of all our friends and classmates. This is what happens when you don't think about the consequences."

"Christ. What crawled up your ass and died?" I regret the words even before the last one is out of my mouth.

Ella winds up and punches me in the arm.

"Dammit!" I rub my arm and give her a wounded look, but it doesn't work.

She crosses her arms and glares at me.

"Sorry about the ass comment, but can we not rehash all my past fuckups? We'll be here until next week."

"Fine. But I'm not apologizing for the hit. You deserved it."

"Fair enough." Girl can throw a punch. No wonder Jordan backed down. "Can you go beat Felicity up so she stops this bullshit?"

Ella snorts. "No."

"Why not? It worked with Jordan."

"No, it didn't. What worked last year is that we all stood together and said enough was enough with the bullying."

"So let's all stand together again and say enough is enough with Felicity."

"Do you have proof that she's the one who framed Hartley?"

"Yup. She admitted it in front of Claire and a couple other girls."

Ella tips her head from side to side, considering this tidbit. "She must be pretty confident they aren't going to say anything," she finally concludes. "At this point, it's your word against hers, and your word is crap. You're constantly getting in trouble. Felicity is in Honor Society and is a perfect student from a great family."

"Thanks for the ringing endorsement," I grumble, but we both know she's right. *Trouble* is my middle name. "Maybe I should call her."

"And say what?"

"'I'm sorry'?"

Ella shoots me an annoyed look. "Seriously? You haven't said that yet? That's the first thing you should've done!"

"Maybe I did." I think back and then grimace. "I don't remember."

"Then, yeah, I think you should call her and tell her you're sorry." Ella shakes her head a few times, as if she can't believe she's sharing the same space as such a moron. "In fact, buy some flowers and go to her house and tell her you were stupid and thoughtless and a jackass and that every bad thought she's ever had about you is true, but please don't take it out on Hartley."

I wince. "All of that?"

"Yes," Ella replies sternly. "All of it."

"Fine." I curse ungraciously and launch myself off the bed. At the door, I turn around. "I still prefer the idea of you beating her up."

Ella throws a pillow at me. "I'm not beating her up!"

I head downstairs and jog outside to my truck. At the end of the driveway, though, I find myself turning left instead of right.

I didn't like the way Hartley ran off. What if her parents are at her apartment, yelling at her? She probably needs moral support.

I decide to check on Hartley first and hit up Felicity on my way back.

I swing by a gas station and buy a pint of ice cream along with a couple of sodas and popcorn. At the checkout, I throw in two candy bars. There's a bucket of single roses at the front and I throw one of those on top, too.

"Pissed someone off, did you?" the clerk says as he rings me up.

"How'd you guess?"

"This is the 'I'm sorry' starter package," he jokes.

I snicker. Technically, only the flower is part of my apology to Felicity, but I'm still curious enough to ask, "What's the success rate of the starter package?"

"Depends on the scale of your wrong. Big wrong requires big apology."

I grab the rest of the flowers. "Let's go big, then."

He swipes my card. "Good luck," he says.

From the tone of his voice, it's clear he thinks I'm gonna fail.

Ten minutes later, I park in front of Hartley's apartment and kill the engine. I grab the bag of goodies and three of the flowers—Felicity doesn't need all of them—then climb the rickety stairs two at a time. I'm raising my hand to knock on the door when I hear voices.

"Whatever you hoped to accomplish before isn't going to happen now. Daddy's been ranting for the past hour."

I freeze. Oh shit. That's Parker. I glance over the railing to see where I missed her Mercedes, but it's nowhere to be seen. She either parked down the street or took an Uber.

"I didn't do it," Hartley says flatly.

"You are always so full of excuses," Parker scoffs. *"I didn't mean to spy on you, Daddy. I didn't mean to ruin your campaign. I didn't mean to embarrass this whole family. I didn't mean to ruin the family."*

Silence falls.

Hartley doesn't respond. I guess there's nothing she can say to make Parker believe in her.

I almost knock. I almost barge in. I almost try to reason with Parker.

But something, some divine force, stops me from doing any of that.

I swallow, trying to force air past the rock that's appeared in my throat. This is my fault. I got drunk and embarrassed a girl I knew better than to mess with, a girl whose claws naturally came out in retaliation. I was a thoughtless jackass. And I'd be even more thoughtless if I got in the middle of Hartley's family feud.

I need to fix this with Felicity. *That's* my only play here. Once I fix it, Hartley will be able to get back into her family's good graces and then it'll be smooth sailing for the two of us.

I can fix this. I can.

Twenty-Seven

THE NEXT DAY at school, everyone is talking about Hartley's suspension. You'd think nobody at Astor Park Prep had ever been busted for something before. The thing is, Hartley didn't deserve to get busted—she didn't do a damn thing wrong, and the person who did is strolling down the hall like she's the queen of Astor.

I catch Felicity before first period. She's at her locker with her girl crew. Luckily, Claire's nowhere to be seen. Good. I hate the idea of my ex getting all chummy with Felicity. Who knows what Claire has on me? I was drunk a lot when we went out.

"Leave," I bark at Felicity's friends.

My expression must tell them I mean business, because they scurry off like rats fleeing a sinking ship. Felicity remains, looking amused.

"Well, aren't you the tough guy, scaring away all the innocent girls," she mocks.

I scowl at her. "There's nothing innocent about any of you."

Rolling her eyes, she slams her locker door. I grab her forearm before she can march away.

"Did you get the flowers?" I grumble. I'd swung by her house on my way home from Hartley's, but nobody answered the door, so I left the flowers on the porch.

"Yes. I did."

"And the note?" I left that, too. A note with three simple words: *I'm sorry—Easton.* "Did you read it?"

"Yes."

"And? Are we cool now?"

She starts laughing. "Wait. You thought that sad excuse for an apology would make us cool? Oh, Easton."

Frustration jams in my throat. "For fuck's sake, Felicity. What you did to Hartley was not right."

"Are you seriously going to lecture me about right and wrong? You, Easton Royal?"

"Yeah, I'm a total shit," I readily agree. "I'm a bad, selfish person. I drink and I fight and I screw girls I shouldn't screw. I'll own that. But Hartley didn't do anything to you. So, please, just tell Beringer that the cheating thing was a total misunderstanding and . . ." I halt, because I realize I'm wasting my breath.

Felicity will never confess to planting those notes in Hartley's locker. That would mean admitting she set up a fellow classmate, and risking punishment herself. So as much as I don't want to, I have to let this go. Hartley got a three-day suspension. That sucks, but she'll survive and she'll be back at school on Monday. The "exonerate Hartley" ship has sailed. All I can do now is wave a white flag at Felicity before she does any more damage.

"How can I make this right with you?" I ask through clenched teeth.

Her blue eyes take on a disbelieving glint. "You can't."

"Come on," I plead. "There's got to be something I can do."

She directs a pointed glare at my bracelet. I fight the urge to cover it. "Something I can buy you," I clarify.

"Like a Candy Machine necklace?"

"Done."

"How about the limited-edition Dior bag?"

"I have no fucking clue what that is, but it's yours."

"It's thirty-five thousand." Somehow she manages to look down her nose at me.

I don't know how I'm going to explain this to the family accountants, but okay. "Great. Every girl needs a limited-edition purse." I stick out my hand. "It's a deal. When Hartley comes back, she's off-limits."

"No."

"What?"

"There is no deal. This is payback, and I'm not done yet."

Her icy stare, combined with the tiniest of smirks on her lips, makes me want to slam my fist into a locker. I can't believe she stood there negotiating about jewelry and purses just to shoot me down. Is it only Astor girls who carry out vendettas, or are all chicks this bloodthirsty?

"If you want me to beg, I'll beg. On my knees."

Felicity's smile widens. "That'd be nice to see. But . . . no, thank you. I have even nicer things planned."

With that, she shoves my hand off her arm and flounces off.

I swallow a groan as I watch her go. What the hell is wrong with that girl? I get that I embarrassed her, but get over it already. Grow the hell up.

The irony of me ordering someone else to grow up doesn't escape me.

With a tired breath, I pull out my phone and shoot a text to Hartley.

U ok this morning?

She responds right away.

No.

Guilt pricks at me. I lean against Felicity's locker and type out another message.

I'm sorry, H. All my fault

This time there's a long delay. I stare at the screen and will her to answer.

"East," someone says.

I glance up to see Sawyer and Lauren drawing near. Seb's not with them. "Hey," I say absently. I look down at my phone. Still nothing. "I'm good. You?"

My little brother snickers. "Didn't ask how you were, but I'm glad you're good."

"You're going to be late for class," Lauren says unhelpfully. "The first bell already rang."

Screw the bell and screw class. Hartley still hasn't answered my text. Why hasn't she answered?

Is it because she agrees that the suspension is my fault?

It is, a little voice says.

Fuck, I *know* it is. That's why I apologized to her. But . . . I kind of expected her to wave it off. To say, *I don't blame you, Easton. Felicity is the one who blah blah blah.*

Instead, I'm getting radio silence.

"Sure, we'll talk later," I mutter to my brother. "See you at home."

As I race off, I hear their bewildered voices behind me.

"Is he drunk?"

"I don't think so?"

I leave the building through the side doors and sprint to the parking lot. I need to see Hartley and apologize in person. I need her to forgive me for dragging her into this Felicity mess. It's not like I did it on purpose. She has to know that.

The drive to her neck of the woods is quick. But, just like yesterday, someone's already beaten me there.

From the bottom of the stairs, I can see a man's back clad in an expensive gray suit jacket. A head of salt-and-pepper hair.

". . . kicked out of the number-one prep school in the country. You're a disgrace to the Wright name," the man is saying, his words laden with disgust.

Hartley's father.

Crap.

I edge toward the side of the staircase and hopefully out of view.

"I didn't get kicked out" is the surly reply. "It was a suspension."

"For cheating!" he barks. "Cheating, Hartley. What in the hell is wrong with you? What kind of child did I raise?"

"I wasn't cheating, Dad. A girl who hates me planted the test answers in my locker. I'm *not* a cheater."

"Your headmaster is a member down at the club, did you know that? All my peers and colleagues know about your little scandal. That's all I was asked about over breakfast this morning."

"Who cares what a bunch of old men at the country club think?" Hartley sounds frustrated. "All that matters is the truth."

"For the love of God! You and that goddamn word! 'Truth.' Enough, Hartley!"

His sharp tone makes me flinch.

"Enough," Mr. Wright repeats. "You're going back to New York. Today. Do you understand me?"

"No!" she protests.

"Yes." There's a rustling sound, as if he's reaching for something. "Here's your ticket. Your flight leaves tonight at midnight."

"No," she says, but it's with uncertainty this time.

"All right." He pauses. "If you don't leave, I'm pulling Dylan out of school and sending her in your place."

"Why?! Why do you always have to threaten her? She's a baby, Dad."

"No, she's thirteen and she's already being influenced by you."

"She's been on medication since she was eight. She's fragile, and you know it. You can't take her away from her family."

He ignores that. "If you don't leave Bayview, then we'll protect Dylan by sending her out of state. It's your choice."

My hands fist by my sides.

"If I go . . . will you let her see me?" Hartley speaks so quietly, it's hard for me to hear.

"If you get on the plane, you can spend time with her from here to the airport."

What a shithead. The airport's thirty minutes away.

"I . . . I'll think about it."

No, I want to yell. *Don't think about it. Fight him.*

"I'll pick you up at ten. Dylan and I will accompany you to the airport, where we will smile and wave while you go through security."

"What if I don't come with you?"

"I'll be driving to the airport regardless," Mr. Wright says in a clipped tone. "Someone will be getting on a plane tonight. It will either be you or your sister." He pauses. "I trust you'll make the right decision."

Twenty-Eight

MY PLAN IS to wait ten minutes before knocking on Hartley's door. I want to give her time to recover from her father's visit and his brutal ultimatum. But only two minutes pass before her door swings open and Hartley stumbles outside.

If I wasn't parked in front of the two-story complex, Hartley might've walked into the middle of the street. Instead, she nearly bangs her nose against the side of my pickup.

"You look like you either drank too much or just got run over by a truck." I reach out a steadying hand.

Surprisingly, she takes it. "Truck. Definitely run over by a truck."

"Let's go for a ride." I don't give her time to answer. In a few moves, I have her inside the cab and buckled up.

"Any special requests?" I ask once I'm in the driver's seat.

"I don't care. Just away from here." Looking defeated, she rests her head against the window and closes her eyes.

"No problem." I play it easy. Like my own insides aren't tied up in knots. I hate this. I hate feeling like this. I hate seeing her like this.

I don't ask her any questions and she doesn't volunteer

anything, so the entire drive is spent in total silence. Funny how the quiet can be deafening. What'd she say before? In the quiet, you can hear the heart beat? You can also hear it break. The air in the cab of my truck grows thick and heavy.

We end up at an old marina not far from the pier. I turn into the gravel lot and park the truck. When I glance over, I realize that Hartley's crying. They are noiseless tears. Just endless drops streaming down her face. I swear when they land it's as loud as a clap of thunder.

It's why I keep the engine running. I need something to mask those tears. She sits beside me, staring out the window. I wonder if she can even see through the veil of tears.

I try to lighten the mood. "Dad said that this used to be the hottest place in town back in the seventies. I told him I didn't realize they had boats in the medieval days."

She cracks a tiny smile.

"Come on, let's walk by the water," I suggest.

I help her out of the truck. The old marina is run-down. The cedar plank siding is washed gray by the sand and the salt of the ocean. There are only a couple of docks still above water. The rest are sunken or have broken off.

It's an overcast morning to match our mood. Hartley looks stricken. I'm sick to my stomach. We're like two survivors wandering around in a daze after an explosion. But hey, at least we're together, right?

I take her hand. The moment I do, she stares at our interlaced fingers. Suspicious. "Why aren't you at school?"

"Because I was worried about you." *Because I want you to forgive me.*

As always, Hartley calls me on my bullshit. "Worried that I was mad at you, you mean."

I swallow.

Her sharp gaze continues to pierce into me. "You were outside my house. Did you see my dad?"

"Yeah," I admit.

"Did you hear what he said to me?"

I consider lying, but then decide against it. "Yeah." I take her arm and we make our way close to the water. There's no railing, just a rocky slope about six feet wide that leads to the water's edge. "You're not getting on that plane, though. Right?"

"I . . . don't know."

I tamp down a jolt of panic. "Damn, Hartley. What the hell happened with you guys? Why does he ha . . ." I stop before the word *hate* pops out. I don't think she'd appreciate me saying her father hates her. "Why is he so pissed at you?"

Her gaze stays fixed on the pebble-covered bank. "It's a long story."

I hold out my arms and gesture to the open air. "We've got nothing but time."

She stares in silence for a long time. I want to fidget, kick some rocks, bellow at the ocean. Nah, what I really want to do is drive over to Hartley's house and kick her dad and bellow in his face. I do neither, and my patience is finally rewarded.

"Four years ago—I guess maybe it's almost five now—I was having trouble sleeping one night, so I went downstairs to get a glass of water. My dad was in the living room, talking to some woman. They were quiet, but she sounded mad and she was crying in between sentences. I think that's why I didn't interrupt or let him know I was there."

"What were they talking about?"

"He was telling her he could take care of the problem but

that it would cost her. The woman said she'd pay whatever he asked as long as he helped her son."

I frown. "What did he say to that?"

"I don't know. I snuck back upstairs because I didn't want him to know I was eavesdropping. He's got a temper, so we all try not to make him angry if we can help it." She scowls. "Anyway, two days later I heard him arguing on the phone with his boss that he'd used 'prosecutorial discretion'—whatever the hell that is—in dismissing the charges against the Roquet kid."

"Who's the Roquet kid?"

"Do you know Drew Roquet?"

"No."

"He's older than us. He was nineteen at the time and got busted for heroin possession. It was his third offense, and they were going to charge him with trafficking because of the amount he had on him. That's five to twenty-three years in prison." Hartley's tone fills with disgust. "But what do you know—the heroin he had on him was lost in the evidence room, so my dad dismissed the charges."

"I don't like where this is going."

"I didn't, either, but I tried to forget about it. At the time, I didn't think my dad would do anything wrong. He was a DA and he hated drug offenders. Called them lowlifes who didn't contribute to society, and he said drugs were the reason for everything wrong in this country. Murders, domestic abuse, theft. All of it could be traced back to drugs, according to him."

"Okay. So you let it go."

"Yes, and everything seemed fine, but . . . it bugged me. So I started nosing around where I shouldn't. I went on his computer one time. He always uses the same password, but he changes the last number every month or so, so it was pretty easy to guess. And when I was on there, I found this anonymous account where people would email him requesting a special favor and they'd say who referred them. There were no details and no responses other than 'Let's meet.'"

My eyebrows shoot up. "They came to the house?" That seems risky as hell.

"No. He usually met them in public places. I think the house thing was rare and that's why he was so angry with that woman. I have no idea how many cases he 'fixed,' but there were so many emails, Easton. Like, a lot of them." She bites her lip, looking miserable.

"Did you confront him?"

"No. I went to Parker instead. She told me to stop making up stories and to keep my mouth shut and not say a word about it to anyone."

"Parker knew what your dad was doing?"

"I don't know."

I think she does know but doesn't want to believe it. I wait for her to continue, but she doesn't. She bends down and picks up a few rocks and throws them in the ocean. I join her and say nothing for a minute. But then I have to ask the one question that's been bugging me since we first met. "How'd you break your wrist?"

The question startles her. She drops the little rock and it hits the water with a splat.

"Hartley," I press. "How'd you break your wrist?"

"How did you know I broke it?"

"You have a surgical scar on the inside of your wrist."

"Oh, that." She rubs a hand over the scar. After a moment of hesitation, she exhales an unsteady breath. "A few months after I talked to my sister, Dad announced he was running for mayor. We got lots of lectures on how to behave in public. Some woman even came to the house and actually showed us how to stand, smile, and wave."

"Yeah, we had one of those, too," I admit. "PR's important down here in the South."

She gives a scornful laugh. "I can't believe how anxious I was to be the perfect daughter. I actually videotaped myself in the mirror. Anyway, right before my freshman year, I broke a string on my violin and ordered a new one online. I'd been tracking it and saw that it was going to be delivered, so I ran down to the end of the street to ask the postman if he had it. That's when I saw Dad sitting with a woman in a car."

Hartley stops abruptly. I can tell it's hard for her to talk about this stuff. I don't blame her. Learning what kind of man Steve is still haunts me. I looked up to him. He flew planes, drank like a fish, had the best cars, the hottest chicks. He was living the best life, and I wanted to be him. But my role model is one of the worst human beings in the world, and now what am I left with?

"I watched them for a long time." Hartley finally picks up where she left off. "They talked. She handed him a phone and some papers, and then he got out of the car, carrying his brief-case and a backpack. The backpack was weird, you know? He never carried anything like that. I was so busy staring at him that I didn't realize the car I was hiding behind was leaving. I started running back to the house. He caught me right out-side the front door, grabbed my wrist, and pulled hard on it. He was so angry. That's why he didn't realize how much force he'd used."

Is she really trying to explain away her father's violence? That makes me angry. I form a fist and then tuck it against my side so she doesn't see it. It hurts not to yell or hit something, but now I get why she hates violence. Why she freaked out the night I dragged her to the dock fights.

"He asked me what I saw. I denied it at first, but my wrist hurt so bad that I started yelling about how I'd seen everything and that it was wrong and that he shouldn't be doing what he was doing and I was going to tell Mom everything." Her bottom lip trembles. "He slapped me across the face and sent me to my room."

"What about your wrist?"

Her mouth quivers again, and then her face collapses. "That's why it didn't heal right. I didn't see a doctor right away."

"What's 'not right away'?"

"Three weeks."

"What?" I explode.

She gulps. "The next morning, Dad came to my room and told me I was going away. I guess I didn't really understand what was going on. I was fourteen. Maybe I should've stood up to him."

"You were only fourteen," I repeat. "And you were scared. Hell, my mom took my pills and said she was going to flush them down the toilet. I handed them over knowing she had a drug problem. We want to make our parents happy, even if we think we hate them."

"I guess. But . . . yeah, I was on a plane and in upstate New York before I could really think. When I got to my dorm room, I called home and begged Mom to let me come back, but she said that Dad was the head of our household and you can't disobey the head of the household." Sarcasm rings in her voice. "She said that once I learned to be a good daughter, I could return. I didn't know what that meant, but I said okay.

I guess that's why I didn't say anything about my wrist right away. It got worse, though, and one of my teachers noticed and took me to the ER. I had to have surgery to fix it."

"What'd you tell them?"

She looks away. "That I fell."

I turn her chin toward me. "Don't be ashamed."

"It's hard not to be."

"Don't be."

"I was so good that first year. Mom reminded me that Dad was running for mayor and that if I behaved, I'd be able to come home."

"But he didn't win."

"No. Parker said that shipping me off to boarding school made it seem like Dad couldn't take care of his own house-hold, let alone run Bayview." Tears cling to Hartley's eyelashes. "And they wouldn't let me come home. Dad wouldn't talk to me. Mom said I hadn't shown that I was a good daughter, and that because I was bad, I had to be kept away from my sister. That I was a bad influence."

"I don't get it. How are you the bad influence?" Hartley cares a shit ton about her family. More than her sister, from what I can see.

"My baby sister is . . . complicated. She's the sweetest girl, but sometimes . . ." Hartley trails off.

I fill in the blanks. "Sometimes she wants to scream at the world for no reason? She's happy one day and frustrated the next? She can get violent and aggressive without warning?"

Surprise flares in Hartley's eyes. "How did—" She stops, understanding dawning. "You, too?"

"Mom was like that. I get it from her. I'm guessing your sister doesn't like her meds, either."

Hartley nods back. "She's bipolar, or at least that was the diagnosis a child psychologist gave. I heard my parents arguing about it because Dad refuses to believe that mental illness is a thing. He thinks she just needs more discipline."

Where have I heard that before? "Poor kid."

"Is that your diagnosis?" she asks hesitantly.

I stare at the water, not ready to see any judgment on Hartley's face. "I don't think so. It was ADHD for me. I started taking Adderall when I was seven. It was supposed to mellow me out, but after a while it didn't work. I didn't want to tell my mom that it wasn't helping and that my head was getting noisier, because she was pretty messed up herself. It's easy to get those drugs at school. Someone's always willing to sell their share of their prescription. And from there it was an easy slide into oxy and other stuff." I mumble the last admission.

"Our parents are supposed to be there to help, not hurt us."

There's a prickling behind my eyes. I blink a few times. "For real. When's the last time you saw your sister?"

"Three years ago. I've talked to her a handful of times, but that's only because she answered the phone before one of my parents got there. Sometimes she misses me. Other times she hates me for abandoning her. They can't send her to a boarding school, Easton. Boarding school is terrible. I was so lonely there. I haven't had a Christmas or Thanksgiving or birthday with someone who loved me in three years. Do you know what that's like?"

"No," I say hoarsely. "I don't."

Beside me, her body trembles. "I wouldn't wish that on Felicity, let alone the person I love most in this world. She'd be destroyed there. No one would understand her or take care of her the way she needs."

"How were you able to come home, then?"

"I found out last year about that trust I told you about, the one from my grandma? The Bayview Savings and Loan oversees it, not my dad. But food and rent isn't considered educational, so that's why I work at the diner." Her expression becomes sad. "I thought if I went to the best school in the state and kept my nose clean without saying anything about my dad's shady dealings, they'd let me back into the family."

"But then you got suspended for cheating." The guilt rips into me again, burning a path up my throat.

"Yes."

"This is all my fault."

Hartley tips her head to meet my eyes. "Yes."

That one syllable tears me apart. It's brutal. Fucking brutal.

"I told you, trouble follows you wherever you go, Easton."

I have to break the eye contact before the shame eats me alive. I stare hard at the water and mentally punch myself for all the bullshit I've put this girl through. The bullshit I put *everyone* through. Ella, my brothers, my dad. I'm a screwup. They all know it, and they all love me in spite of it.

What is wrong with them?

"But this was bound to happen, with or without your involvement."

I look over in surprise. "You think so?"

Hartley nods glumly. "The minute I moved back to Bayview, my whole family was on the alert. Parker's probably spying on me for Dad. Mom's doing everything to keep Dylan away from me. My parents were just waiting for me to mess up, I guarantee it. Waiting for any excuse to get me out of Bayview again."

That makes me feel better. Just a tiny bit. But it doesn't stop me from accepting responsibility for my part in all this.

"Felicity wouldn't have fucked with you if it wasn't for me, Hartley. That means it's on me to fix this."

"You can't fix it."

"Sure I can."

She tips her head in challenge. "How?"

I pause. "I don't know. But I'll figure something out."

She gives a humorless laugh. "Yeah, well, you'd better figure it out before ten o'clock tonight. That's when my dad's showing up to take me to the airport."

"You're not going to the airport," I say firmly. "You're not going anywhere."

She just shrugs.

Dammit, she's actually planning on leaving. I can see it in her eyes. Hartley will do anything to protect her little sister, even if it means going back to the boarding school she hated.

"I need to get back," she tells me, stepping away from the pebbled waterfront. "Can you take me home now?"

I nod.

We climb into the truck and once again make the drive in silence. I study her profile at every stop sign, every red light. The first time I saw her, I thought she was kinda plain. Pretty but plain. Nice legs, sweet ass, kissable lips.

Now that I know her better, it's her face that draws me in. All those disparate features come together to form one beautiful image. She's not plain. She's unique. I've never seen anyone like her before, and I can't believe I might never see her again.

The desperation triggered by that awful thought is what

drives me to kiss her. The truck barely comes to a full stop in front of her apartment before I'm yanking her toward me and covering her mouth with mine.

"Easton," she protests, but soon she's kissing me back.

It's intense. Her lips are warm and taste a bit salty, probably from her tears. I thrust my fingers through her soft hair and pull her even closer.

Soft arms wind around my neck. Her beaded nipples press against my chest. I raise a hand between us to cup her breast in my palm, rubbing my thumb over one of those peaks. She shudders. My own body quakes in response.

I kiss her harder. My hands rove desperately around her body, trying to keep her anchored to me. Somehow her legs straddle mine. I stroke a hand up her thigh and around the curve of her ass before pressing her tightly against me.

I'm beyond aroused. And I'm a guy. Guys don't always do or say the right thing when they're turned on and their brains are overpowered by their dicks. Still, I regret the words the moment they leave my mouth.

"Let's go inside where we can be more comfortable."

Hartley jerks her mouth away from mine. Her eyes narrow. "Comfortable?"

"Yeah. You know . . ." My breathing's kind of labored from all the heavy-duty kissing. "Comfortable," I repeat lamely.

"You mean naked." Her tone is flat.

"No. I mean, sure, if that's what you want." *Shut up, man. Shut the hell up.* "I just . . . we're sitting out in the truck, and you said you were worried about your dad watching you—"

"Right. I'm sure that's exactly why you wanted to go inside," she mutters. Shaking her head, she unbuckles her seatbelt and shoves it aside. "You're unbelievable."

I frown. "Are you seriously pissed at me right now? You kissed me back."

"I know I did, because I was upset and I needed . . . comfort, I guess. But as usual, you make it all about sex."

Indignation ripples through me. "I only suggested going inside."

"Yeah, so we could have sex." She throws open the passenger door but doesn't get out of the truck yet. "Thanks for the offer, but I'm going to have to pass. I need to pack."

"You're not leaving town!" I growl. "And I don't care about sex right now. We were making out and I said let's go inside—big fucking deal. Don't turn this around and act like I did something wrong."

"You got me suspended!"

I swallow my frustration. "I know I did. And I'm trying to fix that, dammit!"

"How? By sticking your tongue in my mouth? How is that fixing anything?" A weary look creeps into her gray eyes. Sighing, she slowly slides out of her seat. "Go home, Easton. Or back to school. Just . . . go."

"What about your dad's threat? What are you going to do about that?"

"I don't know," she mumbles. "But I'll figure something out. *I'll* fix this. Alone. I don't need your help."

I clench my fists against my knees. "Yes, you do."

"No. I don't. I don't need anything from you." Her expression fills with irritation. "You've caused me nothing but trouble from the moment I met you. So, please, for the love of God, don't try to help anymore. Don't help, and definitely don't fix. You're not capable of fixing things." Sadly, she shakes her head. "All you do is break them."

She leaves me with that. A knife to the heart. An accusation that, no matter how badly I want to, I can't defend myself against.

All I can do is drive home. I can't go back to school, not when I feel like I've been gutted. I can't face Ella or my teammates or that bitch Felicity. So I go home, and I grab a drink from the liquor cabinet, which my dad has blessedly restocked. Getting drunk isn't my endgame. I just need to loosen up. To clear my head so I can come up with a solution to this problem. The problem *I* created. The mess *I* caused.

I owe that to Hartley.

Twenty-Nine

AT NINE O'CLOCK, it hits me.

The solution.

I hurl myself out of bed, but it takes a few moments for my body to stop swaying and the head rush to go away. Whoa. Okay, maybe I shouldn't have gotten up that fast. I'd been lying flat on my back for hours, nursing the bottle of bourbon I lifted from Dad's study. Note to self: ease into this vertical thing slowly.

I'm not drunk, though.

Nope, not drunk. Just buzzed. Buzzzzzed.

"Easton, you okay?" Ella pops her head into my open doorway, looking worried.

I break out in a smile when I see her. "I'm A-okay, baby sis! A-fucking-o-fucking-kay."

"I heard a crash. Did you fall? Break something?"

"You're hearing things," I tell her. "Because I didn't fall and nothing broke."

"Then why is there a broken bottle on the floor?"

I follow her accusatory gaze to the foot of my nightstand. Huh. She's right. There's a whiskey bottle on the carpet and it's in two pieces. Must have hit the corner of the night table and broken in half on its way down. Whiskey, though? I was drinking bourbon.

My gaze travels to the bedspread, where I left the bourbon bottle. Oh. Guess I was drinking both.

"Are you going somewhere?"

"None of your bizness." I tear my eyes away from the bottle and look for my keys. Crap, I don't remember where they are.

I riffle through a pile of clothes. A jingle in the back pocket of a pair of jeans catches my attention.

"Aha," I crow, pulling out the key fob. "There you are."

"There's no way you're going anywhere." Ella grabs for the keys. "You're in no condition to drive."

"Fine." I let her take them and pull my phone out of the other pocket of the same jeans. I tap a few times and smile at the screen in satisfaction. "There you go. Got a car coming."

The little map informs us that my driver is fifty-five minutes away. Or . . . wait, maybe that's *five* minutes. I swear I saw two fives. It better not be two fives, though, because I need to catch Hartley's dad before he leaves to take her to the airport.

"Good," Ella says, looking relieved. "But just in case, I want your bike keys."

"They're in the mudroom. I won't take them with me, I promise."

She trails after me anyway, as if she needs to see with her own two eyes that my keys are staying home. I make it easier for her by tossing them over when we get to the mud-room.

"For safekeeping," I tease.

"Tell Hartley I said hi," she says wryly.

I jog down the driveway and reach the front gates just as the Uber driver is pulling up. I give her the address and then settle in the backseat to call Hartley.

"What do you want, Easton?" I guess that's her version of *hello*.

"Hey, babe. I just wanted to tell you not to go with your dad when he comes to get you tonight." A thought occurs to me. "*If* he comes to get you. He might not anymore."

"Why wouldn't he?"

"I'm not saying he would or he wouldn't," I babble. "But if he does, don't go with him. 'Kay?"

"I don't understand what you're saying, but I've got to be in the car or Dylan goes to the boarding school. Dad doesn't make idle threats. If he says something, he'll follow through."

"Don't worry about it. I'm taking care of everything."

There's a brief pause. "What do you mean?"

"I'm taking care of it," I repeat, smiling to myself.

"Oh God. Easton. What the hell are you up to? What's going on? Actually, you know what? Don't answer that. I don't care what's happening, just that you stop it. You need to stop it right now."

"Can't. Already on my way."

"On your way where?"

"To your dad's house. I'm gonna have a talk with him."

"What! Easton, no!"

"Don't worry, baby, I've got you. Got this."

"Easton—"

I hang up, because all the shouting is making my temples throb. It's okay that she's mad at me. She won't be mad after I convince her father to let her stay in Bayview. I have a plan. Mr. Wright takes bribes. So I'm gonna bribe him.

I'm Easton Royal. I've got money coming out of my ass. All I have to do is give Hartley's dad some money and he'll leave us alone. Money has solved every problem in the past. Money and a hard fist to the face. I'm happy to add in the second part if I need to. I'm not sure how I'll get him to leave Hartley's sister alone, but I'm planning on winging that part.

The driver stops next to the curb. I start to get out, but then realize the driveway looks really long. Too long to walk, especially when I have wheels.

I tap the driver on the shoulder. "Drive up to the door."

"We're not supposed to go on private property," the gal says.

I pull out a few bills and wave them at her. "They're expecting me."

She hesitates but pulls forward. See? Problem plus money equals no problem. Heh.

I stagger to the front door and lean on the doorbell. Inside, I can hear the chime repeat itself over and over. It's annoying. Someone should come to the door soon.

When I see some movement, I start pressing the doorbell repeatedly to get their attention.

It works. The door opens and a man looks out at me. He's about my dad's age, only with more gray in his hair.

"How you doing?" I greet him with a nod. "Got a minute?"

"Who the hell are you?" Mr. Wright asks me.

I straighten to my full height and peer down my nose at him. He's shorter than I expected. Looked way taller when I saw him at Hartley's door earlier.

"Easton Royal." Should I salute? Nah. Let's get this dog and pony show over with. I reach into my back pocket and pull out my dad's checkbook. "What's it gonna cost, John?" I smile at my baller move in adding his first name.

"Who the hell are you?" he repeats.

"Man, I already told you." This guy is slow. Is he really a lawyer? "I'm Easton Royal. I'm here to make a deal with you."

"Get off my porch and leave."

The door starts closing, but I'm quick and I dart inside the front hall before he can block me.

"Now, that's no way to make a deal, John." I wave the checkbook. "I've got a lot here. Name your price."

"Easton Royal, you say?" Wright crosses his arms and narrows his eyes at me. "Let's see. Your oldest brother got in trouble for the distribution of child pornography. Your second-oldest brother was the chief suspect in the murder of his father's mistress, because he, too, had been conducting a sexual relationship with said mistress. Your father nearly bankrupted a century-old family business, and your mother was a drug addict who took her own life. And you're here to make a deal with me?"

My mouth falls open. "What'd you just say?" I can't believe this asshole. I came here with the best intentions and he has the nerve to insult my entire family?

"You heard me." He throws open the door. "Take your fake Royal ass and get gone."

"Fake Royal? I'm fake? You're the fraud. You've got no

honor. You're fixing cases. Taking money, losing evidence. You're dirtier than any criminal you ever put behind bars." I get up in his face. Spittle's flying out of my mouth.

Wright laughs at me. "You don't even know, do you?"

"Know that you're an asshole?" I push his shoulders. He stumbles back and the smile is gone. "Actually, you're worse than an asshole. Assholes would be insulted to be associated with you. You're a child abuser. The worst of the worst. Even prisoners would spit on you."

Red-faced, he charges toward me. "You wouldn't be so brave if you didn't have the Royal name, would you?"

"I do, so we'll never know, will we?"

"Just like we'll never know if you're Steve O'Halloran's bastard or Callum Royal's seed, right?"

What?

I stumble, barely catching myself before doing a header onto the wood floor.

He chuckles. "But we do know, don't we?"

"Kn-know what?" I croak.

"That your whore of a mother spread her legs for your fake daddy's business partner."

There's a shove in my side and I lose my balance, falling to my knees.

I shake my head and look up. What the fuck is he even saying? I'm not Steve's bastard. I'm Callum Royal's son. I'm a *Royal*.

"You have five seconds to get your sorry ass off my property before I call the police," Wright seethes.

Somehow I find myself on the other side of a slammed door. I stare at it. What just happened there? Did he really just . . .

Breathing hard, I raise my fist to the door and pound. For some reason, the knock sounds like a car door slamming.

"What the hell, Easton!"

I spin around in surprise. Hartley is charging up the manicured front lawn toward me. A beat-up brown Volvo sits in the driveway—I guess that's the car door I just heard.

"Whose car is that?" I ask in confusion. Nothing makes sense to me right now. My head is a jumbled mess. There's too much booze in my system. And Wright's accusation has left me shaken and chilled to the bone.

I'm not Steve's bastard.

I'm *not.*

"The car is Jose's," she snaps as she reaches me. She grabs my forearm and holy shit is her grip lethal. "Let's go."

I rub the back of my neck and try to focus. "Who's Jose?"

"My landlord. Now get the *fuck* away from the door and *let's go.*"

My jaw falls open. "You said 'fuck.' You never swear. Why did you swear?"

"Because I am so fucking pissed right now!"

I almost fall over from the force of her response. That's when I notice that her face is beet red. Her hands are clenched into small fists and she's using one to hit me on the shoulder. Hartley is furious.

"You're mad," I mumble.

"I'm mad? Of course I'm mad! I want to *kill* you right now! How *dare* you show up at my parents' house and—and what?" Her wild eyes dart toward the closed door. "Please tell me you didn't talk to them yet!"

I can lie. I can totally lie. I don't have to tell her that I threatened her father and he threatened me back and that I tried to hit him and he told me I wasn't a Royal and slammed the door in my face. It's not like he's out here to contradict me. I can lie.

But I don't lie, because I'm too confused, too disturbed to craft a story for her.

I'm not Steve's bastard.

I'm *not*.

"I tried to bribe him."

Her mouth opens. Then closes. Opens. Closes. And she's breathing hard, like she just finished a marathon.

"You tried to bribe him." She pauses in disbelief. "You. Tried to bribe. A district attorney."

"Hey, we both know he's cool with bribes," I protest.

Hartley stares at me. For a long, long time. Oh shit. She's going to explode. I can see the storm clouds in her eyes. The thunder is going to come any second.

Before she can get out any words, the front door opens and Mr. Wright appears with Dylan at his side. The girl looks frightened, but shock replaces her fear when she spots her older sister.

Her gray eyes widen. "Hartley?"

"Take a good look at your sister," Wright barks, pointing a finger at Hartley. "She's the reason you have to leave the family."

Hartley gasps.

I charge at the asshole, only to be brought up short by Dylan's confused voice.

"Hartley?" she repeats. "What's happening?"

"Dylan, come here." Hartley gestures for her sister to leave her father. "You aren't going to get sent away. Come with me and I'll—"

"You're not going to do anything but leave, Hartley. You are no longer part of this family. Dylan, go inside and pack." Wright's voice is cold and hard.

"No. Please, Daddy," Hartley pleads. "Please don't do this. I'll do anything you want. Anything." She scrambles forward, but her father holds up his hand and she stops in her tracks.

"Go inside, Dylan," he orders.

Dylan's frantic gaze swings from her sister to her father.

I make a last-ditch effort to stop this craziness. "Hey, I'm telling you, I'll pay whatever price you want," I urge Mr. Wright.

"Shut up!" Hartley screams. "Please shut up." She turns back to her dad. "*Please*."

"If anything happens to Dylan, it'll be on your head. You should think about that before you open your stupid, stupid mouth." With that parting threat, Wright slams the door shut.

When the wood hits the frame, it's like a bullet to Hartley's chest. She collapses on the front lawn and starts to cry.

I rush over to her. "Baby, I'm sorry." The buzz in my head is wearing off and the gravity of what's just happened is settling in. The gravity of everything. Hartley. Her dad. Her sister. Me.

Steve.

"Why? Why did you come here?" Tears fill her eyes, but they don't spill over. Her breaths are quick and shallow.

"I was trying to help." I bend close to her. "Tell me what to do?"

She takes a deep, quavering breath. "You're drunk," she

accuses. "I can smell it on you. You came over here drunk and told my dad everything I confided in you?"

My throat closes up, clogged with guilt and anxiety. "No. I mean, I had a little, but I wasn't drunk."

She searches my eyes, sees my lies, and rises slowly to her feet. Her lower lip is trembling and her voice is shaky, but there's a seriousness in her expression that sends a spiral of fear down my back.

"You *are* drunk. And you broke your promise. You made a bad situation worse. Maybe you had good intentions, but you acted to make yourself feel better. You thought of yourself first and this is what happened." The tears start coming now. They course down her face, a tsunami of unhappiness.

Embarrassment fights with remorse inside me. I don't like what she's saying and how these words are making me feel. I tried to do the right thing. Is it really my fault that her dad's a first-rate jackoff? Is it my fault that he didn't take the money? Is it my fault that he made up horrible lies about my mother and my father and some fucking asshole who's *not* my father—

I start to get angry back. "I'm the one who tried to make things right for you. You were just going to run away and avoid the problem. At least I confronted him. You should be thanking me."

"Thanking you?" she screeches. "*Thanking* you? Are you kidding me? You're not the white knight in this picture. You're the villain!"

"What? Me?" I'm pissed now.

"Yes, you." She stumbles away, her black hair whipping behind her. "Stay away from me. I never, ever want to talk to you again."

Her words sound so final. Panicked, I call after her. "Wait. Hartley, come on. Wait!"

She ignores me.

I take a step forward, and although her back is to me, it's like she senses that I've moved. She whirls around and jabs her finger in the air.

"Don't," she commands. "Don't follow me. Don't come near me. Don't anything."

She spins again and practically hurls herself at the rusted door of the ugly Volvo she drove up in. The rearview mirror isn't even attached to the windshield—I can see it dangling at a weird angle through the window.

The sight of the beat-up car makes me sick to my stomach. I picture Hartley knocking on her downstairs neighbor's door, pleading with him to borrow his shitty-ass car so she can come and stop my shitty-ass self from ruining her life even more than I'd already ruined it.

But she didn't get here in time. As always, Easton Royal screwed everything up.

I watch helplessly as she reverses out of the driveway. I want to shout for her to come back, but I know she won't hear me from all the way over there. Plus, the engine of that Volvo is loud as fuck. And so is the squeal of tires from the other car on the road and— What other car?

I blink a few times.

Maybe it's because I'm drunk that the pieces don't fall into place right away. My brain registers each thing separately.

The flashing headlights.

The crunch of metal against metal.

The body lying on the side of the road.

My legs start pumping. I sprint, falling to my knees next to a girl that my mind dimly registers as Lauren. Why is she here? She doesn't live here.

No, she does. She lives down the street. But right now she's curled over on the pavement as she tries to shake my brother awake. He's lying half on his side, half on his stomach, as if he dove onto the ground from a great height. His white T-shirt is torn and streaked with blood. There's blood on the pavement, too.

So much blood.

I feel sick but somehow manage to choke down a rush of vomit.

Something digs painfully into my knees. It's glass. The windshield, I realize. The Rover's windshield is gone.

"Sawyer," Lauren begs. "Sawyer."

"It's Sebastian," I choke out. I can tell the twins apart in my sleep. Even when I'm drunk.

Lauren wails harder.

As my pulse careens wildly, I look at the Rover again to check for my other brother. Sawyer's slumped over the wheel, the seatbelt cutting into his neck, the airbag pushing against his face. A line of blood drips from his right temple toward his chin.

I turn toward the Volvo. It's mostly intact, except that the back door and bumper are completely dented in. My heart lodges in my throat when the driver's door flies open.

Hartley stumbles out of the car. Her face is white, like Seb's T-shirt used to be. Her eyes are wide, but there's something almost vacant in them. Like she's gone completely numb.

Her gaze lands on Sebastian. It rests on his terrifyingly

still form. His bloodied, crumpled body. She just stares and stares, as if she can't comprehend what she's seeing.

Finally, she opens her mouth and a desperate, strangled scream comes out. And mingled in with her screams are three gut-wrenching words that make my blood run cold and my entire body feel weak.

"I killed him."

Acknowledgments

As always, we could not have written, completed, or survived this project without the help of some pretty awesome people:

Early readers Margo, Jessica Clare, Meljean Brook, Natasha Leskiw, and Michelle Kannan, who gave us valuable insight, encouraged us to not hold back, and read the book twice!

Our publicist, Nina, who works tirelessly on our behalf and makes it look easy.

Meljean Brook, for the amazing cover concept.

Nic and Tash, for all their work behind the scenes.

Authors friends Jo, Kylie, Meghan, Rachel, Sam, Vi, and more for their support and enthusiasm for the Royals.

All the bloggers/reviewers, who continue to support this series and spread the word.

Finally, we were totally blown away by the readers who fell in love with *Paper Princess* and shouted it out to the world. The fan art has been incredible. Readers have compiled playlists and taken the time to write and post reviews. Members of The Royal Palace on Facebook keep us entertained on a daily basis. You guys give this series life and we cannot thank you enough!

Exclusive Bonus

EASTON'S PLAYLIST

"Nice for What" by Drake

"Hotel Room Service" by Pitbull

"No Hands" (feat. Roscoe Dash & Wale) by Waka Flocka Flame

"Fire Burning" by Sean Kingston

"Sacrifice" by The Weeknd

"Jimmy Cooks" (feat. 21 Savage) by Drake

"Cash In Cash Out" (feat. 21 Savage & Tyler, the Creator) by Pharrell Williams

"Way 2 Sexy" (feat. Future & Young Thug) by Drake

"Fkn Around" (feat. Megan Thee Stallion) by Phony Ppl

"Best Interest" by Tyler, the Creator

HARTLEY'S PLAYLIST

"Castaway" (feat. Tyler, the Creator) by Yuna

"The Chain" by Fleetwood Mac

"Pink + White" by Frank Ocean

"On & On" by Erykah Badu

"Low" by SZA

"Figure It Out" by Blu DeTiger

"PRIDE." by Kendrick Lamar

"Same Ol' Mistakes" by Rihanna

"Dead to Me" by Kali Uchis

"No Role Modelz" by J. Cole

Keep reading for an excerpt of

Cracked Kingdom

The next book in the Royals series by Erin Watt

One

EASTON

EVERYONE IS SCREAMING.

If I weren't in a state of shock—not to mention drunker than drunk—I might've been able to hear the individual shouts, connect them to certain voices, make sense of the caustic words and angry accusations being hurled around.

But right now, it sounds like one unending wave of sound. A symphony of hatred, worry, and fear.

". . . your son's fault!"

"Like hell it is!"

". . . press charges . . ."

"Easton."

My head is buried in my hands, and I rub my eyes against my callused palms.

". . . even here? . . . should have you taken out in handcuffs, you son of a bitch . . . harassment . . ."

". . . like to see you try . . . not afraid of you, Callum Royal. I'm the district attorney—"

"Assistant district attorney."

"Easton."

My eyes feel dry and itchy. I'm sure they're bloodshot, too. They always get bloodshot when I'm wasted.

"Easton."

Something smacks my shoulder, and one voice breaks through the others. I jerk my head up to find my stepsister regarding me with deep concern in her blue eyes.

"You haven't moved in three hours. Talk to me," Ella begs softly. "Let me know you're okay."

Okay? How could I be okay? Look at what's happening, for fuck's sake. We're in a private waiting room at Bayview General—the Royals don't have to wait in the real ER waiting room with the rest of the peasants. We get special treatment everywhere we go, even hospitals. When my older brother Reed got stabbed last year, he was rushed into surgery like he was the president himself, no doubt taking an OR slot from someone who needed it more. But Callum Royal's name goes a long way in this state. Hell, the country. Everyone knows my father. Everyone fears him.

". . . criminal charges against your son—"

"Your fucking daughter is responsible for . . ."

"Easton," Ella urges again.

I ignore her. She doesn't exist to me at the moment. None of them do. Not Ella. Not Dad. Not John Wright. Not even my younger brother Sawyer, who was just allowed to join us after getting a couple stitches on his temple. Massive car accident and Sawyer walks away with a scrape.

Meanwhile, his twin brother is . . .

Is what?

Fuck if I know. We haven't received an update about Sebastian since we got to the hospital. His bloody, broken body was whisked away on a gurney, his family banished to this room to await the news of whether he's alive or dead.

"If my son doesn't survive, your daughter will pay for this."

"You sure he's even your son?"

"You goddamn asshole!"

"What? Seems to me like all your boys need DNA tests. Why not get all the testing done now? We're at a hospital, after all. It'll be easy enough to draw some blood and confirm which of your boys are Royals and which ones are O'Halloran spawn—"

"Dad! SHUT UP!"

Hartley's anguished voice cuts into me like a knife. The others might not exist to me right now, but she does. She's been sitting in the corner of the room for three hours. Like me, she hadn't spoken a word. Until now. Now she's on her feet, her gray eyes blazing with fury, her voice high and ringing with accusation as she lunges toward her father.

I don't know why John Wright is even here. He can't stand his daughter. He sent Hartley to boarding school. He wouldn't let her move back in once she returned to Bayview. He shouted at her tonight, told her she wasn't part of his family and threatened to send her little sister away.

But after the ambulances took Hartley, the twins, and the twins' girlfriend away, Mr. Wright was the first person to leave for the hospital. Maybe he wants to make sure Hartley doesn't tell anyone about what a piece of shit he is.

"Why are you even here?!" Hartley screams out my thoughts. "I wasn't hurt in the accident! I'm just fine! I don't need you here and I don't *want* you here!"

Wright yells something back, but I'm not paying attention.

I'm too busy watching Hartley. Since her car collided with the twins' Range Rover outside her father's mansion, she's insisted she's fine. Not to me, of course—nope, she hasn't looked my way even once. I don't blame her.

I did this. I destroyed her life tonight. My actions drove her to get into that car, at the exact moment my brothers were speeding around the curve. If she hadn't been upset, maybe she would've seen them sooner. Maybe Sebastian wouldn't be . . . dead? Alive?

Goddammit, why aren't there any updates?

Hartley keeps insisting she's not hurt, and the EMTs obviously concurred because they examined her and then let her come to the waiting room, but she doesn't look so good right now. She's swaying slightly on her feet. Her breathing is short. She's also paler than the white wall behind her head, creating a shocking contrast between her skin and jet-black hair. There isn't a drop of blood on her, though. None. It makes me weak with relief to see that, because Sebastian was covered in it.

Bile coats my throat as the scene of the accident flashes through my mind. Shards of the broken windshield littering the pavement. Sebastian's body. The red puddle. Lauren's shrieks. The Donovans already picked up Lauren and took her home, thank God. The girl didn't stop screaming from the second she got to Bayview General to the second she left it.

"Hartley," comes Ella's quiet voice, and I know my stepsister has noticed Hartley's ashen state. "Come sit down. You're not looking too good. Sawyer, go get Hartley some water."

My younger brother disappears without a word. He's been a zombie since his twin was taken away.

"I'm fine!" Hartley spits out, shoving Ella's small hand off her arm. She turns back to her father, still wobbly on her knees. "*You're* the reason Sebastian Royal got hurt!"

Wright's jaw drops. "How *dare* you insinuate—"

"Insinuate?" she interrupts angrily. "I'm not insinuating! I'm stating a fact! Easton wouldn't have been at the house tonight if you hadn't threatened to send my sister away! I wouldn't have come after him if he hadn't come to see you!"

That makes it my fault, I want to object, but I'm too weak and too fucking cowardly to do it. But it's true. I'm the reason this happened. I caused the accident, not Hartley's dad.

Hartley wobbles again, and this time Ella doesn't hesitate— she clamps a hand around Hartley's upper arm and forces her into a chair.

"Sit," Ella orders.

Meanwhile, my father and Hartley's father are staring each other down again. I've never seen my dad so pissed.

"You're not going to be able to buy yourself out of this one, Royal."

"Your daughter was driving the car, Wright. She'll be lucky if she doesn't spend her next birthday in juvie."

"If anyone's going to jail, it's your son. Hell, all of your sons belong there."

"Don't you dare threaten me, Wright. I can have the mayor here in five minutes."

"The mayor? You think that sniveling pencil-dick has the balls to fire me? I've won more cases in this godforsaken county than any other DA in the history of Bayview. The citizens would crucify him and you—"

For the first time in three hours, I find my voice.

"Hartley," I say hoarsely.

Mr. Wright stops midsentence. He whirls around to face

me, daggers in his eyes. "Don't speak to my daughter! You hear me, you little bastard? Don't say a word to her."

I ignore him. My gaze is glued to Hartley's pale face.

"I'm sorry," I whisper to her. "This was all my fault. I caused the accident."

Her eyes widen.

"Don't say a word to her!" Shockingly, this comes from my father, not hers.

"Callum," Ella says, looking as astonished as I feel.

"No," he booms, his Royal-blue eyes fixed on me. "Not one word, Easton. Criminal charges could come into play here. And *he*"—Dad glances at John Wright as if he's a living manifestation of the Ebola virus—"is an assistant district attorney. Not another word about the accident without our lawyers present."

"Typical Royals," Wright sneers. "Always covering each other's asses."

"Your daughter hit my sons' car," Dad hisses back. "She is the only one responsible."

Hartley makes a whimpering sound. Ella sighs and strokes her shoulder.

"You're not responsible," I tell Hartley, ignoring everyone else. It's like we're the only two people in the room. Me and this girl. The first girl I've wanted to spend time with without getting naked. A girl I consider a friend. A girl I wanted to be more than friends with.

Because of me, this girl is facing my father's wrath. And she's racked with guilt over an accident that wouldn't have happened if I wasn't in the picture. My older brother Reed used to call himself The Destroyer. He thought he ruined the lives of everyone he loved.

Reed's wrong. I'm the one who screws everything up.

"Don't worry, we're leaving," Wright growls.

I tense up as he stomps toward Hartley's seat.

Ella wraps one arm around Hartley's shoulder in a protective gesture, but my dad briskly shakes his head at her.

"Let them go," Dad barks. "Bastard's right—they don't belong here with us."

Panic lodges in my throat. I don't want Hartley to go. And I especially don't want her to go with her father. Who knows what he'll do to her.

Hartley obviously agrees, because she instantly balks when her dad tries to grab her. She shrugs off Ella's arm. "I'm not going anywhere with you!"

"You have no choice," he snaps. "I'm still your legal guardian whether you like it or not."

"*No!*" Hartley's voice is like a crack of thunder. "I'm not going!" Her head swivels toward my father. "Listen, my dad's a—"

She never finishes her sentence because in the next second she topples forward, crashing to the floor. The sound of her head thudding against the tile is going to live with me until I die.

A hundred hands seem to reach for her, but I get to her side first. "Hartley!" I yell, pulling on her shoulder. "Hartley!"

"Don't move her," my dad barks, and tries to shove me away.

I jerk out of his grasp but let her go. I lie down on the floor so my face is next to hers. "Hartley. Hart. It's me. Open your eyes. It's me."

Her eyelids don't move.

"Get away from her, you punk!" screams her father.

"Easton." It's Ella, and her voice is lined with horror as she gestures to the side of Hartley's head, where a thin stream of blood is spidering out. I feel like throwing up, and it's not just because of the alcohol still buzzing through my veins.

"Oh my God," Ella breathes. "Her head. She hit her head so hard."

I swallow my terror. "It's fine. It's going to be fine." I turn to Dad. "Get a doctor! She's hurt!"

Someone grabs my shoulder. "I said get away from my daughter!"

"You get away from her!" I spit at Hartley's father.

Suddenly there's a commotion behind me. Footsteps. More shouts. This time I let myself be wrenched away. It's like Sebastian all over again. Hartley's on a gurney, and doctors and nurses are barking orders at each other as they wheel her away.

I stare at the empty doorway, numb. Stunned.

What just happened?

"Oh my God," Ella says again.

My legs can no longer support my own weight. I drop into the nearest chair and gasp for air. What. Just. Happened?

Hartley was hurt this entire time and didn't say anything? Or maybe she didn't realize it? The paramedics cleared her, dammit.

"They said she was okay," I croak. "They didn't even admit her."

"She's going to be fine," Ella assures me, but her tone doesn't hold much conviction. We both saw that blood, and the purple bruise forming at her temple, and her slack mouth.

Oh fuck. I'm going to be sick.

Gotta give Ella credit—she doesn't jump away when I bend over and throw up all over her shoes. She simply strokes my hair and smooths it away from my forehead. "It's okay, East," she murmurs. "Callum, go get him some water. I don't know where Sawyer wandered off to when I sent him to get some. And you"—I assume she's talking to Mr. Wright—"I think it's time you left. You can wait for news about Hartley somewhere else."

"Gladly," Hartley's father says in disgust.

I know the moment he's gone, because the air in the room loses some of its tension.

"She's going to be fine," Ella says again. "And so will Sebastian. Everyone's going to be fine, East."

Rather than feel reassured, I throw up again.

I hear her murmur under her breath, "God, Reed, would you just *get* here already."

The waiting game begins again. I drink water. My dad and Sawyer sit in silence. Ella throws her arms around Reed when he finally shows up. He had to drive all the way from college and he looks exhausted. I don't blame him—it's three in the morning. We're all exhausted.

News of Sebastian's condition is the first to trickle in. His head injury is the biggest concern. There's swelling in his brain, but the doctors don't know how serious it is yet.

My oldest brother, Gideon, arrives a bit after Reed, in time to hear the part about Seb's brain. Gid throws up in the wastebasket in the corner of the room, though unlike me, I don't think he's drunk.

It's hours later when a different doctor appears in the doorway. It's not the one who operated on Seb, and he looks incredibly uneasy as he glances around the room.

I stumble to my feet. Hartley. This has to be about Hartley.

Two

HARTLEY

A BRIGHT LIGHT aimed at my face wakes me up. I blink groggily, trying to decipher actual shapes from the blobs of white in front of my eyes.

"There she is. Sleeping Beauty has awakened. How are you feeling?" The light flashes again. I reach up to wave it away and nearly black out from the pain that washes over me.

"That good, huh?" the voice says. "Why don't we give her another thirty milligrams of Toradol, but make sure to watch for bleeding."

"Yessir."

"Great." Someone snaps two pieces of metal together, making me wince.

What happened to me? Why am I in so much pain that even my teeth ache? Did I get in an accident?

"Steady there." A hand presses me back onto something soft—a mattress. "Don't sit up."

A mechanical whir buzzes and the back of the bed raises. I manage to unstick one of my eyelids and, through my lashes, I see a bed rail, the edge of a white coat, and another dark blob.

"What happened?" I croak.

"You were in a car accident," the dark blob at my side says. "When the airbag deployed it broke a couple ribs on the left side. Your eardrum burst. As a result of the vestibular imbalance along with some dyspnea—that's shortness of breath—you passed out and hit your noggin pretty hard. You have a concussion and some mild brain trauma."

"Brain trauma?"

I raise my hand toward my chest, wincing the whole way, until I can press my palm over my heart. I gasp. That hurts. I slowly lower my arm back to my side.

"It's still beating, if you're wondering." That's from the original voice. He must be the doctor. "You shorter girls need to try to sit as far from the steering wheel as possible. A deploying airbag is like getting punched in the face with a one-ton truck."

I let my heavy lids fall shut again and try to remember, but there's nothing in my head. It feels empty and full at the same time.

"Can you tell me what day it is?"

Day . . . I recite them one by one in my head. Monday, Tuesday, Wednesday—but none of them register as being accurate. "How long . . . been . . . here?" I manage to ask. My throat feels raw, but I don't know how an accident would cause that to happen.

"Here," the female voice says, pushing a straw against my lips. "It's water."

The water feels like a blessing, and I gulp until the straw's removed from my reach.

"That's enough. We don't want you getting sick."

Sick off water? I lick my dry lips but can't muster up any energy to argue. I slump back onto the pillows.

"You've been here for three days. Let's play a game," the doc suggests. "Can you tell me how old you are?"

That one's easy. "Fourteen."

"Hmmm." He and the nurse exchange a look that I can't figure out. Am I too young for the drugs they're giving me?

"And your name?"

"Sure." I open my mouth to answer, but my mind goes blank. I close my eyes and try again. Nothing. A big fat nothing. I glance at the doctor in panic. "I can't . . ." I gulp and give my head a fierce shake. "It's . . ."

"Don't worry about it." He grins easily, as if it's no big deal that I can't remember my own name. "Give her another dose of morphine and a Benzo cocktail and call me when she wakes up."

"On it, Doctor."

"But I— Wait," I say as his footsteps fade.

"Shh. It'll be fine. Your body needs the rest," the nurse says, placing a restraining hand on my shoulder.

"I need to know— I need to ask," I correct myself.

"No one's going anywhere. We'll all be here when you wake up. I promise."

Because it hurts too much to move, I let myself be reassured. She's right, I decide. The doctor will be here, because this is a hospital and that's where doctors work. Why I'm here, how I got hurt—that can all wait. The morphine and Benzo cocktail—whatever that is—sounds good. I'll ask more questions the next time I'm awake.

I don't sleep well, though. I hear noises and voices—high, low, anxious, angry. I frown and try to tell the worried ones that I'm going to be all right. I hear a name on repeat—*Hartley, Hartley, Hartley.*

"Is she going to be okay?" asks a deep male voice. It's the one I've been hearing say that name—Hartley. Is it mine?

I lean toward the voice, like a flower seeking the sun.

"All signs point to that. Why don't you get some sleep, son? If you don't, you're going to be in the same bed as her."

"Well, I'm hopeful," cracks the first voice.

The doc laughs. "That's definitely the right attitude to have."

"So I can stay, right?"

"Nope. I'm still kicking you out."

Don't go, I plead, but the voices don't listen to me and all too soon I'm left with the dark, suffocating silence.

About the Authors

PHOTO BY AMANDA NICOLE WHITE   PHOTO BY TIME OUT LLC

A *New York Times*, *USA Today*, and *Wall Street Journal* best-selling author, ELLE KENNEDY grew up in the suburbs of Toronto, Ontario, and holds a BA in English from York University. She is the author of more than forty titles of contemporary romance and romantic suspense, including the international bestselling Off-Campus series.

JEN FREDERICK is a Korean adoptee living in the Midwest with her husband, daughter, and rambunctious dog. Under the pseudonym Erin Watt, Frederick has cowritten two #1 *New York Times* bestselling novels.

Ready to find
your next great read?

Let us help.

Visit prh.com/nextread

Penguin
Random
House